LONG LOST

CORA BRENT

LONG LOST

"Not until we are lost do we begin to understand ourselves."

-Henry David Thoreau

❋ Created with Vellum

CONTACT ME

Sign up for my newsletter and get early news on releases, cover reveals and special giveaways…
CORA BRENT'S NEWSLETTER SIGNUP

I always love hearing from readers so contact me at:
corabrentwrites@yahoo.com.

Check out what's happening on Facebook:
www.facebook.com/CoraBrentAuthor

Join my exclusive reader Facebook group:
https://www.facebook.com/CoraBrentsBookCorner

Add future releases to your TBR list:
https://www.goodreads.com/CoraBrent

Follow me on Instagram: CoraBrentAuthor

LONG LOST (BLURB)

We should have been enemies from the beginning.
But we were children when we met and children tend to ignore such
rules.
Even if the rules exist for a reason.
Because Jonathan came from a family of savage killers.
While I was born into the broken aftermath of their victims.
For one short season we were inseparable.
All it took was one terrible day to turn us into strangers.
I've spent a long time chasing him from my mind.
And I assumed he was gone forever.
Until he shows up here.
So far from where we started and so changed from the friend I once
knew.
The gentle boy I loved has grown into a volatile man with dangerous
secrets and a different name.
He won't admit to who he is.
Or where he comes form.
Or who we are to each other.
And I knew I shouldn't have provoked him.

I knew I shouldn't have touched him.
Most of all I knew I shouldn't have offered him my heart.
Yes, Jonathan and I were born to be enemies.
And maybe that's how our story will end after all…

PROLOGUE

CARIS, AGE 13

The last day of summer

know I won't be here tomorrow.

In fact there's a good chance I'll never be here again. My dad is already on the road from Dallas. My mom won't be with him. Any day now she's supposed to be released from the facility where she's been healing for the last two months. But she'd be too fragile for a return to Arcana, especially after everything that's happened. It's possible she doesn't even know, that this will just be something else I'll be instructed to add to the 'Don't upset your mother' list.

I'm supposed to stay in the waiting room, which smells like rubber and sadness. The blood spots on my yellow shirt have dried in the pattern of a flower and I remember the bunch of wildflowers I plucked from the rim of a roadside ditch last week.

Asters, they were called. I hadn't known that. Johnny told me.

The dried blood makes me want to throw up. Earlier I asked a nurse if she had an extra shirt so I could change but she looked at me like I had soup for brains and said the hospital doesn't keep shirts for little girls just lying around for god's sake. She didn't need to be so rude. She probably felt bad about her attitude and that's why she handed me two limp dollar bills with instructions to go down the hall and get something to eat from the vending machine whenever I get hungry.

There's a cop standing by the reception desk with a clipboard and a frown but he only glanced at me once before losing interest. He won't care if I walk out. I have been left here to await the life or death verdict because there is no one else and because they don't know what to do with me. I am not even a witness. I am a minor nuisance. I am 'Suzanne's daughter'. I am 'the poor Chapel girl', even though Chapel was never my last name but my mother's. I am to be pitied and whispered about and otherwise avoided.

Even before I came here to Arcana this summer I understood something about people. They might smile at you and offer their sympathies but in the end they'd prefer you to stay at arm's length. They don't like to be too close to disaster. Like it's a virus. Something invisibly spread from one person to another just by getting too close. Johnny knows this too. He had the nerve to say it out loud once while it's something that only ever ran through my head.

Thoughts of Johnny no longer make me happy. They make my heart thud painfully and my eyes squeeze shut. My fingers curl and the short nails dig into my palms. The ache in my chest is real. I suspect this is what a broken heart feels like. I hope I never feel it again.

The cop continues to scribble on his clipboard. The nurse's name is Rachel and he asks her if she's going to rodeo night at Cradle, which is this raunchy bar off the highway exit to town. Aunt Vay complains that it's where paychecks and morals go to die.

Thinking about Aunt Vay should make me feel even worse than thinking about Johnny but that's not the case. I have my reasons.

Rachel likes the Clipboard Cop. I can tell by the way she throws her shoulders back and points her boobs in his direction as she says that she'll be on shift tomorrow but she has no plans the following night. Clipboard Cop smirks and clicks his pen. With every second that passes as I sit here in a scratchy red chair with my knees pressed together I want to scream a little more.

That would be something they would notice.

That would be something they would need to pay attention to.

Rachel glances over when I stand up but I wave the dollar bills she gave me to show that I'm just going to get a snack. I know it'll be a while before she wonders why I haven't come back.

It's easy to slip out of the side door. A man in mint green scrubs is gulping a large energy drink while his thumb scrolls through his phone. I'd be using my phone right now too if I knew where it was. In all the turmoil I must have left it behind at the house.

The color of the sky surprises me. The pinkish orange of summer twilight still cups the horizon. It's not even late enough to be dark. Waking up to the sight of bright pink walls in my mother's childhood bedroom feels like something that last happened a week ago and yet it was only this morning.

My destination is not far, perhaps a twenty minute walk if I cut through parking lots and the tumbleweed-choked field that Johnny told me used to be a piece of his family's land. It's a good thing it's not far because the bus service here in Arcana is infrequent and unreliable and the only money I have is Rachel's two vending machine dollars.

I'm tired and I dislike walking alone in the near darkness but this is my only chance. I won't get to talk to him later. Once my father gets here it will all become impossible to explain.

The sun keeps creeping lower, like an eyelid slowly closing. It's still hot and I should have brought some water but there's no helping that now. I walk quickly, sensing that time is running out with the fading of the light. A car honks at me from the road and a man extends a tattooed arm out the window. This kind of attention is new to me and I hate it. I cross my arms over my chest and veer off through a drug store parking lot, slide through a gap in a property line rail fence and ignore the trespassing signs as I speed walk.

The sandy dirt crunches with each sneaker step and I keep my head up to make sure no one weird is in sight. Back in Dallas there was a girl two grades ahead of me who was practicing her cheerleader jumps one morning on the high school football field when a man approached. He asked her if she knew the way to a gas station and then without warning he threw her on the ground and hurt her. She never returned to school and I heard that her parents moved the whole family to Georgia for a new start. As if a change of scenery fixes the worst thing that ever happened to you. Maybe that's true for some people. It's never worked for my mother. Her awful history lives in her mind and all the passing years and the pills and the doctors can't get it out.

I wonder what that girl is doing right now. I think her name is Angeline. I wonder if she's a cheerleader in her Georgia high school or if cheerleading is just a reminder of something she can't bear to remember.

If I see a strange man coming too close I'll run. I'm not the fastest runner but I'm not the slowest either.

A peculiar sensation is crawling up my spine, sort of like a sense that once I've been here doing this exact thing, maybe in a half forgotten dream that exists in pieces inside my head. I can't remember walking through this dim parking lot before but it's possible I ran through here with Johnny at some point this summer.

Or perhaps my brain has discovered an inherited memory, if such things are possible. It could come from my mother or my grandparents or my great grandparents. My Arcana connections are infinite. They press down on me more than ever.

I've never been to Johnny's house but I know exactly where the trailer park is. Once he told me that he's glad the trailer he lives in is located close to the entrance so he doesn't have to walk through the whole place to get home. I also remember him saying that his place is really old and has ugly turquoise trim.

The trailer park isn't as crowded as I thought it would be. I pictured trailers stacked in neat rows but they are placed more haphazardly with wide spaces between them. I have no problem finding Johnny's. He's standing right outside. He doesn't seem shocked to see me show up here and there's something different in his posture. A look of carelessness. And strangely, he's smoking a cigarette.

"I thought you'd be gone already," he says and tosses the lit cigarette into the dust.

"I will be." I'm watching the burning tip of the cigarette, annoyed that he refuses to put it out. I step forward, intending to crush it under my shoe but he beats me to the job and stomps the light out before I can get there.

"My dad's on his way here," I tell him.

"Lucky you." He stomps on the ground hard again. There's fury in his every move. "My mom's gonna get out of town. This thing with Rafe is the last straw. She wants to go to Arizona."

"You're going with her?"

"Not like I have a whole lot of options."

I swallow hard. "I was at the hospital."

He stuffs his hands in his pockets. His jaw moves, almost like he's gritting his teeth. "So I guess she'll live, huh?"

"It's touch and go tonight," I say, echoing the words I heard Rachel tell Clipboard Cop.

Johnny's response is to light another cigarette. I wonder when he began smoking.

"He'll be charged with murder if she dies," I blurt, my voice layered with the anger that I can't hide.

He inhales, blows out smoke, and gazes out beyond the park into pitch blackness. I get the feeling I'm boring him.

"Why the hell are you here right now?" he asks with an irritated sigh.

"Just wanted to tell you goodbye I guess."

"Oh." He snorts, taps out ashes even though there are no ashes yet. "Bye."

I don't move. There are thoughts swirling around in my head of the things I ought to say. This shouldn't be the last time we speak.

"We're not them, Johnny. We're us."

That was my promise to him one afternoon as we stood at the threshold of the meteor crater and I slipped my hand into his. I'd thought about kissing him before and I thought we might kiss then but we didn't. Now we never will.

Grief thickens inside my chest, a different kind of grief than I was familiar with. This isn't the grief of a baby sister's death or watching your mother look right through you because her mind is broken. This is losing someone in a different way.

He laughs at me, like he's guessing my thoughts and has decided to torture me with them. "What are you waiting for, a farewell kiss?"

"No! I don't want to kiss you." And I don't. Not anymore. But my cheeks are full of heat and I'm grateful for the twilight because I know I'm blushing.

Johnny smirks with the knowledge that he's successfully pissed me off. "Couldn't pay to me to do that anyway."

How could he have changed so much in so short a period of time? It's almost like the violent actions of his brother have crushed every bit of kindness in his heart.

"You're just like *them*," I spit out because I'm hurt by his coldness and I want to hurt him back.

But he's not hurt. He simply shrugs. "So are you. Just like them."

My 'them' is different from his. His are cruel and terrifying. Mine are fragile and ruined.

Johnny, determined to forever destroy the bonds of our friendship, comes closer. The gathering darkness doesn't hide his contempt.

"Go back to your fucking family," he says. "So you can all play bitch ass victims together. It's the only thing you're good at."

The sudden sour taste in my mouth warns me of forthcoming tears. I bite down hard on my lower lip to chase them off. My eyes water anyway.

"Why are you trying to make me hate you?" I ask and I can't stand how my voice cracks. I sound pathetic.

"Because you should," he says and the corner of his mouth quirks up in a wicked smirk that turns his face into Rafe's. "Now why don't you get lost before something bad happens to you?"

He doesn't shove me but I feel like he has. I feel like he's pushed me, kicked me to the ground and left me flailing in the dust while he laughs and makes plans to do worse.

I don't believe that he'd physically hurt me. Not even this new and awful version of Johnny would do that. But what he's doing is almost as bad.

I tip my head up and stare him down. I'm an inch taller so the move feels effective.

"I never ever want to fucking see you again, Jonathan Hempstead!"

I drop the words and run. I'm already scrubbing him from my mind as my legs begin pumping. I don't want to hear anything else he has to say but I'm not fast enough. I hear his bitter chuckle.

I also hear the last thing he decides to tell me.

"You never will, Caris!"

And I'm sure he's right.

JAY

My bones know that I'm back in Texas.

Before I spot the sign on the Interstate, twin feelings of dread and familiarity begin crawling through my blood, reminding me that nine years have passed since I was on this side of the state line. The moment might be sentimental, thinking about the long line of Texas sons that came before me, but in my case they are nothing to be proud of. At least the route I chose doesn't require me to pass through Arcana. The choice is deliberate.

A buzz from my phone, which sits in the closest cup holder, accompanies a text from Shane. I called him while stopped at a New Mexico gas station and told him to expect me before the sun sets.

Stay hungry. Got meat ready to grill.

My map ETA tells me I'll be in Hutton within the hour so I just answer with a thumbs up.

I have no memory of ever being in the panhandle before, that geographic wedge jutting up out of the western quadrant of the state. Besides a childhood visit to San Antonio, my Texas experiences were pretty well confined to Arcana and the surrounding hardscrabble towns where fortunes rise and fall on oil. The sights are all new to me and yet not much different from the haunted places of my childhood.

I never planned to see Texas again. And I might have kept that plan. But then my best friend asked for a favor.

About a month ago Shane was crashing on my sofa by night and by day grudgingly doing hard labor on a framing crew at a housing development east of Phoenix. And then came the phone call. A godmother he hadn't seen in fifteen years had died, leaving behind a house and a business. She wasn't the kind of godmother who was willing to take in an ornery teenager after his mother died, not even following a near fatal incident in a foster home. But she thought of him when she was handed the news that her latest bout with lung cancer was destined to be terminal and she had no close family who deserved a place in her will. Shane had been born in Texas too, although he didn't think of himself as being from Texas. This godmother named Ruby had been a kindly employer when Shane's mom got pregnant by a married cop with a side business dealing meth. He was knifed in the throat during a deal that turned violent. It was a fucked up situation and must have something to do with why Shane remembers nothing of Texas. He'd grown up in Arizona.

So there's Shane, sleeping on my couch, working twelve hour days in the sun while his car plays a daily match of hide and seek with the repo man, when he finds out that he now owns a house and a bakery. He gets to Hutton and learns that the bakery is in crappy financial shape because Ruby had been too sick to run it properly for a while. Shane doesn't know what to do about this so he calls me and asks if I'll come out for a few months and help him figure out how to make the place turn a profit.

Of course my own years of construction work have nothing to do with mixing cookie batter, but I'm good at organizing and I know how to get things done. I didn't even consider rejecting him. Shane and I have been through too much shit together. I don't have family and there aren't many guys in my circle even worth grabbing a beer with. Shane's the only person who could make me go to this kind of trouble. Besides, I've been worried about him. Things tend to go side-ways for Shane when he's left on his own for too long. The old demons come scratching at his door. Addiction. Depression. He can only hold them at bay for so long before needing a hand to lift him back into the light.

There are all kinds of signs now promising that Hutton is within reach. The road signs boast 'Hutton State University' with cartoons of howling coyotes. Residential neighborhoods are thickening on all sides and in the distance looms an unremarkable clot of downtown buildings. I've already gathered that there isn't much to Hutton, aside from the university. It's just another small western city that's too far outside a major metropolitan base to attract much notice. No one would go out of their way to visit Hutton.

I'm aware that his house is within walking distance to campus. Squinting at tiny maps on phone screens while driving is something I like to avoid so the directions were memorized before I left Phoenix. I swing right at the next light and drive slowly as I turn this way and that through the narrow streets. The neighborhood is neither shabby nor decadent. Some of the yards could use a trim but the evenly spaced tract homes look comfortable. The next left will be Shane's street.

A minute later I'm braking in front of a single story red brick house with powder blue shutters. A lush oak tree accents the front yard, spidery branches fanning out over the uncut lawn. From here I can see the roofline of the house behind it, meaning the yards are shallow, yet Shane had mentioned that a pool has been squeezed into the backyard. It's a far nicer place than I'm used to living in.

A college kid rolls by on a motorized scooter and slows down to eye the way I'm idling beside the curb. I don't flinch under his gaze and notice he's probably about my age. But the way he drops his eyes, hunches his shoulders and slinks away indicate that he's younger, or at least weaker, in all the ways that matter.

Shane must have been keeping a lookout for my truck because I've barely hopped out of the driver's seat when the front door swings open. He's shirtless and even from here I can see his wiry frame has gained a few pounds since he left Arizona a month ago and I'm glad. Relieved. He swears he hasn't been using since moving to Texas and now I'm ready to believe him.

Shane saunters to the center of the yard, raises his arms and whoops an ear piercing rebel yell.

"Hell yeah!" He punches the air. "My boy's here to liven up the place."

I snort and move to the truck bed to dig the old army surplus duffel bag out of the back. I didn't pack a ton of stuff because I don't own a ton of stuff and because I'm only planning to be here until August. Shane said the guest room already contains a dresser and a bed and I can't imagine I'll need much else.

"What's with the southern drawl?" I holler to my best friend but I'm grinning. My smile never comes easily but Shane always manages to bring it out.

He's moving in for a fist bump now, then changes his mind and squeezes my rib cage in a hug. The rocks of dread that have collected in my stomach since crossing the Texas line are slowly dissolving. The town haunting my memories is still two hundred miles away and I was someone else when I lived there. Shane knows more of that backstory than anyone else but even Shane's knowledge is skeletal at best. I ought to relax. These hang ups are mine alone. No one cares about the Hempstead boy from Arcana. No one would even recognize him. Or give a damn if they did.

Shane tries to take on the burden of my duffel bag but I brush him off and prop it on my shoulder. I'd never let anyone else carry my garbage and besides, I'm easily twice as strong as my best friend, although I'd never brag about it out loud.

He gestures that I ought to follow him into the house. "How was the drive?"

"Boring as hell." I'm getting a kick out of the fact that Shane is walking into a house that belongs to him. Of course no one is happy that his poor godmother is dead but the guy has never caught a single break in life. This is his chance to stay on the straight and narrow.

Maybe Shane hears my thoughts because he comes to a sudden stop just outside the doorway and swivels to meet my eye. "Look, thanks for coming, man. I know this is a favor I'll probably never be able to repay."

There is nothing in my history that points to a talent for saving small bakeries. But his faith in me is unwavering and maybe he just needs someone around who also has faith in him.

"I don't mind the vacation from the desert. There will still be plenty of houses to build when I return in August."

He keeps hesitating there in the doorway and I kind of want to get moving. The bag on my shoulder is becoming awkward to hold and a bead of sweat slides down the back of my neck. But Shane's looking uncertain and the way he rakes a hand through his mop of hair confirms that there's something on his mind. People often ask if we're brothers and it's true we both have the same nondescript shade of brown hair, along with ordinary brown eyes. Plus neither one of us are everyday shavers so there's always a bit of visible jaw scruff. But Shane's more the vulnerable pretty boy type that girls want to fold into their arms. Meanwhile, I hit puberty late but eventually acquired the big, muscled form and squared off features that made the men in my family look as dangerous as they really were. I don't think Shane and I look alike but people somehow see a parallel between us. Maybe there's something similar about the way we carry ourselves in the world; two castoff boys forced to test our wits at a young age with mixed results.

Shane glances behind him, peering through the screen door. "I just want to give you a heads up. Lana's here. She's out back, keeping an eye on the steaks."

I know about Lana. Ruby's house came with two college girl roommates who'd already signed a lease for the next year. One of them instantly became Shane's girlfriend.

"Things are good with you guys?" I ask him. Shane's never had a problem getting girls but from the way he always goes on and on about Lana, I know he's already pretty attached.

The grin on his face is full of eagerness. "Things are crazy good. She's something else, Jay. You'll like her."

"I'm sure I will."

His smile fades a little. "I've been pretty up front about shit but, you know, I left out a few details." He shrugs. "She's from a different kind of world."

He means a world where you're not required to slip a knife into your sleeve at dinner in order to fight off a midnight attack from the scumbag who receives state checks to keep you under his roof. A world where it never crosses your mind to behave like an animal and stalk the dumpsters at a nearby diner in order to seize the moment when trash bags filled with uneaten food scraps will be carelessly tossed away. That's the world Shane and I know.

That, and worse.

If Shane's worrying that I'll spill some of his secrets then he ought to know better. "No judgment here. I'm not in the habit of sharing details myself so I won't be ratting you out."

He shakes his head. "I didn't mean it like that, Jay. I was just thinking this could be more than a chance for me. It could be a chance for both of us. To start over."

I've started over before. It's not as neat or clean as it sounds. I don't feel any ambition to try again. Besides, my life in Phoenix isn't awful. I'll be able to step back into a construction crew upon returning. The apartment that I'm currently subletting to a friend whose girl kicked him to the curb will still be there.

But now Shane's looking all hopeful with his 'start over' plans lighting up his eyes and I don't see a reason to kill his good mood.

"Yeah, maybe," I tell him and try to sound cheerful. He gestures for me to follow him into the house and I cooperate without sermonizing.

There are things I've learned the hard way. You can change your hometown and your name and the idea of who you are. But you can't change where you've been and who you've known.

You can't change what it's already done to you.

JAY

The dark paneling is a dim contrast to the summer sunshine and I have to blink a few times to get oriented. There are flashes of orange everywhere; orange fake flowers and an orange chair and orange glass bottles lined up on a windowsill.

Shane is pointing out things that are obvious and not so obvious. We are standing in the living room. The kitchen is on the left. The hallway leading to the bedrooms and bathroom is on the right and the guest room is at the end. There's a flat panel door awkwardly located on the far wall of the living room, the doorway cutting right into the paneling pattern. Shane says it leads to the second set of living quarters where Lana and her roommate live. He explains that the house had been split that way before Ruby bought it and she'd rented out the apartment for years.

Shane suggests that I should just drop my bag where I stand for now. He's already shoving a sliding glass door open. On the other side a girl in a red bikini has her back to us in front of a smoking grill. She emits a squeal of surprise when Shane grabs her from behind and growls into her neck. Then she laughs, notices me and waves a long two-pronged fork in greeting.

"So you're the famous Jay Phoenix from Phoenix."

She's blatant about appraising me, looking me over as if I'm auditioning for something.

I don't like the scrutiny but I can hardly blame her for being curious. And I know how to act properly when I should.

I force my voice to sound light and cheerful. "Yep, according to my driver's license I'm Jay Phoenix from Phoenix."

She laughs again with a natural kind of energy that's woven into some personalities. "I'm Lana," she says, leaning into Shane when he slides a comfortable arm around her waist. "And I'm already a fan of yours because this guy never stops talking about you. It's JayJayJay all the time. If you were prettier I'd be jealous."

I doubt Lana ever had a reason to be jealous of anyone. She has to be one of the most beautiful girls I've ever observed up close. Her smile is Miss America quality, her richly brown complexion is flawless, and her thick black hair cascades to her waist.

Shane plucks the fork out of his girlfriend's hand and pokes at the sizzling blobs of meat on the grill. He's overseeing enough steak to feed a sizable frat house.

"You still insist on eating your meat burned to a crisp, Jay?"

I sink into a cushioned chair at the umbrella-shaded patio table. "Blackened without a trace of pink."

"You got it."

Lana decides that we should eat outside. She begins setting out paper plates and napkins. She likes to talk a lot. She's from Hawaii and I can't guess why she traded island paradise for the Texas panhandle but she must have her reasons. She's on the college swim team. She majors in psychology but won't be graduating when she should because she changed majors so many times. She's lived in the house for a year and feels bad that she never knew how sick Ruby was until hospice care showed up.

And she's wild about Shane. She doesn't even have to say it. I notice the way her eyes spark every time she looks at him.

But now she's sitting across from me and leaning on her elbows while she inspects me once more. "Such a weird coincidence," she says. "The fact that your last name is Phoenix and you live in Phoenix."

There's nothing coincidental about it. My last name is Phoenix because that's the name I chose. Shane shoots me a look. He knows I don't like explaining things.

"Pretty big coincidence," I agree and Lana drops the subject because her phone buzzes.

"Jay, my Care Girl will be home soon. You'll love her. She's just your type." Lana taps the back of my hand to reassure me that although she's known me for a lengthy time span of fifteen minutes, she knows what kind of girl I go for.

"I wasn't aware I had a type," I say and hope the comment doesn't come off as rude.

Shane arrives with a plate piled with glistening steaks. "Jay's just been looking for a challenge. That's why he's never settled down." He drops into Lana's chair because she has left the table to dig around in a red and white plastic cooler.

"You want a beer, baby?" Lana asks as she paws through ice. "And what about you, Jay?"

"Sure, I'll take a beer." I kick Shane under the table. "What the hell do you mean I'm looking for a challenge?"

He forks the top steak and tosses it onto my plate with a smirk of amusement. "You know, a ball buster who will make you work for it."

I don't know how he got that idea. I don't want my balls busted and I sure as hell don't want to crawl around at some girl's feet begging her to do the job. There's no one waiting for me to return to Phoenix because that's my preference. I'm no manwhore player, hopping from one girl's bed to the next, but I'm not boyfriend material either. Sometimes my hookup situations go on for a while and that's where it ends. Shane probably thinks I can be tempted because I've been living like a monk for the past six months after the girl I'd been steadily fucking got sick of hoping for a real relationship and told me in a nice way to shit or get off the pot.

Needless to say, I got off the pot.

Last week I heard she's sporting a brand new diamond from a high school boyfriend she reconnected with. Good for her. These days it's easier to get satisfied with my own hand and some amateur internet porn. I'm the problem. All I have to offer is dick and no matter how dirty she tries to be, a girl eventually wants more than dick. She wants heart too and she won't find that in me.

Lana objects to the idea that her friend is a ball buster. "Don't go scaring him off. She's a total sweetheart, Jay. I swear."

Lana exchanges a look with Shane and I figure out what's going on. I'm going to be set up with 'Care Girl' in the hopes that we'll coexist as a happy, wholesome quartet. This must be part of the whole starting over package. At some point I'll need to break the news that I have no plans to be domesticated.

"Wait." Shane smacks his thigh. "Does she still have something going on with that piece of shit in the Acura?"

Lana groans. "Oh god, I can't stand Alden. He's a total tool and she needs to unload him for good." She turns thoughtful eyes on me. "Jay over here doesn't seem like a tool."

Shane shoves the steak sauce in my direction. "Jay's no tool for sure."

I don't feel the urge to confirm my tool status one way or the other and no one's waiting for me to chime in anyway so I cut up my steak and stay quiet. Shane pulls Lana into his lap and the two of them start sucking face because apparently it's too much to expect that they can keep their hands off each other for eight seconds.

The time may come when I'll need to articulate that screwing a pouty roommate who may be attached to an angry Acura-driving ex won't be a leading item on my agenda. I'll have to find a way to get the point across without seeming like an asshole. Shane's used to my attitude but Lana and her friend aren't and just because I don't want to fuck around where I sleep doesn't mean I want to be hated. If Care Girl makes a move I'll just pretend my dick doesn't work. I'll invent a medical condition if I have to.

Shane leans over and rummages in the ice cooler until he comes up with a beer. I raise an eyebrow while he twists open the bottle. Alcohol has never been his primary weakness but it is a gateway to other bad decisions. He takes only a few sips and sets it down on the table, obviously content to nurse the bottle for a while. I ought to give him the benefit of the doubt. Looking out for Shane is an old habit.

Lana remains perched on Shane's lap and now she's cutting her steak up into dainty little pieces, none of which she eats. She notices my stare.

"Recovering vegetarian," she explains with a grimace. "Sometimes I'm still squeamish."

"Yeah, me too," Shane says and stabs his fork into a juicy cut of ribeye. He tears off a bite with his teeth. "Totally fucking squeamish."

Lana elbows him with a smirk. He winks at her. I have to admit they're cute together.

A buzzer sounds and Lana jumps in her chair, looking this way and that. She locates her phone on a nearby chair and hops over to seize it.

"It's just Care," she announces and taps out a text with impressive speed. "She's almost home."

I decide that's my cue to finish my beer and steak. Shane has never said much about Lana's roommate other than she's a college girl from Texas. But when it comes to being social, I don't have a lot of stamina. Especially after all these hints that there might be expectations involved.

"Listen, buddy," I say as I crumple up my napkin and drop it on my empty plate. "I appreciate the meal but I'm tired as hell. You mind if I knock off early and get settled in?"

Shane nods and raises his hand in a wave. "Yeah, man, I totally get it. Leave the dishes. I'll take care of them."

"Whatever you say."

A small frown crosses Lana's pretty face when I rise from the table but then she brightens and flips her hair over her shoulder. "I guess we'll have plenty of time to initiate you into the Hutton party scene."

I nod even though I'm not a fan of any party scene. Lana flashes one more smile and then moves away from the table to the edge of the rectangular pool that runs nearly the length of the small yard.

Shane calls "Hold on, Phoenix," before I take another step toward the patio door.

When I turn he sidles up to me and shoots a glance at his girlfriend. She extends a shapely leg and dips a toe into the water.

The look on my best friend's face is a little sheepish. "I know I've said it already but I owe you big time for giving up your summer to come out here."

I nudge his shoulder. "You don't owe me nothing."

That's the truth as far as I'm concerned. There's no need to keep score. We found ourselves trapped in a crappy system at the same time and learned to rely on each other for survival. I know Shane would take a bullet for me. He's far more of a brother to me than my own brother, wherever the hell he is.

A cold finger touches the base of my sweaty neck at the thought of Rafe. I haven't seen him in years. Chances are high we'll never see each other again. That ought to bother me more than it does.

Shane delivers another grateful look and I watch him join Lana by the pool. Shane deserves a fairy tale ending in life. If there's any way I can help him get it then I will.

The sliding glass doors are pushed open and a girl steps outside. She's enthralled with something on her phone and squints into the early evening sunlight. Her hair is parted in the middle and straight; a light honey color, falling just past her shoulders. She wears glasses, black-rimmed frames cut in a trendy cat's eye shape that she probably selected to look quirkier than she really is. If she smiles there might be a gap between her two front teeth unless she'd caved to suggestions to correct it with braces.

The last time I saw her the gap had been there.

I'm only standing about six feet away from her but she is distracted, fussing with her phone while trying to keep a bulging red backpack from sliding off her shoulder. She spots Lana and Shane and takes a few steps in their direction, still taking no notice of the stranger on her patio who has stopped breathing.

"Hey girl," Lana calls. She's balancing on the edge of the pool, holding onto Shane's arm as she swings her foot out and kicks up a splash of water. "You're just in time to meet Jay Phoenix. Jay, this is my roommate, Caris."

Caris turns to look at me but I move my face to the side. Let her think I'm shy. An asshole. Whatever.

Fuck.

"Hi, Jay." She lets the heavy backpack slide to the ground with a slight thud. "And it's Caris Marano if we're adding last names."

I already know that. I know her last name and I knew she loves butter pecan ice cream. I know she can find every constellation in a clear night sky and that she wants to be a veterinarian.

Lana shrieks with laughter because Shane has swept her into his arms and now threatens to jump into the pool with her.

"My hair's going to get wrecked," she giggles.

Caris watches the poolside struggle and tucks a strand of hair behind one ear, an old habit that stabs at cold places in my heart. She hasn't really given me her full attention yet. I'm not eager for that to change. God has a really fucked up sense of humor.

Caris Marano.

What are the odds?

Better left uncalculated.

I might assume that some sick hand of fate has delivered us to this backyard nine years after we last laid eyes on each other and I don't believe in such mystical shit.

I believe in fury and grief and bitterness. I know them all well. And once I knew her too.

I steel myself for a direct look into the grey eyes that are now surveying me but there is no surprise there, no recognition, just a polite level of curiosity as she takes me in. She's waiting for me to say something.

"Nice to meet you."

My words sound sharp.

She notices and is puzzled, cocking her head to the side and then looking back at the pool as a gigantic splash signals that Shane has made good on his threat and jumped into the water, girlfriend and all.

I should forgive her for failing to know me. She hasn't changed significantly but I have. A skinny thirteen year old boy who could hardly throw a punch even to defend himself has been replaced by a scruffy grown man who has long since learned to draw blood when he has to. I don't look the same. I don't sound the same. Even my name isn't the same.

So yes, I should forgive this girl for looking my way and seeing nothing but some unshaven ogre with an attitude.

I should.

Yet I couldn't.

Because of that one sweet, painful, fucked up summer. The summer I met her. The last summer I was still Jonathan Hempstead.

It's not reasonable to hope that a light bulb will never go off in her head when we'll be living in the same house for the next three months. She was never stupid. But for tonight I'm going to be keeping my distance.

Shane and Lana don't notice that anything is up. They're messing around in the pool and I am grateful for all the commotion because it keeps Caris from staring at me for more than a few seconds.

"Come on you guys!" Lana, now soaking wet, is perched on Shane's shoulders and she waves at us. "Jump in. Chicken fight!"

Caris never closed the patio door. I pretend like the invitation hasn't made its way to my ears and walk right into the house without looking at anyone.

That must have caught everyone's notice because Shane feels like he has to explain on my behalf.

"He gets quiet like that sometimes."

Ruby's orange living room looks even more orange than it did earlier. I don't stick around in there and so I don't hear if Caris has an answer to Shane's comment. I head straight to my room, although later on I start to wonder if she stared after me in confusion after I ran inside.

Or if she'd forgotten me the second I was out of sight.

I hope for the latter.

CARIS

Some book I read years ago began with this sentence:
"The day was off to an inauspicious start."
That line has been running like a marquee through my brain ever since realizing I'd slept through my morning alarm and had only fifteen minutes to cover my body in semi-clean garments, run a comb through the hair that still reeked of the greasy diner food I'd been serving until midnight, and pretend I'm an Olympic sprinter as I dodge the slow moving student obstacles on a race to the exam room.

I reach the finish line three seconds before the door to the testing room closes and try to stop panting like a dog because (ahem, spoiler alert!) I am actually NOT an Olympic sprinter and this kind of exercise first thing in the morning is not my idea of a good time. Then I catch my breath, look at the exam and realize that before I passed out in the wee morning hours following an unproductive last minute cram session, I really should have paid more attention to the Whiskey Rebellion. I bite my lip to keep the curses from flying out and cross my legs while my bladder howls for relief.

The class was chosen to fill space as an easy elective and should have been a cakewalk this semester; an introductory American History class in the middle of grueling upper division accounting coursework. I would have preferred The Sociology of Star Wars but it was full. With only two semesters left after this one I was eager to get an easy requirement out of the way. I might have misjudged.

After that disaster of a test I take a desperately needed trip to the rest room, become disgusted by my limp-haired, waxy reflection and try to calculate how much damage I've just done to my GPA.

The math is depressing.

"The day was off to an inauspicious start."

I need to hang around campus for a meeting with my Computerized Accounting group to finalize our project but there's a two hour gap, which I decide to partially fill by dozing off in a fuzzy blue tapestry chair in the Student Union. When I wake up there's some guy with a carefully groomed goatee and a fishing hat sitting on the floor at my feet and rummaging through my backpack.

"Dude." I snatch my bag out of his hands. "What the hell?"

He seems hurt. "I need a pen."

"You need a pen?"

"Yup."

"I don't have a pen."

"Oh. Do you have some gum?"

My head throbs. He seems so earnest. It occurs to me that I might be the subject in someone's psychology project. That happened to a friend of mine. She was minding her own business and eating waffle fries out on the quad when a pair of distraught girls approached and asked her to help them search for a lost ferret. Though the request was odd, my friend disliked the thought of misplaced ferrets and crying girls so she helped. For three hours she combed the campus and asked everyone in sight if they'd noticed a confused ferret running around. No one had. Because no such ferret existed. After pressuring her to abandon her waffle fries and waste her afternoon, she was proudly informed that she'd been an unwitting participant in an academic experiment. Something about strangers helping strangers. She was thanked for her contribution and presented with a coupon for a free scone at the Student Union coffee stand.

"Fuck you," she said and stalked off to buy more waffle fries.

I'd like to say I would have done the same thing but I probably would not have had the nerve.

My goateed beggar is still staring at me so I break the news that I don't have any gum and then excuse myself to go buy a churro for lunch. I'm holding a handful of warm sugary perfection when a thick elbow jostles me from behind and knocks it out of my hand. It lands on a patch of dirtily discolored tile.

"Sorry," grumbles the hulking brute who abused me and then he disappears into the crowd.

I snatch the churro up and consider whether the five second rule applies to the grimy floors of the Student Union. I decide it does. And that was definitely less than five seconds. I take a bite. Then I notice that I'm being watched with disgust by a nearby suntanned blonde wearing a one piece outfit the color of a yellow highlighter.

"Don't judge me," I say and take a bigger bite.

She rolls her eyes and scrolls through her phone.

I exit the double glass doors to the quad and prepare to relax on a grassy patch. Balancing the uneaten churro portion on one knee, I withdraw my phone to see what kind of earth shattering developments have occurred in the ninety minutes since I last looked at my phone.

Alden has texted a pic of himself, shirtless and sweaty and pressing weights at the gym. He's added a caption.

Muscle God.

A snort of laughter bubbles out of me but I stare at the image for a few long seconds. Alden is easy on the eyes, always has been. We started out in veterinary medicine together before he switched to political science while I changed to accounting. We've been hanging out off and on for a while and I could only guess that his motivation for this cheesy skin shot is to persuade me to reconsider having sex with him. Sometimes I want to and more than once we've come damn close.

Alden is all right. Most of the time. But I already know I'll never fall for him. Aside from Alden, my relationship experience is limited to three short term boyfriends, two of whom were silly high school romances. I would describe my virginity as a technicality. I've done just about everything else and I know how to get off while also getting the guy off. The first time I ever admitted my status to my roommate, Lana, I explained it like this:

I'm afraid I'll enjoy *actual* sex much less than I enjoy *thinking* about sex.

And I enjoy thinking about sex *a lot*.

It is one of my favorite past times. Becoming disillusioned with my many and sundry sexual fantasies would be a major bummer.

Lana, however, was outraged.

She'd placed her hands on her perfect hips and informed me that my perspective was nothing short of ridiculous. After all, if I didn't like the way sex worked out with one guy then I could just try another one. Lana feels this way because Lana is gorgeous and filled with sensual confidence.

But me?

I'm bespectacled, small breasted and the frequent recipient of jail bait accusations. But really, I suppose I could be considered cute in an unblemished, girl next door kind of way. Not all of us could make mouths water just by strutting down the sidewalk. Nobody is likely to gag with disgust at the sight of me. That's better than nothing.

Alden's sweaty smirk is still taunting me from the phone and I'm tossing around the idea of texting back a filthy response. After today my school responsibilities are pretty much finished and a long hot summer of scribbling burger orders and balancing chicken wing baskets stretches ahead. Some entertainment might be nice. And Alden is entertaining. As long as our conversations don't run too deep or go on for too long. Then he begins sounding like a complete jackass and I get annoyed.

I notice that besides Alden's text I've missed a voicemail alert. My stomach clenches when I see the caller is my father. He's never gotten the hang of texting and still leaves long winded messages that sound like he's dictating a business letter. He's following up on my call from yesterday. My mother's panic attacks have returned. She hates taking the meds that always leave her feeling depleted and empty headed but there are consequences when she stops taking them. Two days ago a neighbor had to escort her home from the grocery store after she started hyperventilating in the produce section.

My father's voicemail is cheerful. He says Mom is doing much better today. He says there's absolutely no need for me to rush home to Dallas during finals week. They are both looking forward to my planned visit for my birthday next month. I listen to his message a second time and try to decode the meaning behind the bland sentences.

Sometimes I wonder if he ever resents the role he's played for nearly thirty years as Suzanne's caretaker. If he has such feelings he never allows them to show. He is endlessly patient. He is eternally devoted. He's much better at being a husband than I am at being a daughter.

The thing is, I really do adore my mother. I always have. It just hurts to be around her too much. It hurts to see when she spirals downward and grieves for the lost more than she allows herself to enjoy the living.

My mother answers her cell phone on the second ring. She's in the middle of an at home luncheon with the dog rescue group she volunteers for and I'm glad to hear she's not just sitting around, sadly awaiting my father's return from work. She asks about my exams and if I'm enjoying the homemade canned peaches she mailed to me three months earlier. The questions sound forced, as if they have been invented for the benefit of her luncheon guests. I'm not sure she listens to the answers because she advises me to study hard this weekend even though I've just told her that I finished my last exam this morning. It's not an ideal moment to inquire about her mental health and I'm never good at choosing my words on that topic anyway. The call ends quickly and afterwards I sit there in the grass, picking at the remains of my churro and wishing I had a better gift for knowing the right thing to say.

I'm no longer in the mood to have sexy thoughts about Alden and yet I don't want to insult him by ignoring his text. I finally answer with a lame smiley face because I can't think of a better response.

Then I lie back in the grass with my arm over my eyes. The sun is right overhead and the hottest season is close enough to touch. The prickly sensation of grass on my skin and the particular scent of summer conjures carefree emotions; of childhood, of lazy serenity, of simple happiness.

I have no clear idea of how many minutes pass as I sprawl on the quad with formless images floating behind my eyelids but the buzzing of my phone probably saves me from a bad case of sunburn. It's Lana. She wants to confirm that I'm not working tonight and will be around for the grand arrival of Shane's best friend.

Shane is Lana's new boyfriend and he's also technically our landlord. The death of his godmother, Ruby, left him with an inheritance that includes a local bakery and the house where Lana and I rent rooms. We were shocked and saddened when we learned that the quiet elderly woman who rented half her home to us and generously supplied us with the delectable leftovers from her bakery was dying. Shane proved to be an even bigger surprise. Ruby had never mentioned a godson. He arrived a week after her death and assured us he had no problem honoring the continuation of our lease. We were relieved. It would have been tough to find another place in Hutton that was this cheap, this close to campus, and even boasted private backyard pool access. Shane and Lana hit it off right away and their hot and heavy love affair was giving me a lot of alone time in our side of the house. Shane's best friend Jay will be crashing here for the summer and from what I understand, he's coming at least in part to help Shane rescue Ruby's Bakery from financial collapse.

Ever since she found out about Jay, Lana has been eager to set me up with him because she thinks Alden is trash and because she believes I ought to have better orgasms and because happy people who are in love want everyone around them to also be happy and in love.

The other night she shoved her phone in my face and insisted that I should 'look look LOOK at how hot he is!' but it was hard to get a read on Jay Phoenix from the photo. He seemed to be in the process of deliberately turning his head to the side, like he was annoyed that his picture was being snapped. The shot was outdoors and he stood in a stiff pose beside a pile of dusty concrete rubble while the harsh glare of evening sunlight obscured the details. All I could make out was some dude with tattoos and muscles who gave off a tangible angry vibe.

I've never been one to swoon over bad tempered rebels so I doubt we'll have much to talk about but I do wonder about his name. Jay Phoenix. It sounds like the result that might spit out of one of those 'What's My Porn Name?' puzzles. Maybe it is. Lana once hinted that he was kind of a rough character, although if she thinks that clue would tempt me then my own best friend doesn't know me as well as she should. I have no interest in reforming a bad boy. My plan is to be polite and that's all.

I promise Lana I'd be home later to say hello to Jay Phoenix. Then I realize I'm two minutes late to meet my Computerized Accounting group so I hustle over to the library.

Three hours later I am the unhappy owner of a raging headache and I'm convinced that whoever invented college group projects is fundamentally evil. One member of the group was a no show and another failed to complete her portion of the project because, in her high pitched whiny words, "I still gotta get my laptop back from my shitty ex."

Thanks to shitty exes and absent participants I had no choice but to take the lead and scramble to get the gaps filled in before the five o'clock deadline. I knew before I sent it to the professor that the project wasn't worthy of an A but my grade is already high enough in the class that the damage should be minimal, unlike certain Whiskey Rebellion failures.

I leave my group and the words, "Nice working with you" kind of trip over my tongue. Lying doesn't come naturally to me. I do hope that out there in the corporate world, people aren't such hapless flakes when it comes to collaborative efforts. Rumors suggest otherwise.

Speaking of work, I'm exiting the library when my manager from Beefcake Charlie's calls with some unexpected and rotten news. The county health inspector stopped by this afternoon for a surprise visit and discovered enough violations to shut the place down until further notice. I'm not shocked at the violations because I've seen what goes on in the kitchen and I would not even dare to nibble a pickle that originated there. However, my summer plans don't include unemployment. Despite the public health risks and the fact that it's been shut down twice before, Beefcake Charlie's is always busy and tips are decent. I can't afford not to have a job. My scholarship covers only half my tuition and living expenses still remain. I've taken some student loans already and prefer not to take anymore. Asking my folks for money is out of the question. My dad was laid off last year and only started a new job a few months ago. They don't have any cash to spare.

Finding another job right now will be a challenge. Summer is kind of a lean time in Hutton. The university empties out and there are no tourist attractions to draw the vacationing crowd. The situation sucks all around.

Feeling somewhat conquered, I stop to lean against a nearby pillar and pout for a few minutes. All around me, people laugh and skip off to their Friday night destinations, happy that the pressures of school are over for the semester.

Lana texts and reminds me about my promise to be home this evening. She and Shane are barbecuing steaks. I can't think of anything better than enjoying a decent meal and a few beers with some friends. I'll even muster up some cheerfulness for newcomer Jay Phoenix because I promised Lana I would. After detaching myself from the pillar I begin to trudge toward home.

"The day was off to an inauspicious start."

I don't realize I've spoken my mantra out loud until a hand holding couple stop walking in front of me and turn around.

They stare at me.

I stare right back until they become uncomfortable and walk away.

Inauspicious indeed.

*M*y car is a year older than I am and in dire need of repairs that I don't have the money for. My solution is to drive it as little as possible. Luckily, I live within walking distance of school and work.

Well, I lived within walking distance of my job when I *had* a job. This realization makes my headache worse and I dig out the bottle of aspirin I keep in my backpack. It's likely I'll need to get my car situation fixed sooner rather than later.

Lana and I lucked into our living arrangement. We've been roommates since freshman year and it was Lana's idea to move off campus. The residence halls are universally noisy and devoid of privacy and the hallways always smell like wet cheese. Lana said all the cool people were renting off campus and I've always wanted to be considered one of the cool people. I agreed we should follow the trend as long as the rent was manageable.

She happened to share a sociology class with a girl who was transferring to University of Texas in Austin and was giving up the two bedroom apartment she'd been renting in the house of the sweet old lady who owned Ruby's Bakery on Hutton Street. The house was only a mile from campus and there was a pool in the backyard. I doubted

I'd be able to afford the rent but it turned out Ruby just wanted to find decent tenants without the chore of interviewing a hundred ditzy college students. Lana's idea was to show up at the bakery and charm her to pieces. Lana's charm exceeds mine by a mile but Ruby was satisfied enough with both of us to offer a one year lease at a more reasonable rate than I was expecting.

There were a few rules. No wild college parties and no live in guests. Lana is a far more social creature than I am but she was fine with partying elsewhere. And Ruby was a doll, always dropping off leftover cinnamon rolls from the bakery and allowing us to use the pool whenever we pleased. She spent most of her waking hours at the bakery and never mentioned any family. Nor did she mention the fact that she was battling advanced lung cancer and had refused treatment. I wish she had told us but she didn't. She kept right on working until collapsing at the bakery one Saturday morning. Two weeks later she was gone. We found out about Shane the day after her burial. He showed up at the front door with the news that a lawyer called to tell him that he was the sole benefactor of Ruby's will. I figured he'd want to sell off the house and business but he didn't. He wanted to stay.

Shane is our age and even though his mop of brown hair always needs combing, he's eye catching and wears a constant, genuine smile. From the beginning he struck me as fun and friendly, perhaps a little erratic. Lana was immediately crazy about him. Lana could probably have her pick of any guy in Hutton but I've long noticed her fascination with the unrefined wild cards. Shane fits that description. Lana confided that he's spent time in a juvenile detention facility and suffered a few of life's bruises along the way but he really wants to take this chance that Ruby has given him and turn his life around. Nobody could fault the guy for trying to take a step up in life. Plus, he's in absolute awe of my best friend, which earns him my respect.

When I get to the house I find a silver pickup truck with Arizona plates parked at the curb. I'm really hoping there's no reason to be wary about this Jay Phoenix guy. There's a door between the two living spaces, but still. We'll be technically living in the same house together.

Usually I would enter through a side door that leads straight to my apartment rather than traipsing through Ruby's house, but today the front door is cracked open so I walk right in. I can see them in the backyard through the sliding glass doors. Lana and Shane are goofing off by the pool.

I'm in the middle of the pushing the slider open when a text arrives from Alden.

Beaters tonight. Then...???

That's Alden speak for saying he'll be hanging out at his favorite sports bar. And that his late hours are free for a hookup. How romantic. I don't have the energy for Beaters or Alden tonight. Quickly I text back a response.

Hanging with Lana.

That's technically true.

Lana calls, "Hey, girl," and begins passing out introductions. That's when I realize I've somehow missed seeing the guy standing a few feet away from me on the patio. Either he's embarrassed or just plain anti-social because he's showing zero interest in this encounter. He's not even looking at me.

The weight of my backpack is killing my shoulder so I slide it off. "Hi, Jay."

I make an effort. I keep talking, trying to activate a conversation. Unfriendliness doesn't need to be contagious. However, Jay Phoenix just seems irritated.

"Nice to meet you," he manages to choke out, sounding anything but excited. He's still keeping his eyes directed at the more interesting view of the back wall of the house.

I wait for a few seconds and he finally turns his head.

And glares.

For a split second I think I'm imagining it. But no, that's definitely a coat of ice in his eyes as they survey me before shifting away.

What the hell is his problem?

I'm just trying to be nice.

If he's worried that the nerdy girl roommate might try to jump his bones then he should relax. Alden the Muscle God is standing by if my hormones need an urgent fix. Or maybe his personality really is this awful no matter who he's talking to.

Shane and Lana have tumbled into the pool together and I find myself laughing at them. After a tedious day, their enthusiasm for each other is a pleasant thing to behold. It's probably an even more pleasant thing to have but I'm too happy for Lana to feel any jealousy. A big reason she left Hawaii and sought this dusty corner of Texas was because the boy she loved in high school drowned in a drunken surfing accident. She never talks about him much but she kept his picture on her dresser until she met Shane. For the last three years I've watched her play the field and occasionally get her heart broken. I've never seen her this happy before.

Lana is being carried across the pool on Shane's shoulders and she throws down a challenge for a chicken fight. This is the moment when Jay Phoenix decides the scene is not to his liking and dashes into the house with supernatural speed.

His sudden rude exit must have caused a 'What The Fuck?' look to take charge of my face because Shane feels the need to call out an apology on behalf of his friend.

"He gets quiet like that sometimes."

I stifle a sarcastic response.

Whatever.

If Jay Phoenix wants to keep his sullen hot guy mysteries to himself then I won't be bothered at all.

I fall into a cushioned patio chair.

"Jump in, Care," Lana begs from where she's still balanced on Shane's shoulders.

The thought is tempting. I'm sweaty and gross and neither Shane nor Lana will bat an eye if I just dive right in wearing my clothes. But other than my lunchtime churro I haven't eaten a thing today and the pile of steaks on the picnic table looks more inviting than the pool right now.

I help myself to the largest cut of meat, drown it in steak sauce and twist the cap off the beer I grabbed from the cooler. I'm still finishing my steak when Shane and Lana emerge from the pool and join me at the table. I share my unfortunate news about Beefcake Charlie's and Lana promises to ask the diner where she works part time if they have any openings. There's way too much food and Lana packs it away in one of Ruby's green Tupperware containers. By this time the sun is on its way down but the two of them are full of energy and they want to go out. Lana tries to persuade me to join them but I've had enough of people for the day. I just want to take a hot bath, slip on my ugliest, most comfortable pajamas and watch something dumb on my laptop until my eyes close.

Lana stops by my room before leaving. She looks excellent in a red satin dress that shows off her splendid rack while her glossy black hair falls loose and straight. I'm already sprawled on my bed and searching for something funny to watch. There's a show about talking dogs and it's not a cartoon. That looks funny.

Lana sets her hands on her hips. "It's Friday night."

"Yes."

"It's the end of the semester."

"Yes."

"Why don't you come out with us?"

I point at my sleepwear, which is splashed with illustrations of laughing cows. "I'm pretty sure I'd attract the wrong kind of attention in this sexy getup."

She laughs. "Shane wouldn't mind waiting for a few minutes if you want to change."

"Thanks, but you guys go ahead. Oh, but can you do me a favor?"

"Maybe."

"Steer clear of Beaters. Alden said he was going to be there tonight."

"So?"

"So when he texted me earlier I told him I was busy hanging out with you."

Lana gives me a pitying look. "Why do you bother? You don't even like him."

I make a limp attempt to defend Alden. "He's not *all* bad."

"Care, you can do so much better than some narcissistic man boy who's not half as funny as he thinks he is."

I cluck my tongue. "Alas, the best specimens are not exactly falling at my feet."

She's still looking at me and we've been friends long enough for me to guess that she's got something she wants to say.

I toss a throw pillow at her. "WHAT?"

Lana presses her lips together in thought. "I don't know. Sometimes it's like you're willing to take less than you deserve because you're afraid to risk putting yourself out there."

I groan. "Did I ever mention that sometimes having a psychology major for a roommate can be exhausting? Next you'll be asking me to search for an imaginary lost ferret."

Lana snorts, picks up the pillow I hurled at her a moment ago and throws it back in my face. Then she crosses the room and takes a seat on the edge of my bed. "Caris, you have never been in love. One of these days that's going to change and I want to be there to see it."

"Do you love Shane?"

Lana fidgets and runs her hands back and forth over her legs. "Okay, don't think I'm pathetic but I'd marry that boy tomorrow."

I smile at her. "Shane's a good guy."

"Yeah." She bites a corner of her lip. "He's afraid you think Jay was being rude tonight. He says that's just the way Jay is. Doesn't have the social graces down pat."

"I'll say he doesn't," I grumble. Something about Shane's best friend bothers me and I can't put my finger on what it is. We spent less than two minutes together and his behavior wasn't *that* off the wall. Perhaps I'm just letting my crappy day color my perspective.

Lana raises an eyebrow. "You've got to admit he's not bad to look at."

Anyone with eyes could admit that. Jay looks the part of the classic rugged hottie. The type that comes equipped with a treasury of secret complications.

"His last name probably isn't really Phoenix," I point out.

She shrugs. "Probably not. But he wouldn't be the first person in the world to change his last name. Those two boys have both had a rough time."

"What do you mean?"

Lana glances at the doorway and listens for a moment. There's the distant sound of water running from the kitchen sink. And over that, the faint echo of Shane's singing voice. He's a fan of the Beatles and he often sings when he's going about his business.

She smiles to herself and then edges closer. "You know Shane was born in Hutton, right?"

"Yeah." It explains his connection to Ruby. Shane's mother was an employee at Ruby's Bakery when she got pregnant. Things didn't work out with the baby's father but Ruby acted as a support system for Shane's mother and in gratitude she was named as his godmother.

"He was just a baby when his mom picked up and moved to Arizona with him. She wasn't the best mother; always battling addiction and acquiring crappy boyfriends. She didn't have any family left in Hutton and she and Ruby had lost touch by the time she died when Shane was fourteen. There was no one else willing to be his guardian so the state sent him into the foster care system. That's where he met Jay, at the last foster home he was sent to."

Lana pauses and her expression falls.

"It wasn't a good situation. The guy was violent, abusive. He and his wife were major drug users so there were all kinds of garbage people hanging around the house. One night when Shane is getting beaten to the point where it doesn't look like it's going to stop, Jay steps in and fights back. Jay's a good fighter. He nearly kills the guy but the wife makes up some bullshit story and both Jay and Shane wind up getting carted off to a juvenile detention center. Their only stroke of luck was being placed in the same room together. They looked out for each other. They've been on their own together since they were seventeen."

"Oh," I say, hugging the pillow to my chest and wondering how bleak life must have seemed to those boys when they had no family, no resources, no one to give a damn what happened to them.

I can sort of forgive Jay Phoenix for glaring at me. If the guy possesses some character quirks, they might be thanks to a terrible childhood.

Lana chews her lips for a moment before continuing. "Anyway, Shane thinks of Jay as a brother so I'm reserving judgment. I think he'll be fine after he gets more comfortable. Shane would love for him to stay in Hutton but admits that's a long shot so he'll just be around for the summer. We can all find a way to get along."

"Sure we can. I promise to continue inflicting my sparkling personality on him whether he appreciates it or not."

She gives my hand a grateful squeeze before rising from the bed and checking her hair in the mirrored closet door.

Shane is now calling her name from Ruby's kitchen. I still think of the house as Ruby's. Shane hasn't altered a thing about the outdated décor yet even though Lana's been urging him to make some changes. It's no insult to Ruby's memory. Obviously she wanted him to have her house.

Lana is laughing while Shane sings 'Here Comes The Sun' and then a door shuts, plunging the house into instant silence. I watch two hours of dogs getting into all kinds of hysterical pickles in their immaculate suburban neighborhood. The longer the show goes on the dumber it gets. I can't believe important people sat around a conference table and decided *this* was something the world needed to see.

I shut my laptop and consider how nice it would be to have a talking pet of my own. I've never had a pet at all. Perhaps Shane and Lana wouldn't mind if I adopted a cat. A cat won't judge me for sitting at home on Friday night in my cow pajamas. A cat would just be happy to see me.

I peer into the pink tumbler I keep on the table beside my bed. It's empty. I want a snack.

Lana and I have our own kitchen, although it's less equipped than a real kitchen. In a little alcove that probably was once a cozy reading corner we have a small fridge and a short counter that lifts up to reveal a small sink and electric stovetop.

I'm considering the options my limited food inventory has to offer when I notice that the door separating the two living spaces has been left partially open. Keeping it closed was always standard practice out of respect for Ruby's privacy but Lana has gotten into the habit of leaving it open now that she drifts between her room and Shane's.

It dawns on me that I'm not alone in the house, which is something I've kind of forgotten over the last few hours. I don't hear anything but it's barely ten p.m. Jay might be awake. He might be right there on the other side of this door, scowling on the sofa.

I feel sneaky as I creep over to the door and peek into Ruby's living room. The lights have all been left on, however there's nothing to see but furniture and orange table lamps. I pull my head back in, somewhat relieved that I'm not going to be required to interact with a strange guy while clad in baggy cow pajamas.

Nudging the door closed, I think of the details Lana shared about Jay's history. Obviously there were not instant sparks between us but I'll gladly be his friend. I must have imagined the disdain in his eyes. To my knowledge, Shane thinks I'm all right, so why would Jay immediately dislike me?

He wouldn't. Or at least, he shouldn't.

I have every reason to believe that tomorrow we'll be on friendly terms.

And yet I know we won't be.

A tiny puzzling storm stirs deep in the recesses of my mind.

It has nothing to do with Jay. Of course it doesn't.

I'm exhausted after a long week of final exams. I'm worried about my mother. I'm stressed about earning a paycheck now that Beefcake Charlie's is closed.

And I've still got talking dogs on the brain. I'm not thinking clearly right now.

Instead of snacking on junk food, I fill my tumbler with ice water and head to the bathroom to get ready for bed. After I spit toothpaste into the sink I stare at my wide-eyed reflection in the vanity mirror. I look no different than I did in high school. I wish I could at least get rid of these glasses but my allergies won't cooperate with contact lenses and the idea of getting my vision surgically corrected makes me want to cry.

I should be ready to pass out but I feel like I'll be staring at the ceiling of my bedroom for hours. Lana's bottle of herbal melatonin is waving at me on the shelf. I shake three tablets into my palm and wash them down with a gulp of water.

Fifteen minutes later I am indeed staring at the ceiling but a pleasant fuzziness is beginning to eat the edges of my mind. This is why I would never use real pills and why I rarely drink more than two beers. I'm a lightweight, ready to go unconscious from three melatonin. I'm thinking of this afternoon, of lying on the quad while scratchy blades of grass tickle their way beneath my shirt. Something about that scene conjures the past. My eyes close and pictures appear; still shots of things that have long been shoved into a back door in my mind.

Blistering summer days and dry dust. The delicate stems of yellow wildflowers. Their centers are brown, a soft brown the same shade of permanently tousled hair belonging to a boy. The boy has a habit of sifting fingers through his hair so often I doubt he realizes he's doing it. He smiles when I bump his shoulder and laugh at him because we're friends and friends can laugh at each other's messy hair and friends can share butter pecan ice cream cones and friends can help nurse bruises after a beating and friends can keep each other's secrets safe.

He can't do that thing with his hair anymore because it's too short now and when I understand this I bolt upright with a silent scream that nearly shakes my soul loose.

A desperate gasp greets the darkness and it has a meaning.

"JOHNNY!"

Somehow it's fitting that right now the room is so dark I can see nothing in front of my face.

It serves me right.

Because earlier, out there on the bright patio with all the sunshine in the world to help me see I'd been blind, so blind, *so utterly fucking blind*.

And now I'm going to suffer for it.

JONATHAN, AGE 13

There's something like nine thousand people in Arcana and I don't know them all but I know all the kids my age. There's only one elementary school, one middle school, and one high school so there's not much chance that I'd run into a kid I don't recognize.

But this girl I've never seen before.

I'm walking out of Ice Dream with a cone in my hand when I spot her over by the bicycle racks that no one ever uses.

Her hair is kind of blondish and tied back in a messy ponytail. The ugly black glasses she wears are too large for her face and even I can tell that her kitten-patterned t-shirt and frayed cutoffs wouldn't impress the cool girls. But underneath all that she's sort of cute.

"Piece of shit," she mutters to an old bicycle with a flat tire and a sagging chain. She gives the frame a small kick for emphasis. She's got a temper. She's interesting.

And yet I was planning to walk right past her without saying a word. It's not my thing to approach some strange girl and start talking. But when my shadow falls she looks up and sees that I'm staring at her.

"Hey there," she says. "Do you know how to fix a bike?"

"Sometimes," I admit. "But I don't carry around an air pump in my back pocket so I can't do anything about your tire."

She wrinkles her nose. "You think anyone will steal it if I just leave it right here for now?"

"Not unless the junk collector stops by."

She laughs. I'm not used to making girls laugh. Usually their laughter is awarded to fuck ups and football kings. Guys at the top of the food chain. Guys like Rafe. My brother could collect enough for his own cheerleading squad just by picking the girls who are always trailing after him and giggling. Maybe they wouldn't be so quick to follow him everywhere if they knew his dangerous act isn't an act.

Or maybe they would.

"What's your name?" the girl says. "I'm Caris."

"Jonathan."

"And you live here?"

"On the sidewalk? No."

Caris finds that funny. She flashes a wide grin that shows off a small gap between her two front teeth.

"I've lived in Arcana all my life," I explain. "Did you just move to town?"

She shakes her head. "No, I'm just staying with my aunt for the rest of the summer. She doesn't believe in the internet or even television so her house is boring as hell."

The news is a slight relief. She's not from Arcana. She won't care about who my family is. My last name would mean nothing to her.

Caris cocks her head and looks me over.

"How old are you?" she asks.

"Thirteen."

She nods and I wonder if she's thinking that I look younger than thirteen. I do. I know that. She's slightly taller than me and it's impossible to guess her age. She's not as filled out as some of the other girls in my class but that means nothing. I'm glad she's wearing a kitten t-shirt and has uncombed hair. The girls who layer makeup on their faces and show off their chests in tight shirts make me nervous.

"Guess what, Jonathan?" she asks and I like how she says my name as if we're already friends and she's sharing a secret.

"What?"

"We're the same age. Today is my birthday."

"No shit? Happy Birthday."

"Thanks. My aunt gave me five bucks and told me to come down here and find something to do. I think she just wanted me out of the house for a while because her sleazy boyfriend is coming over. God, he's so gross. I don't think he showers. Like, ever. What's there to do around here for five bucks?"

She talks fast and I need a few seconds to process her jumble of words.

I hold up my cone, which has now begun to drip down the sides. "You could get some ice cream. Or else you could buy some nails at the hardware store. That's about it."

"I'll choose ice cream." She grabs my elbow. "Come with me, okay?"

I'm already being pulled down the sidewalk. I don't mind at all. "Sure."

Caris orders a butter pecan double scoop waffle cone. Once it's in her hand she immediately begins devouring it with impressive speed. There are only five tables in Ice Dream and they're all taken so we go outside and finish our cones while leaning against the side of the building in the shade.

She talks up a storm in between bites of ice cream. She's from Dallas. She'll be starting eighth grade in the fall, same as me. She likes school and loves animals, although she's never been allowed to keep a pet. Her father gave her a phone for her birthday and she removes it from her back pocket to show it to me. It's one of those new iPhones and it's covered with a sparkly purple case. I feel a stab of envy because I'll never have the money for one of those. Rafe doesn't even have one and he's in high school.

I've tossed the remains of my ice cream cone in the trash because it's mostly melted and I don't feel like dealing with it anymore but

Caris consumes every bit of hers and then wipes her sticky fingers on her denim shorts.

She gets real quiet when I ask her why she's not spending the summer in Dallas with her parents. Arcana isn't a place people visit just for fun. There's nothing here to see except the meteor crater with its dismal little science museum. If not for oil and the high school's state football record, it's likely nobody would have heard of Arcana. Unless they're interested in old murder stories. But I'm not going to bring that up to Caris. I'm not at all proud of where I come from but the people around here make sure I don't forget about it.

Caris fiddles with a frayed piece of string that hangs from her cutoff shorts. She swallows hard and keeps looking down.

"Three months ago my mom had a baby girl and she died."

That's a lot more horrible than anything I might have imagined she'd say. I feel my mouth fall open.

Caris takes a deep breath. "She was born way too early and was stillborn. My mom has always had problems but after that she really lost it. She slept for days at a time. She broke all the mirrors. And she kept trying to hurt herself. She had to go stay in a hospital and my dad is busy with work so he decided to send me here to stay with my Aunt Vay for the rest of the summer."

"I'm sorry." I don't know why people say that when a person tells them about something awful. It's the right thing to say if you accidentally step on someone's foot. It sounds stupid right now. I reach out and touch Caris's shoulder, giving her a little pat like you might give a dog. That seems worse than mumbling dumbass 'I'm sorry' words all over the place. I yank my hand back and stuff it in my pocket. Maybe she never noticed.

But Caris raises her head and gives me a slight smile. Her eyes are watery and she briefly removes her glasses to wipe at her eyes with the heel of her palm.

"Thanks, Johnny. Can I call you Johnny?"

Nobody calls me Johnny. I hate that nickname. Usually. "Yeah, that's fine."

"I don't want to go back to my aunt's house for a while. Can you hang out some more or do you need to go?"

The way she looks at me is funny, like she's nervous about how I'll answer because she's not sure I will want to hang out with her. I've got a few friends but none of them are girls. Then again, I can't remember meeting any other girls like Caris.

"I can hang out all afternoon," I say and don't add that I could probably hang out all night too and into tomorrow and possibly the next day before anyone in my house would notice. My mom is off with her new boyfriend most of the time and only comes home to get clothes and give me a few bucks for food. It's a safe bet that my older brother Rafe is currently raising hell somewhere because that's what Rafe does.

Caris claps her hands together like I've just delivered the best news ever. She's actually really pretty.

"Great! Let's go somewhere."

If I lived in a nice house, or any house, I'd invite her there. Ever since the bank took our house three years ago my mom's been renting a place in the trailer park. I don't want to show it to Caris, especially because there's no guarantee that Rafe's not lurking around somewhere.

"Have you seen the meteor crater yet?" I ask because I suspect that it's the kind of thing that would appeal to her. There aren't a ton of options in Arcana. The nearest decent mall is twenty miles and three bus changes away. Maybe we can do that next time if we hang out again. I hope we do.

Caris is all over the meteor crater idea. She's got a few dollars left and buys two bottled waters from the gas station. She won't accept any money for mine when I try to pay her back, which makes me feel kind of weird, like she's taking me out to dinner or something.

The walk to the crater will take less than half an hour if we cut through a couple of fields instead of sticking to the road but I choose a roundabout path because there's one spot in Arcana that's worse than any other spot. The location is marked by large bronze memorial plaque. My mom once told me that the families of Richard and Nancy

Chapel took up a collection to pay for it. She told me that fact with some bitterness. She couldn't understand why anyone would want to mark the site of a gruesome murder that happened decades ago. I'm not sure I understand it either. We'd probably feel differently if our connection was to the victims. She said my father never went there, not once in all the years he spent growing up in Arcana. Rafe told me high school kids go there sometimes to drink and screw around and hold these weird little rituals where they try to contact the dead. *'Nancy, are you there? Are you in pain or are you at peace? Is Richard with you?'* Rafe goes there too but not because he's trying to contact ghosts. He bragged that he's fucked ten girls right on that spot, the spot where Nancy Chapel was found, and the thought makes me physically sick but I couldn't tell him that or he'd keep talking. He'd pin me down and force me to hear all the details that I never wanted to know.

As for me, I won't go there.

Not ever.

"Hey, Johnny." Caris nudges me when we're walking through a field of wild asters. "Who did that to your face?"

I touch my fingertips to the sore spot beneath my left eye. It's not really swollen anymore so I'd kind of forgotten about it but she must be able to see the bruise. "Eh, I was in a fight, that's all."

She's interested. "Did you win?"

No. I always lost when I fought Rafe. I never start the fights.

"I got in a few good punches," I tell her and she looks impressed so I feel like less of a loser. My teachers never ask why I often show up at school with bruises. I don't think they care. Every now and then my mother will take notice and scream about kicking Rafe out but she never does. When she accuses him of growing up to be just like the worst of the Hempstead men he just laughs at her.

Being a Hempstead doesn't bother Rafe. At least not anymore. When he was younger he used to have a hard time because the kids at school would say shit about our father and our grandfather. But he got older and bigger and people are afraid to make him angry now. On the football field he's a monster and around here Friday night games are everything. The annual hunger for a state title means all his other flaws get overlooked but in Rafe's case no one's doing him any favors by refusing to rein him in. Someday he'll go too far. I hope I'm not around when he does.

There was a time when the name Hempstead meant something different but you'd have to reach back about a hundred years to find it. I'm told my family used to own half the land in town. I wonder what that was like.

Caris is fascinated with the meteor crater. Thanks to all the rain this past spring, there's a lot of green ground cover at the moment and it makes the view a lot prettier. It's too bad the museum is closed today because Mrs. Turlington is always at the front desk and on summer days she lets me in for free. She used to be on the cheerleading squad with my mother in high school. That's the kind of town Arcana is.

I have the crater's dimensions memorized and I rattle them off to sound smart. Caris mentioned she was good in school. I'm not but I don't want her to know that.

"This is really cool," she says. "Do you come here a lot?"

"Yeah. It's nice at night. Really quiet. When you look up you can see more stars than you can see in town."

"Which one is your favorite?"

"Which what?"

"Star."

I never really think about what the stars are called. I just like looking at them and thinking about how there are far away places than no one down here knows a thing about. I mumble some dumb answer and Caris asks a question about the crater.

"There are much bigger ones," I tell her. "There's a huge one in Arizona."

She's snapping dozens of pictures with her phone. "Have you been there?"

"Nope, never been out of Texas."

"Me either. My dad is from New York and he has to go there for business once a month but my mom hates to travel."

She abruptly pivots and snaps a photo of me. Then she squints at her phone and giggles. "You didn't smile, Johnny."

"You didn't warn me you were taking a picture."

"Well, now I'm warning you." Caris stands right next to me, shoulder touching shoulder, and she holds her phone up to take a picture of the two of us together with the crater in the background. She lowers the phone and turns it around so I can see. Fuck. I look gross. At least it's a cute picture of her.

She notices the time and lets out a groan.

"Crap. I didn't realize it was after four. My aunt told me to be home by five. Do you know the best way to get to Dunstan Street from here?"

"It's easiest if we double back the way we came. It's only a few blocks from the town square but you probably knew that part."

She nods and starts walking beside me. "Is that close to where you live?"

Nope. Dunstan Street is where the old, pretty houses are. The people who have at least a little bit of money live on streets like Dunstan. I live in a trailer park halfway across town and out of sight.

"It's not too far from where I live," I say and hope she doesn't ask for details.

On the walk back to town Caris exclaims suddenly, "Oh look, a butterfly!"

I look up in time to see vivid orange wings with splashes of black and white.

"It's a Monarch," Caris tells me.

"A what?"

"A Monarch butterfly. It's the Texas state butterfly."

I don't care much about butterflies but I think it's cool that she knows them by name. She makes me wish I was better in school so I'd know about more things than just the meteor crater and the quickest Arcana shortcuts.

When we get to the town square, Caris assures me that she knows the way from here. She retrieves her broken bicycle and I offer to wheel it over to Dunstan Street for her but she grabs the handlebars and says she can deal with it.

We're kind of awkwardly facing off in front of a monument dedicated to all the Arcana boys who died in wars in the last century. The names of dead soldiers are all inscribed at the base of a galloping horse statue. No one has ever been able to explain the meaning of the horse to me. I don't think people were riding horses in World War 2.

"So, um…" Caris says and for the first time she seems kind of shy. She holds onto the broken bike with one hand and tucks her hair behind her ears with the other.

It's weird how I don't want to say goodbye to her. Being around Caris makes me feel like talking a lot more than I usually talk. That's probably why I decide to be brave enough to ask her the next question.

"You want to hang out again tomorrow?"

She lights up and a warm glow spreads inside my chest. She asks me where I want to meet and when.

On the walk home I'm actually smiling even though there's nothing worth smiling about at home.

This is the best day I've had in a long time.

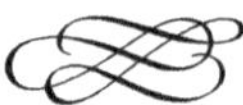

Shane was hung over first thing in the morning but after a few cups of coffee he was conscious enough to head over to the bakery with me. There's a ton of work to do. And, more importantly, I needed to get the hell out of the house before I come face to face with Caris again.

Ruby's Bakery is located in a small strip mall that fronts one of the main arteries crisscrossing through Hutton. The university athletic fields are in sight and the location is promising but the crumbling brick facilities should have been renovated years ago. Beside the CLOSED sign on the door there's a note prettily written in calligraphy explaining that due to the death of beloved owner Ruby Wagner the bakery is currently closed. Shane told me Caris had written the note.

Once inside, Shane begins explaining things. He's already tried to put in an effort but he doesn't have a clue what he's doing. One of the part time employees has already found other work. The other one is an eighty-year-old woman named Delia and she's worked here since Ruby opened the doors nearly thirty years earlier. She remembers Shane's mother and she's eager to help him resurrect the bakery. Ruby had entrusted her with all the recipes and Delia's been teaching Shane how to bake mass quantities of cookies and sweet rolls.

The first thing I do is to test all the equipment. Machinery is something I'm comfortable with even if I'm unsure what everything here is used for. When I point out that one of the tabletop mixers isn't working, Shane just nods.

Shane is good at reading my moods but I can mask them when I choose to. He has no idea that I tossed and turned all night atop the blue quilt in the guest room and thought about someone I assumed I'd never be required to think about again.

Meanwhile, Caris was in her own room a couple of walls away, probably blissfully dreaming with no clue who she was living with.

This is really fucked up.

Like needle in a haystack, Twilight Zone kind of fucked up.

If anyone other than Shane was counting on me I would have packed up and been halfway back to Arizona before daylight.

But Shane *is* counting on me so I can't go anywhere, at least not until he's got a handle on running the place. I'm sure there are bills that still need to be paid even if no business is coming through the door so right now the bakery is just bleeding money. Shane had been hoping to get the doors reopened next week but after a long morning I don't believe that's realistic. There's got to be health inspectors and other bureaucratic shit to deal with. I need to figure that out. When I tried to search for 'How To Run A Bakery' online there wasn't a whole lot of useful information that came up.

"What do you think?" Shane asks when we break for lunch at a Mexican food truck parked down the block.

I squirt hot sauce into my plate at the condiment table and grab some napkins. There's no place to sit so we end up propped against a flat wall halfway in the shade. It's hot out and kind of muggy but a cloudy haze covers the sun and that makes sitting outside bearable.

"We've got our work cut out for us," I tell him in all honesty before taking a big bite of my food.

"I know," he says but sounds rather cheerful about the prospect.

When I've swallowed and can talk again I ask him an important question. "You sure this is what you want? I don't know how much you could get if you sell but it would be something."

He's just shoved two street tacos into his mouth and he looks thoughtful as he chews.

"Eh, the thought is tempting at times but any money I'd get wouldn't last long."

"It would last longer if you were smart about where you put it."

Shit, listen to me. I sound like a fucking parent.

Shane is shaking his head. "I'd have nothing to show for it once the money ran out. And I owe it to Ruby to give this my best shot. Besides, there's something about being back in the place where I was born, even if I don't remember it. I feel like I'm coming full circle somehow, like the shitty years in between can be erased. By the way, Lana was asking some questions about you. She was wondering if you were mad about something last night."

"I hope you explained to her that I'm always this delightful."

"I did. That won't stop her from trying to get you to break out of your shell."

"Then it's up to you to keep her occupied enough that she doesn't have time to worry about me or my shell."

Shane issues a grunt of laughter. I ought to tell him about my link to Caris.

"Hey, you know that Caris girl? Yeah, my family has kind of a habit of killing her family."

I guess I'm hoping Caris suffers from some form of amnesia that carved that particular summer from her mind. Even if there's no amnesia involved, she might not wish to revisit an ugly chapter of her life. She'd likely prefer that I really am a stranger, just some random guy named Jay Phoenix who keeps his head down and isn't much fun.

Plenty of people insist that a name can't define you but that's a crock of shit. A prince born into royalty inherits the thickest natural armor imaginable. A name can give you power. A name can be a brand of disgrace. Or a name can provide the anonymity that you've always wished for, even if you remain the same person beneath the hardened numb layers visible to the rest of the world.

Shane keeps talking while my mind wanders. He's going on and on about his girlfriend again. Lana has him taking multivitamins and thinking about the future. Like how maybe he'll try to take the high school equivalency exam again. And now that he's a homeowner he wants to learn how to mow the half dead lawn and fix the kitchen sink in case it breaks. Lana has three semesters of school left and she hadn't been sure she wanted to stay in Texas after graduation but now that she's met Shane she's talking about getting a job here in Hutton. Sounds like a fast pace for a one month old relationship but what the hell do I know?

"Lana's amazing," I assure him. I know that's what he wants to hear and anyway, what's not to like about Lana? She's friendly and beautiful and says 'I love you' to my best friend.

In the afternoon Delia drops by because she knew we'd be here today. She's tiny and dressed in purple from head to toe. She doesn't look like she's eighty years old. She's a quick worker and good at explaining things. After two hours with Delia I'm feeling more confident already.

On the way home Shane tells me it'll just be the two of us tonight. Lana made plans to hang out with friends to celebrate the end of the semester before everyone scatters for the summer and she's dragging Caris along with her.

Shane doesn't mention anything else about me hooking up with Caris, like he can sense that I'm not interested. Which I'm not. That would be some Shakespearean level shit.

To my relief, the girls are gone already when we get to the house. Maybe things can be this way all summer; coming and going at different times and any contact with Caris will be somewhere between minimal and nonexistent. She has her own apartment behind a closed door. She can stay over there. I can stay over here.

Shane reheats a couple of the cold steaks from last night and then asks me to help him hang the dartboard he wants to install on the patio. We kill a few hours playing darts and Shane keeps jumping in the pool at odd intervals. Once he stays underwater for so long that I hunker down at the side, about to jump in after him, when he pops up and spits a fountain of water that hits me in the chest.

"Asshole." I make an obscene gesture and return to the patio.

He laughs and flicks his wet hair out of his eyes. "What's the matter, you forget how to swim, buddy?"

I fire a dart from ten feet away and hit the bull's-eye. "I never did like to swim."

Shane hops out of the water and drips puddles all over the patio. There are no towels around so he wanders into the house to dry off. When he returns he's got a red and white striped beach towel draped over his shoulders, a bottle of Jack D and shot glasses balanced on his fingers.

I'm aware that a guy who's been in and out of rehab shouldn't be drinking. Shane's aware of that too. But this morning's hangover and the fact that he's now pouring whiskey into shot glasses point to the probability that his memory has faltered.

He takes note of my raised eyebrows and shrugs. "Just a couple of shots, Jay. We're still celebrating your arrival. Come on, you know a few drinks don't send me reeling."

I do know that. Alcohol isn't Shane's primary weakness.

The glasses bear the Hutton State University logo. They probably belong to Lana, or maybe to Caris.

"One shot," I agree, raising a glass and pouring liquid fire down my throat at the same time Shane swallows his. I don't want to be drunk. I just want all the Caris thoughts and memories to vacate my brain. That requires at least two more shots, which Shane pours gladly.

My next few rounds of darts aren't nearly as successful. Now I'm buzzed enough to strip down to my boxers and fall into the pool. When I'm submerged I understand the appeal of staying under as long as you can stand it. A hypnotic quiet envelopes me when I take a seat on the floor of the pool and stare up at the blurred patio lights beyond the surface, which looks to be a lot farther away than it really is.

"Why are you trying to make me hate you?"

"Because you should."

Urgent pressure builds in my chest.

I remember the look on her face. Anger and hurt and a touch of fear. I remember breathing tobacco into my lungs and exhaling a cloud of smoke. The sensation in my chest was different than this, the burden more oppressive. I should have felt sorrow over the tears in her eyes because they were my fault. That's when I knew there was something wrong with me. I have the Hempstead blood. There's always been a monster inside, waiting to claw its way out. There always will be.

I push off the concrete floor with my palms and rocket to the surface. I take a few seconds to gulp the humid night air before noticing that I have some company in the form of a killer pair of legs. And black heels. I'm a sucker for heels. Especially at the end of a short skirt. Taking all those shots has relaxed more than my brain. My dick vibrates to life and if I look at those legs and those heels for a few more seconds I'll be picturing them propped up on my shoulders.

"Thought you were going for a world record," Shane hoots from the patio. He's holding Lana with one arm. The other one is pouring more shots.

"Hey there, Jay," Lana calls. She giggles when her boyfriend nuzzles her neck.

Now I can see that Caris is the owner of the legs and the heels. The toes of her shoes are pointed right at the edge of the pool and she's staring down at me. The light pink dress she's wearing is short and spaghetti strapped and has a soft, velvety look about it. Her glasses are missing and she wears makeup.

"Hi," she says with a shy smile.

Fucking hell.

She's a seductive angel. She could be my nightmare if I let her.

"Care, come take a shot," Lana begs before clinking glasses with her boyfriend.

"No, I've had enough for tonight," says Caris. Her focus remains on me. There's knowledge in her eyes that wasn't there yesterday.

Lana calls out to me next. "What about you, Jay?"

"I'm good." I'd be a whole lot better if Caris would take her legs and her heels and her sympathetic expression somewhere else.

Lana and Shane are sloppy about knocking back their shots. Shane grabs Lana's glass away and then gives her a hungry, sexually charged kiss with both hands twisting in her black hair. She breaks the kiss and murmurs something to him, taking his hand in hers and kissing the knuckles. Shane promptly throws his towel on the ground and starts leading her into the house.

"Goodnight, kids." He waves and takes a few steps back to grab the whiskey bottle. "We'll try not to shake the walls too much."

Their laughter echoes as they disappear into the house together. An awkward handful of seconds ensues. Caris hasn't budged from the edge of the pool and I'm still standing there in the water.

"You look like you want to say something," she says.

I force myself to sound casual. "Shane shouldn't drink so much."

She tugs on the ends of her hair. She's nervous. "I didn't sleep last night."

"That sucks."

A tiny frown wrinkles the space between her eyes. "Can we talk without you running away again?"

I dislike the way we're positioned. Standing down here in the water while she stares at me from up there makes me feel like her goddamn royal subject or something.

I make my way to the edge of the pool and hop up to sit on the concrete with my back to her. I hear her heels clicking in the other direction and a second later Shane's towel lands on my head. When I finish drying off my face and shoulders I see that she's removed her shoes and she sits beside me. Closer than I'd like her to sit. She drops her bare feet into the pool. If I edge away a few inches it would get my point across but why the hell should I be the one to move? She opens up a purse in the shape of a water canteen and withdraws her glasses. She looks more like herself again when they're back on her face. A completely grown up, extremely sexy version of herself.

"So what do you want?" I ask her, aware that I'm being a prick.

She looks me over carefully, sadly. "I didn't recognize you at first."

I toss the towel behind me and pretend I don't hear her.

"The name threw me off," she explains. She reaches out to touch my bare shoulder. I jerk away before she can get there. Her fingers recoil and curl up. Her hand falls into her lap. "God, you look so different."

My head's too fucked up to have this conversation right now. If she were any other pretty girl dangling her legs in the pool and watching me with big, sad eyes I'd be thinking about fucking her. I *am* thinking about fucking her. My dick agrees with my head that this is a good idea. If I play this a certain way I'm sure I could have that pink dress on the ground and her mouth on my cock within an hour.

"Talk to me," she pleads. "I know you remember me, Johnny."

Hearing her say my name is two things at once.

It's a hard kick in the gut and it's sweet music.

It's a wish and it's a punishment.

No. No. NO!

She can't have a fucking place in my life.

"Shit." I force out some fake laughter. "Did we hook up a while back or something? Sorry honey, I wish I did remember you but you've got a lot of competition."

Caris stiffens and her cheeks grow red. I've surprised her. She figured we'd have a sweet moment of reunion with all kinds of emotional hugs and tears and soulful dialogue. She's probably been fantasizing that we'd kiss under the moonlight and end up making sweet love between the sheets. How poetic.

Caris and Johnny: Two childhood friends who become lovers.

But that's not what we are. That's not what we are at all.

"Stop it," she commands.

I don't stop. I dig the knife in with a shrug.

"You gonna make a scene or something? You know how it is. Sometimes you just want to scratch an itch and you don't care whose pussy you're playing with."

She shakes her head. "You're being a real son of a bitch right now."

I laugh at her. "I won't be bragging to anyone if that's what you're afraid of."

Her arms cross over her chest. She looks even sexier when she's angry. "What is this? What kind of fucking game are you trying to play?"

"There's no game." I stand up and stretch. My wet boxers stick to my skin and my dick is still hard. I want her to notice that it's hard. And that I'm walking away from her anyway.

"Look, uh, *Caris*, right?" I shine a cold grin down on her. "I'm only sticking around here to help out a friend. I don't know you. And I don't want to. Because even though you're kind of cute you seem like a lot of crazy trouble."

"Jonathan." She spits out my name, as if that will make all the difference in the world.

I ignore the effect it has on me. "Look on the bright side. I'm sure you'll have no trouble finding another dick to keep you company if you go out dressed like that all the time."

I grab my clothes from where I'd dropped them on a patio chair and head into the house without looking back. When I hear her choke out the word "Motherfucker", I smile to myself although I don't feel remotely happy.

*I*f Asshole were an academic category he would get an A+++ without studying.

He would be the almighty valedictorian.

The goddamn gold medal champion.

After he cackles his vulgar insults and leaves me sitting beside the pool alone, I refuse to give him the satisfaction of staying out there all by myself and nursing the sting of humiliation.

I retreat to my bedroom, pace back and forth while reliving every crushing second of that pool encounter, and then try to calm down in a lavender scented bubble bath. If it weren't for the fact that I've hardly slept for the last two nights I wouldn't be able to sleep now.

However, I'm exhausted. Too exhausted to dwell on Jonathan Hempstead for another moment. I fall asleep on top of my covers.

My dreams become an odd collage.

Johnny is there. Not the cold-eyed muscled jerk who smirked beside the pool and showed off the fact that cruelty made his dick hard. The Johnny who used to be my friend. We are back in Arcana, in the soft twilight of a summer evening. He holds my hand and shyly recites facts about the meteor crater on the edge of town. We are staring down into the wide chasm when I am abruptly shoved, hard and without warning. I fall into the rocky hole and cry for help but there's no one but Johnny to hear me and Johnny doesn't care. Johnny's the one who pushed me.

The landscape shifts and I'm in front of a small white coffin, small enough to hold an infant. The coffin shakes as if the occupant is alive even though that's impossible. The lid opens and my mother slaps me across the face, screaming 'WHY ARE YOU HERE?'

And then I'm lying in a field. Another summer is coming and I'm sad that I won't be here to see it. I can't understand all the terrible things that have happened to me but I know that they are final and I know that I am lost. I know that I am *her*. I am Nancy...

When I awaken my skin is clammy and my heart pounds. It's barely six a.m. and I feel vaguely sick. The troubling images that ran amok behind my closed eyes refuse to fade. And last night's conversation with Johnny/Jay echoes in my ears while I brush my teeth. I don't believe for a red hot second that he doesn't remember me. His anger is confusing. We didn't part on good terms but that was almost nine years ago for fuck's sake. We were both hurting. We said rotten things. We were kids.

Why would he be so angry after all this time? If he's still furious that I told the police about Rafe then he shouldn't be. He couldn't have expected me to lie to protect his brother. Not after what his brother did.

Anxiety has made me jittery. I decide the best solution is to go for a run. I started running in high school but never competitively. I ran to get out of the house, away from the burden of my mother's perpetual sorrow and my father's concern. I ran because it felt good to have to work so hard that all feelings of confusion were chased from my mind. It's an activity I've largely abandoned in college. Between school and work and frivolous social action, my time tends to fill up quickly.

After digging my running shoes out of the back of my closet, changing to workout clothes and tying my hair back, I'm already feeling better. There's not a sound in the apartment. Lana has to be over on the other side, sleeping peacefully in Shane's bed. As for the house's fourth inhabitant, I have no idea what Johnny is up to.

Not Johnny. Jay.

Over the years I wondered about him. Not very often. Thoughts of him were painful. I might have typed his name into search engines a few times. There's no telling when he ditched his real name to invent this Jay Phoenix identity. And after the way he talked to me last night, I'm sure there's no point in asking.

My keychain has a small canister of pepper spray attached and I keep it in my hand as I jog through the residential streets of Hutton. There are few people around this early on a Sunday. I veer towards the university and then regret it. Jogging through the deserted campus is downright eerie. I'm running the path that surrounds the quad when I notice there's a lone man standing directly opposite. He's young, probably about my age, and he has stopped, perhaps to catch his breath. The front of his yellow Hutton Coyotes t-shirt is damp with sweat. He notices me and is pleased, raising a hand in greeting. He'll probably start up a conversation if I come any closer.

I do not wave back. I turn around and run the other way, pumping my legs as hard as possible. Once I glance over my shoulder to ensure I'm not being followed. In all likelihood the guy in the yellow t-shirt means no harm. He's probably just some college guy who'd be happy to meet a new girl.

Yet I was raised to understand something.

There are terrible people in the world.

Usually they don't look like monsters. Sometimes they even look like someone you know. Remaining on guard and running away from strangers with your tiny pepper spray weapon clutched in your fist is a necessity.

It's because of that last dream. That one in the field. I've had that dream before, though not in years. I don't think it's a coincidence that this particular dream has resurfaced just when Jonathan Hempstead does. Little does he know he has the power to summon ghosts, at least the ones that just live in my head.

My hard breathing sounds as loud as a roar in my ears. I'm not in awesome physical shape. I've pushed myself too far. My chest shrieks and my legs are melted rubber by the time I return to my street. Gasping for breath, I stagger to the front lawn and drop down on the cool grass, which is still damp because it's so early. I could have lurched the last few steps to the door but it feels good to sit here in the damp grass in the soft morning sunlight. I run my fingers over the soft green carpet and gradually my heart rate slows to a more normal pace.

My cotton shirt has become a sweaty mess and it feels unpleasant on my skin. I don't think twice about pulling it over my head. It's not like I'm conducting a striptease. I'm wearing a sports bra underneath and no one is watching me anyway. Pulling the shirt taut between both hands I raise my arms and stretch, bending my torso all the way to the right. The muscle extension feels amazing. A borderline pornographic 'ahhh' escapes my lips. Ever so slowly I bend in the opposite direction and this feels equally fantastic. Perhaps I ought to enroll in a yoga class. This is so much better than running.

Then I swivel my neck and receive a shock. Jonathan Hempstead is staring at me.

The hood of his truck is raised and streaks of grease now paint his powerful forearms. He's not wearing a shirt and although I got an eyeful of his chest last night when he shot out of the pool, it's no less impressive today. Those abs are unbelievable. They should be sculpted into marble. They should be worshipped.

He must have been out here messing with the innards of his truck when I huffed and puffed my way to the front yard. He hadn't made a sound and I didn't notice him because I was busy trying not to pass out.

I certainly notice him now.

And I notice something else.

Even from twenty feet away the look on his face is plain. It's not boredom or defiance or scorn. None of the things he's shown me since his arrival. It's something far more startling.

It's hunger. It's lust.

And it's a thunderbolt straight to my core.

The telltale pull in my belly spreads lower and heat rises in my cheeks. I can't stop my body's reaction. And I'll never admit to it either.

The time we spend with our eyes locked probably doesn't last more than three seconds but it is packed with warring emotions. There's something disturbing about those suspended seconds, something disturbing about the way we stare at each other.

He turns away sharply and bends down under the pretense of examining some mystery beneath the hood. This is the first time I take a really good look at his back. It's broad-shouldered and perfect. There's a tattoo behind his right shoulder. A black bird spreading its wings. I want to ask him if it's the bird of mythology that rises from the ashes. The Phoenix. Like the name he chose. Like the city he lives in. It's a symbol of hope and defiance.

What's happened to you, Johnny?

But this man, Jay, is not willing to answer any questions I might ask. He's made that clear. He prefers to be despised.

Feeling awkward, I climb slowly to my feet and I'm about to leave him alone to toy with his engine parts. He's got a wrench in his hand and his arm moves back and forth, twisting something under the hood with more force than required.

I'm halfway to the side door that leads to my apartment when I stop in my tracks. This is absurd. He's going to be here all summer and he'll have to deal with me at some point. Last night I tried being nice and that was a waste of time. I'm no longer in the mood to be nice.

"Oh, Johnny," I call in a singsong, taunting him with every syllable. He freezes, wrench in mid twist.

A smile spreads across my face.

"I was just wondering how often you visit Arcana," I say with false sugar sweetness. "Your family is so well known in town. I'm sure everyone would be excited for the return of the Hempsteads. You could pay a visit with Rafe, if he's not in prison. Imagine that. The two Hempstead brothers. You would stop traffic."

I wait for him to show emotion. To get angry. To order me to go straight to hell. He does nothing of the kind. Instead he bends down and places his wrench in a grey metal toolbox that sits on the curb. He selects a different tool and calmly returns to his task under the hood without even turning his head to acknowledge that I've spoken. He wants me to feel invisible.

"Weirdo," I mutter under my breath but I'm embarrassed. I don't really want to attract a lot of attention in the front yard so I stalk the rest of the way to the door without looking back.

Lana has never been an early bird if she can help it so I'm not surprised that there's still no sign of her. I cut up a banana into a bowl of cornflakes and pour a glass of cranberry juice because it's the only non alcoholic beverage in the fridge. I haven't been to the grocery store in two weeks. I'll go shopping today. Right after I finish hunting in vain for a job. Yesterday I made a flurry of calls and fired off a stack of Please Hire Me emails. No one has responded yet. Either all the jobs in Hutton have been filled or else no one does any hiring on weekends. Something needs to come up soon. If not, I'll have no choice but to beg my dad for a loan when I visit home next month.

After breakfast I take my time in the shower. The tightness in my muscles fades under the hot water. The loofa sponge rolls over my belly and I remember the hungry rush of desire when confronted with the sight of a half naked sex god in the front yard.

Yeah, Johnny is hot.

So what?

Plenty of guys out there manage to be hot without competing for asshole gold medals.

Alden, for example.

Alden isn't a Johnny-level stone cold beast but he's better than average. When we're out together girls are always looking him up and down. And then he gives them an encouraging wink when he assumes I'm not watching.

Okay, so Alden might be an asshole-in-training. At least he never pretended like he'd forgotten my name.

I set the loofa on the cutout shelf and allow my fingers to stray. I want to get off. Orgasms have a way of cleansing the mind.

A breathy moan fills the confined shower stall when one finger, and then another, slips into the aching cleft between my legs. I can imagine it; the consuming pleasure of being invaded. Better than fingers or a tongue, better than rubbing one out by way of dry humping in a back seat.

My fingers move faster, probe deeper. My fantasy lover is faceless, nameless and brandishes a record sized cock.

"Sometimes you just want to scratch an itch and you don't care whose pussy you're playing with."

Oh, fuck it all.

Can't I even enjoy a few seconds of orgasmic glory without Johnny's interference?

Now my thoughts are all about him. I'm thinking of his mouth watering six pack and the way his wet boxers bragged about the size of his dick.

I yank my hand away and savagely switch off the water. It's unreasonable to be downright pissed as I wrap myself in a fluffy blue towel but I'm pissed anyway.

I mean, who the hell does he think he is, ruining my shower time masturbation fun?

While I comb out my wet hair and glare at my fuzzy reflection in the steamed up vanity mirror, I'm grateful that no one can hear my inner dialogue. I proceed to my bedroom in search of clean clothes and banish all thoughts of throbbing cocks from my mind, at least for today.

With no job to go to and no classes to worry about, I'm starting to feel rather forlorn and restless. My fallback activity when I've got nothing else going on is cleaning. I drag all the supplies out from underneath the kitchen and plan to kill a few hours by transforming the apartment into a sparkling showcase. If it weren't for a certain unpleasant houseguest I wouldn't mind performing some housekeeping on Shane's side as well. I doubt he's cleaned a thing since he moved in and Lana claims to suffer from skin sensitivity to all household cleaning chemicals so she won't be in a hurry to scrub the floors. But Shane's just going to have to clean his own place. I have no desire to encounter Johnny again today.

Inner voice: *Jay. He calls himself Jay now. You need to call him Jay too.*

Also inner voice: *Fuck that guy. He ruined my orgasm. I'll call him whatever I want.*

I'm down on my hands and knees and scouring the grime out of the very dated vinyl flooring when Lana opens the connecting door. Her red bikini is balled up in her right hand and she's wearing only a faded black t-shirt that says 'Suck My Dick'. It's a departure from her usual fashion sense.

She's in the middle of a yawn when she walks in but then she cheers up when she notices me. "Oh, awesome! You're in cleaning mode."

I sit back on my heels. Blood rushes through my lower legs. My knees are killing me. "Yeah, I've got nothing else to do. How pathetic is that?"

Lana laughs. "I'd chip in and help but…"

"I know. Skin sensitivity."

"And I have to be at work in an hour." She takes a peek in the fridge and makes a face. "Slim pickings in here."

"I'm going grocery shopping later. Just tell me what you need."

"Cool. I'll give you some cash before I leave." She shuts the fridge and leans against the door. She looks tired, her hair is tangled and she's wearing an ugly shirt, yet she's still enviably gorgeous.

"I have a favor to ask you," she says, chewing her lip, a sure sign that the favor is of a serious nature.

I toss the wet sponge in a nearby soapy bucket. "Name it."

"Shane needs some help figuring out some of the financial crap with the bakery."

"I thought Ruby always used a bookkeeper."

"She did, but Jay's not impressed with the job the bookkeeper was doing. He thinks Shane ought to get someone independent to take a look at everything and since you're an accounting major I thought you could help."

She pauses and when I say nothing she continues in a rush. "I haven't mentioned it to Shane, though, so feel free to say no."

"I don't mind helping Shane out. But what's Jay's problem with the bookkeeper?"

She shrugs. "Who knows. Jay seems a little tense about some things."

"I'll say," I mutter.

Lana eyes me. "You don't like him."

I deliberately misunderstand her comment. "You know I like Shane just fine."

"And you know who I'm actually talking about." She sighs and takes a seat at the small dinette set in the middle of the tiny kitchen. "It's all right if you don't like him but he's Shane's best friend. If not for Jay then I'm not sure Shane would still be alive."

In spite of my resolve to avoid thinking about a certain gold medal asshole, my attention is captured. "What do you mean?"

She glances over to make sure the connecting door is closed and lowers her voice. "Remember I told you the two of them met while staying at the same foster home? I didn't tell you how awful it was. God, it was bad, Care. Almost unimaginable. They had about half a dozen boys at any one time and when there was a drug debt they couldn't pay they would...um...*rent out* the kids."

Lana's voice falters and she cups a hand over her mouth. I don't need her to be explicit. I can guess what she means. I'm aware that depravity exists everywhere and still, the idea shocks me and I feel suddenly ill.

She removes a paper napkin from the napkin holder and folds it as she collects her thoughts. "Shane was so depressed there, even suicidal at times. He'd been in the house of horrors for about three months when Jay showed up. Jay was bigger and stronger than the other kids. The first time the foster dad went after Jay he got his nose broken. So he left Jay alone after that. But meanwhile things were getting worse for Shane. They'd gotten him hooked on meth and they used it as a way to control him. Shane couldn't take the abuse anymore. He tried to get himself clean and fight back but he didn't stand a chance. One day his foster dad was kicking the living daylights out him when Jay intervened. Jay fought like the devil, even at age sixteen. The guy got hurt pretty bad. But the authorities were skeptical of the story Shane and Jay were telling because no one else would confirm it. As for the wife, she was just as guilty so the truth wasn't coming from her anytime soon. And the other kids were terrified. That's how Shane and Jay ended up in the juvenile detention center. At least the two of them got to room together the entire time. Shane says that Jay doesn't have any family, at least none that he talks to. And Shane was left all alone in the world when his mother died. That's why they're so close. They are each other's family."

Lana sighs after she finishes talking and I can't speak at all for a moment.

"Damn," I finally whisper, rubbing my eyes to hide the tears threatening to roll out. I know nothing, nothing at all. The kind of horror Johnny suffered is alien to me.

"Hey." Lana is concerned and handing me her half shredded napkin to help with the tears that I can't seem to control.

"That's so awful." I blow my nose with the napkin. "I wish I'd known what he went through."

"Who?"

"Um, Jay."

A dent appears between Lana's flawless eyebrows. "Why?"

I'm about to tell her. About me and Johnny and Arcana. About my family and his family. The story about my grandparents is one she already knows. It's not something I often share because people tend to be too interested. They have questions, morbid questions.

But even though Lana knows about my history I'm sure I've never mentioned Johnny's name to her. I'm sure because I've never talked about him with anyone.

And now…

If he feels like he needs to forget he knew me and be a man named Jay Phoenix then I can't rat him out. Not even to my best friend.

Lana's still watching me with worry and confusion.

I sniff and ball up the napkin. "I don't know, I would have been more understanding, that's all."

She smiles. "He's a little rough around the edges. But I haven't seen you be anything but polite to him, Care, and you couldn't have known about his past."

"No," I grumble. "I don't know *anything* about him."

Lana gives me a hug. I guess I look like I need one. Then she scampers away in her 'Suck My Dick' shirt to get ready for work.

The apartment isn't very big and eventually I run out of surfaces to clean. There's a determined moment when I almost knock on the connecting door and then change my mind when I flash back to the encounter in the front yard.

Jonathan Hempstead was my friend.

Jay Phoenix doesn't want to know me.

I'll find another time to talk to Shane about taking a look at his financial records.

Instead of cash, Lana hands off her debit card before leaving for work. She orders me to use it for the entire grocery store trip, claiming that it's payback for some old debt she owed me. I know she made it up but the gesture is nice and I can't really afford to refuse nice gestures at the moment.

While at the store I dawdle for a long time in the brilliantly lit aisles and marvel at how everyone takes the endless selection of glossy packaged foods for granted. During my summer in Arcana I'd been surprised at the small marketplace that served as the only grocery store in town. The store had been there since the forties and was run by a pair of elderly twin brothers. I doubt it's still open. Nine years ago the town was excited about the giant chain grocery store that was being built ten miles away in neighboring Absolom. I can remember walking through the short aisles of the Arcana Market and being charmed by the idea that my mother had shopped at the same place. And then I remember being haunted by the idea that my grandparents certainly must have shopped there as well.

When I return home there are no other vehicles parked in front of the house so the boys must have gone somewhere. I unpack all the groceries and out of gratitude to Lana I bake a batch of cinnamon rolls and leave them for her to find on the breakfast bar, prettily presented on a plate that's been covered in clear plastic wrap.

Once the kitchen is back in order I retreat to my room, sit cross legged on my bed and open my laptop. After a deep breath I type a pair of names and click the search icon. I know what I'll find, although it's been a while since I've considered the details. A few months ago I received a call from a journalist in New York. One of those crime shows planned to dedicate an episode to the Chapel murders. She'd already tried to get a comment from my father but he hung up on her. I did the same.

It's a famous story and it has everything that fascinates true crime enthusiasts.

A small town and the brutal double murder of a beautiful young couple.

An orphaned child and a community in shock.

Nearly fifty years ago on a humid summer evening a young married couple left their two-year-old daughter, Suzanne, in the care of a babysitter and went out to celebrate their anniversary. She was a beauty; a former prom queen and the center of the local social scene. He was from a good family and expected to become mayor someday, just like his father. They were so very much in love and people smiled at them wherever they went.

On this night, following a dinner at a local barbecue shack, they visited a nearby bar. A minor scuffle broke out. The furious drunken patron who was held back from throwing a punch was the boy she dated in high school. He was once the town football hero but his fortunes had fallen and everyone knew he was prone to violent behavior. Under threat of arrest, he left the bar and the happy young couple carried on with their otherwise pleasant evening.

Sometime later, they were on their way home when the passenger side front tire of their car blew. He pulled over to the side of the road and began replacing the mangled tire with the spare. The car was still propped up on its jack when they were found by their killer.

He was bludgeoned to death with a tire iron in front of the horrified eyes of his young wife. She was then dragged to a nearby vacant field. She was raped and strangled and left to die.

Their names were Richard and Nancy Chapel.

And they were my grandparents.

And their killer?

He died in a prison riot before he could be executed for his horrific crimes.

His name was Billy Hempstead.

CARIS, AGE 13

No one has warned me to be quiet all the time and yet I can't stop tiptoeing around like I'm afraid to make any noise, which makes no sense.

After all, who would I be afraid of?

The neighbors?

Aunt Vay?

Ghosts?

Every room in the house is small and dark and I'm staying in my mother's old bedroom where the walls are covered with the most garish shade of pink wallpaper. The sense that I've entered a time capsule is boosted by the felt Arcana High School pennant above an oval vanity mirror. The mirror remains flanked by old magazine pages thumbtacked to the wall. There's no closet, just a white dresser and a metal clothing rack that still hosts a few abandoned items. I don't know why this room was never redecorated. Suzanne is certainly never returning to live here again.

As far as I know, my mother hasn't even set foot in her hometown since before I was born. We don't come here, not ever. Aunt Vay always climbs in her puttering old Volkswagen every Christmas and occasionally on Easter and makes the drive to Dallas. When my mother mentions Arcana it's with the same level of venom that a person might talk about hell. She hates this town. She has good reason. I wonder if anyone has told her yet that I'm here or if she's just staring at a blank wall in the hospital without knowing or caring about a thing.

There's a heaviness to the air inside this house. It's probably my imagination but it bothers me anyway. Taking a deep breath is like trying to breathe through a layer of honey. I swear it feels like I've been here for half a year even though it was only ten days ago that my father dropped me off a few minutes before midnight and refused Aunt Vay's offer to stay over and get some rest. The drive home to Dallas was long and he needed to get back. Aunt Vay played with the strands of my hair and told him not to worry, that she would take excellent care of me just like she'd always taken excellent care of Suzanne after her parents were killed. My dad was barely listening but he crouched down and opened his arms, inviting me in for a hug as if I were still five years old and I ran to him, happy to be his little girl only for a moment.

Daddy, don't leave me here.

I couldn't say that to him. He had too much to worry about already. In my mind, twelve-almost-thirteen was plenty old enough to stay home by myself while he spent his time at work or at the hospital with Mom. If there were other relatives to choose from I'm sure he would have sent me to them instead but there was only Aunt Vay in Arcana.

I promised him I would cause Aunt Vay no trouble and he rose to his feet, kissed the top of my head, called me 'sunshine', which was actually my mother's nickname for me, and then offered Aunt Vay an awkward hug. His hair, already grey at the temples, had begun changing from black to white months ago, right after the baby died. Thinking of him as old was painful.

"I'll be fine," I told him and allowed Aunt Vay to drape an arm around my shoulders because she cared about me and meant well even if she had a hardboiled, sour kind of personality.

For the first few days I crept around the house and tried to imagine my mother growing up here. I thought if I could somehow sense a kinship with the teenage Suzanne who'd once lounged in the pink room, staring at the ceiling and daydreaming about the future, then I'd feel closer to her. I would understand why she was afraid to go outside sometimes or why she would occasionally burst into tears at the dinner table for no apparent reason and run to her bedroom in despair while my father pretended everything was fine, asking me about my day and then preparing a meal tray to bring to his wife.

It didn't take me long to figure out that the house offered few options in the way of entertainment. There was no working television and no reliable internet service. Aunt Vay saw no reason to fix either of these situations. She pointed me to her pressed wood bookcase of tattered paperbacks and I spent a vaguely pleasant two days scanning the pages of *A Tree Grows in Brooklyn*. Aunt Vay was involved with a lot of local committees and she was gone more than she was home, which was fine with me because she hovered. Plus, sooner or later Gary, the rubber-faced 'boyfriend' she'd been attached to for thirty years and yet had no intention of marrying, would find his way over here from down the street. There was something about the flat expression in his eyes that troubled me. And then there was the way he called me 'girlie' and giggled like a hyena at things that weren't even funny.

My mother grew up here so there are plenty of pictures of her around, although most of the ones I've found where she was smiling were taken before she hit her teens. The most prominent photo is an eight by ten studio photo framed in dark wood and it hangs in the living room.

The photo has faded with time, the colors all diminished to a brownish orange. Nancy holds my mother in her lap while Richard stands beside her with one hand protectively on her shoulder. I'd like to know if they chose those poses or if the unseen photographer posed them that way. My mother wears a frilly white dress that she's also wearing in her photos of her second birthday.

I'd seen this picture before, although not at my house in Dallas. I'd seen it on the internet when morbid curiosity drove me to search for some details about something terrible that happened and was almost never talked about at home. Sometimes I'd tell someone, a friend at school, or a kid I met on line at the water slide park. Now and then I just need to say it out loud for some reason. Then as soon as I do I always regret it.

"Your grandparents were killed? Like *murdered* kind of killed?"

And then they want to talk to me all about it because they think it's interesting. I don't want to be interesting in that way.

On my birthday Aunt Vay noticed that I was getting mopey and bored. She gave me some money and told me to take her old bicycle out of the garage and pedal it the three blocks to the strip of low brick buildings that comprised downtown Arcana.

And that's when I ran into the only stroke of luck that's happened to me in months. I met Johnny.

The boys my age tend to be thoughtless jerks that say disgusting things and laugh about sex and farting. Johnny is different. When I'm around him I feel like I can be me because even if I blurt out something stupid he won't mind.

"Caris? Are you going to town again?" Aunt Vay now asks me from the living room sofa where she's curled up with a People magazine and drinking a cup of black coffee.

The living room is my least favorite part of the house. Somehow it always smells like overcooked pasta and the furniture is hideously patterned with green and yellow flowers. Worst of all, there's a sense of being suspended in time as a young, happy family smiles from the wall with no idea what the future will do to them.

"Is that okay?" I ask while tying my hair back in a sloppy ponytail. I'm supposed to meet Johnny at the Arcana Market in an hour. I can't wait to get out of this house.

Aunt Vay glances up from her magazine and gives me a wistful smile. I know it's because I look like my mother. People comment on this regularly, although I think they're being kind. My mother's far prettier than I'll ever be. I'm just a watered down version of her.

"Just be home before six," Aunt Vay warns. She reaches over to dig a fork into the plate of chocolate cake sitting on the polished end table. "And you'll be with your new friends, right?"

"Right," I confirm and feel a minor stab of guilt. Aunt Vay has old fashioned ideas about young girls and young boys spending too much time alone together. I had to tell her I'd found a group of kids to hang out with. If she thought I was with Johnny and only Johnny every day then she might stop letting me out of the house.

Aunt Vay asks if I'll pick up a box of macaroni and cheese from the Arcana Market on the way home. That will be dinner tonight. She withdraws a ten dollar bill from a leather change purse sitting beside the plate of cake.

"Oh, I spoke to your father this morning. Your mother has made some progress."

Her voice is so hopeful it's easy to hear the love behind the words. Aunt Vay is my grandfather's younger sister. After the horrifying murders of Nancy and Richard, she dropped out of college to raise the little girl who had been left behind. She moved into the house her brother had purchased as a hopeful young newlywed and became the only parent little Suzanne would ever remember.

"Yeah, he told me that too." The ache in my heart that has kept me company for months resurfaces as I remember the tired sound of my father's words as he tried to sound positive about the fact that my mother's mind is so confused that she needs round the clock hospital care in order to be safe from herself. There's really no happy way to spin that reality and Eben Newsom, the hateful boy who lives across the street from our house in Dallas, taunted me the day before I left for Arcana.

"My mom says your mother's a fucking lunatic, Caris. She says it's a good thing your dad locked her up before she killed someone."

Instead of firing an insult back at Eben, like the fact that he's not one to talk because his own father was arrested for drunk driving last year, I picked up a river rock from my mother's garden and hurled it with all my might. It bounced in the middle of the street and landed a good ten feet away from Eben, who howled with laughter at my pathetic retaliation.

Thinking of Eben makes me appreciate my luck in finding Johnny. I'm sure that Johnny would never say such ugly things to anyone. He talks about stars and meteor craters and laughs when I tell one of my stupid jokes. Plus it's nice to make a friend who knows nothing about my family's sad times. Even friends like Megan and Ashley, who I've known since first grade, didn't know what to say to me about my mother. Johnny has a way of letting me know that he cares without making me feel like crap. With Johnny, everything becomes fun and adventurous and the summer doesn't seem so depressing now that I can look forward to hanging out with him.

"Caris." Aunt Vay is scrutinizing me with an air of worry. "She *will* get better."

"I know." I try to smile but the corners of my mouth are stuck.

Aunt Vay simply nods and for a second directs her gaze to the hanging photo of her lost brother. She had no other siblings and her own mother died a year before Richard was killed. Their father was inconsolable over his son's murder and died of a stroke a few months after the killings. There were a few scattered cousins but none were close by. The Chapel family had once been very important in Arcana and now I'm struck by a thought. Aunt Vay is the last of them. The last of the Chapels. What a lonely sounding fate.

"I'll see you later," I say, surprising her by leaning over the couch for an impulsive hug. She sort of awkwardly pats my back but when I pull away I see that she is pleased by the affection.

Aunt Vay's last word of advice is to grab a bottle of water from the fridge. I'm on my way out the side door with the cold water in my hand when I nearly collide with Gary.

"Whoa," he says, pretending to reel back and placing his hands on my shoulders as if he's doing me a favor by steadying me. I instantly hate the warm pressure of his fingers.

"Sorry," I mumble and try to take a step backwards. My heel bumps into the concrete foundation of the house.

His breathe exits in a garlicky wheeze and he chuckles. "Where are you running off to, girlie?"

I tip my head back and stare him straight in the eye. I don't want to. The sight of his beady eyes and corn yellow teeth make me want to throw up.

"I'm meeting a friend," I say, loud and clear. "And I'd like you to let go of me now, Gary."

His grin falters. The stench of stale cigarette smoke rolls off him in waves. "Yes, ma'am."

He makes a big show out of taking his hands away and raising them in the air. I just want to get away from him as quickly as possible so I break off into a run. I don't understand why Aunt Vay bothers with Gary. He messes up the kitchen, eats all the food and perspires all over the couch. She's never excited to see him, never jumps up to kiss him or anything. I don't know if they sleep together and I don't want to know. It's like Gary is a permanent habit that she has simply accepted.

I know Gary isn't following me but I don't slow down until I've turned the corner. Somewhere along the way my hair tie fell out, which isn't surprising because they never seem to stay put in my thin, super straight hair. I'm already sweaty and I pluck my shirt away from my skin, trying to air out a little so I don't have to meet Johnny with a sweaty shirt. The humidity here is not as bad as it is at home but it's still plenty hot.

The Arcana Market is at the north end of Division Street. Now that I know my way around a little I'm starting to feel a happy sense of familiarity whenever I walk the streets of Arcana. I've never seen where Johnny lives but he finally admitted to me yesterday that he lives in the trailer park about a mile from the center of town. He told me this shyly, like he expected me to be disgusted or something. I don't know why. Everyone has to live somewhere and for all I know his small home is filled with more warmth and happiness than the stately brick house where I live with my parents.

I'm almost half an hour early to the market. A bell clinks overhead when I step through the glass door. An old man with very dark skin and thick glasses waves at me while I linger just inside the entrance.

"You're Suzanne's daughter," he announces cheerfully. "I'd know you anywhere. Heard you were staying with Varina this summer."

"Yes, I am." I return his smile because unlike Gary, there's nothing creepy about the way he looks at me. He's very talkative. His name is Harold Keyser and he owns the market with his twin brother, Roger. He's lived in Arcana his whole life and he remembers my mother very well. For a split second a look of sorrow replaces his good mood and I have to wonder if he's remembering the rest of the Chapel family. He's definitely old enough to remember my grandparents. It's possible he was right there behind the cash register when he got the news that they'd been killed.

Harold's smile returns and he insists on giving me a bottle of soda and a small bag of chips free of charge, as a welcoming gift. I gratefully accept. Then he has to interrupt our conversation because a woman with a very cranky little red haired boy and a cart filled with groceries is wheeling her way to the register to check out.

There are a few other customers in the market and I don't want to get in anyone's way so I decide to take a seat on a splintery wooden bench right outside. The nacho cheese chips are my favorite and I'm crunching away happily when it occurs to me to save some for Johnny. I roll up the bag and sort of awkwardly hold it, wishing for once that I carried a purse like my mother is always urging me to do. She insists that once I start getting my period carrying a purse will become a requirement because there are certain items a girl can't be without. By the end of the school year every one of my friends had gotten her period, or at least claimed to. I'm in no hurry. Being up to your eyeballs in tampon strings and sanitary pads isn't something to look forward to. But I do kind of hope I'm not still waiting around for it to show up in ten years. That would probably suck.

A peek at my phone tells me that Johnny should be here soon. He's never been late yet. I wish he had a phone too so we could talk at night.

Swinging my legs with impatience, I notice the scrape on my left knee. That happened yesterday because we were scaling piles of rocks that had been left in an empty field by a construction crew. My foot slipped on some gravel and my knee skidded over a jagged point. Aside from a tiny trickle of blood I was fine, but Johnny was concerned and talked me into abandoning the activity. Once we were back on flat ground he tore off the right sleeve of his shirt and poured bottled water on the scrap of fabric before handing it over so I could clean the dirt out of the cut. That's why I like Johnny; he's the kind of kid who will ruin his shirt for you even though from the looks of it he probably doesn't have very many.

There aren't a lot of people walking around on Division Street, but then again it's mid morning on a weekday. The frazzled young mother departs the market with her son and her groceries. She doesn't notice me but the little boy gives me a mischievous toothless grin and pretends to shoot me with his fingers. I can see now that the woman is pregnant and I wonder what kind of big brother the boy will be. I would have been an excellent big sister. At home I still have a dresser drawer full of baby things that I started buying with my allowance as soon as I found out my mom was pregnant. The thought is almost enough to make me cry right here on this stupid bench.

I forget about crying when I notice the couple across the street. They are older, probably in high school. She's got curly blonde hair, long suntanned legs and the shortest denim skirt I've ever seen. He's dark haired, tall, and his muscled arms are roped around the girl's waist. They are kissing. It's a furious level of kissing, nothing like the tentative pecks I used to get from Adam Ruiz last fall when we told people we were together for a solid month because it seemed like everyone was doing the same thing.

No, this boy kisses like he's devouring his favorite meal and she's loving it, pressing herself closer and hooking her leg on his hip when he reaches under her shirt right here in the middle of Division Street. And though a flush of embarrassed heat travels from my belly to my cheeks, I can't look away.

He's got both hands under her shirt now and she's moved on to suck his neck so I can see his face for the first time. He catches me looking and smirks. He's obviously used to this kind of attention. Any one of my friends would squeal about how hot he is and they'd be right. I can't stop staring at him.

All of a sudden he drops his hands and kind of pushes the girl away. He turns around and starts walking south and she's confused, tucking her shirt back in as she follows and begs him to tell her what's wrong. He doesn't answer and I get the feeling he's enjoying her distress. He's bored with her and wants her to know it. She continues to follow him and then they turn the corner so I can't see what happens next. I don't understand why girls do that; chase after boys who treat them with disrespect. It makes me mad. I'll never let any guy treat me like that.

Seconds later Johnny emerges around that same corner. He's got his head down, like he's deep in thought. His hair is a little too long and falls forward so his expression is hidden. He's wearing a plain white tee and a pair of army green shorts that I've seen him wear before. When we stand side by side he's about an inch shorter than me but my mom says that boys hit their growth spurts later than girls.

Suddenly he stops and looks up. He smiles when he sees me waiting on the bench. He really is a cute boy, not that I'm thinking of him like that. But I can see how one day he'll get older and maybe I will think of him like that.

I'm still considering this while he closes the distance between us.

"Saved you my chips," I say instead of hello.

"Thanks." He sits right down beside me and eats the rest of the bag in two mouthfuls. He doesn't think it's weird when I also offer him the rest of my soda. He's not all uptight and immature about things like spit and germs.

After Johnny finishes his snack he asks me what I want to do. We still haven't taken the bus to see that shopping mall he told me about but I don't want to do that today. I want to see the meteor crater again.

It's a long walk but at least a haze of gray clouds is blocking the sun and Johnny doesn't hesitate. I would have been happy to do something else if he objected.

We're past Division Street and I'm showing him a video of three kittens playing with a ball of yarn. I watch this video often, for no reason other than it's something that makes me happy. Our shoulders keep bumping because we are walking so close together.

The sharp, angry voice startles both of us.

"Hey, little fuck face! Get over here."

At first I don't believe we're the ones being yelled at. Then I notice that the boy who was making out on Division Street a few minutes ago is the one doing the yelling. He's standing in an empty parking lot across the street and the blonde girl is still hanging around with him, though she's got her arms crossed and a sullen look on her face.

"Come on," Johnny mutters and starts race walking away. I have to hurry to keep up with him.

We're not quick enough. The sound of pounding footsteps follows.

"Fucking hell, quit running like a bitch you little shit!"

Johnny stops. He shoots me a helpless look, a silent apology for whatever is about to happen. Then he swivels around to face his tormentor.

"What do you want, Rafe?" he asks.

And now I understand.

This is his brother. He has no sisters and only one brother. Johnny doesn't talk about him much but I get the feeling they don't get along. I can see it now, the resemblance between them. Rafe's hair is darker plus he's a few years older and much bigger, but they have the same nose and chin. Their eyes, however, are completely different. Johnny's eyes are a warm, woody brown. Rafe's are blue and cold.

Johnny's posture has changed, his good mood gone. His shoulders have tensed and his hands have balled into fists. Rafe looks the two of us over and is amused.

"I just want to give you a piece of brotherly advice."

He punches Johnny in the shoulder hard and Johnny winces but stands his ground, regarding his brother with wariness

"What advice is that?"

Rafe jerks his head in my direction. "This little piece is your girlfriend?"

"No! She's my friend."

Rafe snorts. "No such thing. Hey, you can let her suck your limp little dick but tell her to get used to swallowing. The good ones always swallow."

Then he cackles like this is the funniest thing anyone has ever said in the history of words. The blonde girl has caught up to us by now and she mechanically laughs with him.

I'm mortified. I don't know where to look or what to say. Sometimes boys at school say disgusting things like that and even worse but there's something infinitely more threatening about Rafe.

Johnny's fury is written all over his face, which has turned an angry red. He steps up, ready to do battle while his brother continues to howl with laughter. I quickly grab Johnny's arm to pull him back. I don't think I could stand watching him get hurt.

"Let's go," I urge, still trying to pull him away, and from the stubborn set of his jaw I'm sure he'll refuse but he finally nods and falls back.

Rafe's arm is around the blonde girl again. He mutters something to her and she looks annoyed but then bites the corner of her lip. She sinks to her knees while Rafe gyrates his hips toward her face in an obscene manner.

"Stick around," he says before yanking on the girl's hair to draw her in. "We'll let you watch how it's done."

"Run," Johnny mutters and he doesn't need to say it twice.

He's faster than I am and yet he jogs by my side until we are sure Rafe is not following. I'm out of breath and I feel nauseous. I want to eliminate this past minute from my mind. I can't imagine living with a person like that and I have to revise my opinion about Johnny's home being a happy place. I'm also thinking about that bruise on his face the day we met. I bet he suffers a lot of bruises at the hands of his nightmare of a brother.

After this incident with Rafe, Johnny is glum and embarrassed. He stuffs his hands in his pockets, stares down at the sidewalk and barely speaks. I want him to cheer up so I suggest we ditch the plans to walk all the way out to the crater and go to the lone movie theater in town. There's only one screen and it's playing one of those super hero action movies where things explode every thirty seconds. The film was released months earlier but Johnny had mentioned how much liked the movie. My dad sent me some pocket money so I have more than enough to treat us both. He mumbles something about paying me back another time and I don't argue although there's no need for him to pay me back.

There are only about ten other people in the theater and it's a pleasantly cool place to pass a couple of hours. There's a moment when I see Johnny's hand resting on his knee and I think about taking his hand in mine but in the end I'm too chicken. Besides, I like the way we're just friends without all the boy and girl complications. Hanging out with Johnny makes me feel like I get to be a kid for a little while longer.

Still, holding his hand for a little while would probably feel nice.

By the time the movie ends it's getting close to the time when I need to head home. I'm worried about Johnny. When I ask him if Rafe will do something to hurt him later on at home he shrugs off the concern and says Rafe probably lost interest three seconds after we ran off.

"I'm sorry, Caris," he says, looking so miserable that all I want to do is hug him. "I'm really sorry for what he said about you."

"Don't worry about it," I assure him. "He probably can't help being a jerk."

"Born that way," Johnny agrees and relaxes into a smile.

The market is more crowded than it was earlier. People are probably stopping on their way home to grab food for dinner. Harold is still ringing up orders at the cash register, but now a young woman is operating the second cash register that was empty earlier. Johnny helps me find the macaroni and cheese and I wait in Harold's line to pay for it.

Harold looks up and when he notices that I'm next in line he gives me a smile. Then he looks at Johnny and his smile fades. His eyes dart back to me and then return to Johnny. He's still watching Johnny when he slowly hands the guy in front of me a receipt.

Johnny hasn't noticed. When I set the blue and yellow box on the counter he drifts away to examine the rack of sunglasses.

"I'm back," I announce as if it's not obvious. I unfold the ten dollar bill Aunt Vay gave me and pass it to Harold. "Just here to pick up dinner."

Harold takes his eyes off Johnny long enough to ring up the food and accept payment. He counts out changes and passes it over. I'm confused because all of his happy cheerfulness has vanished and I get the feeling I've done something wrong.

Harold's brow furrows with concern. "Does Varina know you're hanging out with the Hempstead boy?"

I feel the change drop into my hand and I automatically send it to my back pocket. His question makes no sense to me.

The Hempstead boy.

Johnny has finished inspecting the rack of sunglasses and waits for me patiently by the door.

I've never asked him his last name.

I don't know his last name.

The Hempstead boy.

There's no way it's a coincidence. The name of the man who killed my grandparents was Billy Hempstead. Aunt Vay has never mentioned the Hempstead family and I just assumed they were long gone from Arcana.

I'm still frozen at the counter and Johnny's head tilts as he regards me with curiosity. I feel lightheaded.

"Yes, of course," I tell Harold and I know I sound a little snotty. "Of course she knows."

Before he says anything else I barrel right out of the store with the hideous feeling that there's not enough oxygen in there. Once outside I run halfway down the block and tip my head back to take big gulps of air.

"Caris!" Johnny has chased me and he's worried. He looks this way and that way, trying to figure out who or what upset me.

"What's going on?" he wants to know.

I never asked him what his last name was because it never seemed important.

And it's *not* important.

It's just not.

Because he's still Johnny. He's still my friend.

Nonetheless there's a quaver in my throat as I summon the answer to his question.

"My mother is Suzanne Chapel. I'm the granddaughter of Richard and Nancy Chapel."

His eyes widen. His jaw hardens and he swallows. His head sinks and he stares at a giant crack in the sidewalk. After a few seconds he raises his head and there's pain along with a silent plea in his brown eyes. He understands.

"Caris, if I'd known that I would have told you."

"Told me what?" I'm afraid of the answer.

Even though I already know the answer.

An apology is all over his face as he delivers the news.

"My grandfather was Billy Hempstead."

There's no movement, not even a breeze in the air as we stand there on Division Street facing one another.

JAY

"You're shitting me."

Shane shrugs. "We need the help. She needs a job. What's the problem?"

I bend down to grab a twenty pound bag of flour and toss it on a shelf. "No problem, but does she know a damn thing about working in a bakery?"

"Do we?" he laughs.

I heave another bag of flour onto the shelf.

"It's your call," I mutter. "I just thought someone around here ought to have an idea how to operate the place."

"Delia is still around to help."

"Delia says she doesn't want to work more than fifteen hours a week because of her arthritis."

"You worry too much." Shane shakes his head while gesturing to the mess of supplies and failed muffin batches. "We've gotten a ton of shit figured out already and we'll be ready to open next week."

I'm having my doubts about that but far be it from me to crush Shane's enthusiasm. "Have you scheduled the health department inspection?"

"Caris is going to look into that. She's good with all the paperwork crap. She sorted through the pile of invoices that were stacking up, paid the ones that needed to be paid and called suppliers to talk about terms."

"Terms?"

"Yeah, like negotiating payments and whatever."

My next comment is limited to a grunt. Shane has every reason to hire Caris. She's a business major and she's smart and he needs all the help he can get with the paperwork side of the business. Her presence in the bakery kind of throws a wrench into my plans to avoid her at all costs but that was probably never a reasonable strategy anyway.

There was a moment when I almost broke down and talked to her honestly. It was Sunday morning and I was outside trying to diagnose a rattling noise under the hood of my truck when she came running up out of nowhere and sprawled on the grass, panting from exertion. She didn't notice me at first and I saw her as the girl she'd been in that brief window of time when we were friends. Hair messy, glasses crooked, no makeup.

I had the urge to tell her that I remembered her and my memories weren't bad. Most of them, anyway. But that was then and this is now. We'd be doing each other a favor if we just shook hands and kept a polite distance for the rest of the summer.

Then she ruined everything.

She took her shirt off.

She sat there on the grass in nothing but a white sports bra and stretched this way and that with a moan.

And just like that my dick got so hard I could hardly stand up straight.

What the hell is it about this girl?

She's cute for sure. Just like a million other girls are cute. If I hit the local bar scene I'd have little trouble finding one to spend a few sweaty hours with.

Yet some sexy, confident college girl wouldn't satisfy me. I'd still want this one instead. And there's something too fucking powerful about how bad I want her. If she knew she might be afraid. Maybe she should be.

Shane assumes the subject of Caris's employment at Ruby's Bakery is closed and he begins cleaning up mounds of leftover flour. "I think the last batch of banana muffins came out all right, don't you?"

"They were edible," I agree and start filling the sink with soapy water. Every day that I don't share the truth with my best friend makes me feel a little guiltier. Obviously Caris hasn't said anything to Lana or Shane would know. She must have her own reasons for keeping quiet.

I remove the pair of food handler gloves I'd been wearing. "Hey, can we talk about something serious?"

His head pops up and he looks surprised, then wary. "Are you gonna hassle me about drinking? I told you I've got it under control."

I'm not sure that's true. That's not what I was going to say, though. I've got to tell him. I'll feel better after I blurt out the fact that I knew Caris way back when I was a kid named Jonathan Hempstead. He might scratch his head in confusion over why I didn't just say so in the first place but in the end he won't think much of it. Shane knows I have worse secrets and his loyalty has no limits. Neither does mine.

Before I can open my mouth the door opens and in walks Caris herself. She's wearing jeans and a bright blue polo shirt emblazoned with the bakery name. She doesn't give me a second glance and heads straight for Shane.

"I found a place in town that would print up the shirts today. I'm wearing a prototype." She spins in a circle to model it.

"That's great," Shane says and then turns to me to explain. "Caris and Lana thought everyone who works here should have a company shirt. Lana designed these."

"I ordered some for you, Jay," Caris says with cheerful sweetness. "I guessed extra large."

"That'll work." I'm wondering if she's up to something.

Caris has already moved on to discussing net thirty terms and other business babble that kind of makes Shane's eyes glaze over. He checks his phone.

"Shit, I've got to go meet Ruby's lawyer to sign some paperwork. I don't know how long I'll be gone. Jay, you want to close up or stick around?"

"I'll stick around," I say, eyeing Caris.

She eyes me back. "Jay can show me the ropes since we'll all be working together now."

I glare.

She grins.

"Don't scare her away, pal," Shane warns, patting me on the back on his way to the door.

Caris laughs. "I don't scare easily."

Shane nods at her. "I haven't said this enough but thanks for your help. Glad you're on the team."

"Yeah well, thanks for offering me the job, Shane. I was about to give up and start selling my clothes by the side of the road."

"See you guys later." Shane waves once and then is gone.

Deathly silence reigns for a full minute.

Caris crosses her arms and inspects me before breaking the silence. "It's a mess in here."

Wordlessly I sweep the flour off the prep counter and into a garbage bin and grab a washcloth.

"Before I forget, I have a paycheck for you." She digs inside her purse now and comes up with a paper rectangle. She waves it a few feet from my face. "Shane asked me to figure out how to run payroll."

I don't want a paycheck. I already told Shane I don't want a paycheck.

"I know you don't want Shane to give you a paycheck," Caris says and carefully sets the thing down on a dry section of the counter. "Shane insists that you are getting one anyway."

"Don't need it."

"Then donate it to someone who does."

"All right. You take it."

"No."

"Well, I saw a homeless guy sleeping on the corner this morning. Give it to him."

"Jay."

She's calling me Jay now, not Johnny. We're the only ones here. There's no need to keep up the charade.

I ball the washcloth up and aim it at the sink. "What do you want, Caris?"

She runs her fingertips over the counter. "I want you not to hate me."

"I don't hate you."

She turns her eyes on me and they are so full of sorrow that my gut twists.

"Really?" she asks with all the shy hope in the world.

Damn it to hell.

She's killing me with those eyes. I might be able to think clearly if she'd stop gazing at me like a sad puppy.

"I don't know why you're going by a different name but I won't tell anyone. I haven't even told Lana. There's no way I can understand everything you've been through but I know you must have reasons for wanting to keep your past to yourself. I have no intention of doing anything to screw up your life."

I breathe out a sigh and realize I should be less of an asshole to her. The fact that I'm fucked in the head isn't her fault.

I look her in the eye. "I swear I've never hated you."

She wants to believe me. She chews her soft lower lip and waits for me to say more.

Of course I don't hate Caris. The feelings I do have are worse, so much worse.

"But you don't want to be friends, do you, Jay?"

"Fuck no."

The response is brutal and instant and she blinks in disbelief. Then she's irritated.

"Why the hell not?" she demands.

I turn on the sink full blast in the hopes of drowning her out. She walks over and savagely turns it off.

"Look at me."

I cross my arms over my chest and stare straight ahead at nothing.

"Why not, Jay?" she shouts in my ear. "Why can't we be friends?"

Because I could fucking lose myself in you and there's not much of me left.

Before the situation intensifies I'm saved by the arrival of some dickhead wearing a backwards baseball cap and two hundred dollar sneakers. He strolls right through the door, disregarding the very prominent closed sign.

"Alden!" Caris exclaims and yeah, he looks very much like a guy who would be named something shitty like Alden.

"What are you doing here?" she asks him, taking a step away from me.

He gives her his charming dickhead grin. "Just passing by and wanted to see where you'd be working."

Dickhead takes a stroll behind the counter, plants his hand on her ass and slobbers on her mouth. I feel the intense urge to drop kick him through the plate glass window.

"Um." Caris is obviously uncomfortable as she extricates herself from his grip and shoots me a glance. "This is Jay. Remember, I told you about him? He's Shane's best friend and he's helping out here for the summer. Jay, this is my friend, Alden."

Friend. Interesting. From the way he was manhandling her I would have guessed him to be her boyfriend but apparently not.

Alden acts like he just noticed that I'm in the room. His eyes narrow for a split second before he becomes a politician and offers me a handshake.

"How's it going, dude?"

I have a brand new life goal and it involves inflicting discomfort on people who say 'dude' and wear backwards baseball caps. I squeeze his hand hard enough to make him flinch.

"It's going nowhere," I say, pleased to see how he flexes his hand to make sure it's in one piece after he withdraws it.

"Uh, okay." He bleats out a cough of laughter. "Care, let's get out of here and grab some lunch."

She shakes her head. "Sorry but I can't. I just got in and I'm supposed to be training."

"Go on, *Care*," I urge, trying to be obnoxious and succeeding. "Go have lunch with your friend."

Caris is plainly irritated that I've chosen to chime in. Alden strikes me as an ass clown of the first order but right now he could serve a purpose. The last thing I feel like doing is continuing my one on one conversation with Caris. If she takes off for lunch with this dipshit right now then there is a good chance Shane will be back by the time she returns.

She tips her chin up and gives me a stubborn look. "Fine, Jay. If that's the way you want it…"

"Yup. Get lost."

"Great," she snaps and takes Alden by the hand. "See you later."

I wave at them. "Take your time."

Caris shoots me a final scowl that says, *This isn't over.*

I respond with a stony stare that answers, *Yes it is.*

Once they are outside he puts his arm around her and my teeth grind together, which is nuts. After all, I'm the one who pushed her into his arms. I can already tell he's too brainless to deserve her. But watching her skip away with Alden is better than remaining here alone with her and explaining all the reasons why I can't be her friend.

That's a path leading to places we can't go. Not together. Not ever.

CARIS

unning a bakery is a crazy amount of hard work.

When Ruby was alive I never appreciated how much it must have taken for her to keep the place operating on her own. The last week has been one giant crash course in cookie baking and small business management. I'm certainly not doing all the work, or even most of it. The guys had been spending most of their waking hours there leading up to yesterday's grand re-opening and even though I burned two batches of scones and had to fix a couple of glitches with the payment processing system, the day could be counted as a success. Customers showed up, many of them longtime regulars who were fond of Ruby and eager to give her godson a chance to prove himself.

Today has been nearly as busy but feels less frantic.

Shane decided to keep Ruby's original operating hours so the doors close at three in the afternoon. Shane's in a hyper mood, ready to celebrate, and while we're still cleaning up I hear him call Lana to suggest inviting some friends over tonight.

Working for Shane is fun, if a little chaotic. He tends to fly by the seat of his pants and possesses a short attention span when it comes time to discuss matters of complexity. His saving grace is that he's charming and earnest. It helps that Jay spends every effort trying to keep his best friend focused.

As for Jay, we've come to an understanding of sorts. He likes his role as a hostile douchebag. And since he likes being a hostile douchebag I'm not required to waste any more time on him.

At work we communicate when necessary but with as few words as possible. At home it's easy enough to avoid him. He rejects social activities and according to Lana he stays in his room, emerging only to eat, talk to Shane, go to the gym and work at the bakery.

Shane notices that I'm practically dead on my feet and urges me to leave, saying he and Jay can handle closing up. I'm happy to take him up on that offer. Waking up at five a.m. like I've been doing is for the birds. I have newfound respect for people who make sure that donut and bagel bins everywhere are filled before the breakfast hour begins.

Once I'm home I can think of nothing more fantastic than a late afternoon nap. I change to a soft tee shirt that's more comfortable than the scratchy Ruby's Bakery polo and fall asleep on top of the covers.

When I wake up to the sound of splashing and laugher I sit up and rub my eyes. I can tell by the light filtering in that it's early evening. I hear voices that I don't recognize coming from outside but from the sound of things a raucous good time is going on in the pool. The nap delivered all the rest I need and a burst of energy convinces me to head out there and join them. I'm not especially worried about running into Jay. A gathering like this is the sort of thing his grumpy ass would shun.

Before I leave the room I check my phone. Alden had texted while I was asleep. He wants to hang out tonight.

As soon as I step outside I'm greeted with lots of waving. Some of Lana's coworkers are here with their boyfriends and I only know two of them slightly.

While I'm sinking into a patio chair and scoping out the scene I receive another text from Alden.

What R U doing?

The pool is full of couples and a few seconds out here is already making me feel like a spare part. The summer twilight weather is perfect and Jay is nowhere in sight. I have to guess he's in the house somewhere, probably perfecting his sneer in the bathroom mirror. Alden's not perfect but he's social and sometimes even entertaining. I don't feel like being the single girl accessory tonight so I text him back.

Nothing. Come over.

Two seconds later he responds with a winking emoji, which is kind of dumb but so very Alden.

Someone has abandoned food to cook on the grill without tending it. The chicken wings look crisp and borderline burnt so I remove them from the flame with a pair of metal tongs and lay them out neatly on a platter. Lana's kicking back in a corner of the pool, her elbows propped up on the concrete. Whatever she's saying makes her friends erupt into peals of laughter.

The picnic table looks like someone emptied a liquor cabinet and dumped it out here. There's a bottle of everything imaginable. I'm really thirsty, but the beer chilling in the cooler looks like a better option so I grab one and start sipping.

Shane swims over to the side of the pool, vaults up to the deck and shakes the water out of his hair. He must have been the one to leave the wings burning on the grill because he spots the platter and thanks me for dealing with them.

I tip my beer bottle in his direction. "Congrats on a successful grand re-opening."

Shane is helping himself to one wing after another. He wipes his mouth with the back of his hand and grins. "Couldn't have done it without you guys."

"Did Jay go out tonight?" I ask, trying to sound casual. I don't want to be thinking about him or wondering where he is but I can't seem to help it.

"Nah. He's at the gym." Shane surveys the layout of booze on the table. "Hey Caris, how about a celebratory shot?"

I hate doing shots but Shane's already at work, using two empty red cups to pour a generous mixture of rum and coke. He hands one over with a delightful grin that would brighten anyone's day and we clink plastic cups before he downs the contents of his in one swallow. I take a mouthful but then spit about half of it back in the cup. Shane doesn't notice. He howls like a wolf and then cannonballs back into the pool, disturbing the rest of the occupants with a tidal wave splash.

"You idiot," Lana laughs but she holds her arms out and squeals when he swims over to maul her. They're cute to watch, as usual, but I'm remembering a remark from Shane's best friend.

"Shane shouldn't drink so much."

Based on Lana's stories I know that Shane has had addiction issues in the past and although I thought he'd overcome them, I would have to guess that Jay's worries are genuine. Shane does drink an awful lot. Lana must realize this. At least I hope she does.

I'm finishing off my latest beer when Alden shows up. By now the sun has set and I'm feeling slightly buzzed. Alden looks good tonight. He looks even better when he yanks off his shirt and I don't mind when he swoops in for a kiss that includes an obnoxious level of tongue.

"Hi," he says. He tastes like he's already had a few drinks elsewhere.

"Hi." I have to suppress a sneeze because he overdid it on the after-shave this evening.

He wants to know what's in the red cup and before I can explain that it includes a mouthful of my backwash he tips his head back and swallows the contents like it's water.

A guy paired with one of Lana's friends knows Alden and they share a moment of coarse, nearly indecipherable guy banter before Alden strips down to his boxers and jumps right in the water. He swims like a fish, rocketing underwater from one end of the pool to the other before returning to his jumping off point. He slicks his hair back and rests his elbows on the edge while grinning at me.

"Get in here," he orders.

I stand up and remove my glasses, setting them in the middle of the table where I hope they won't get knocked off. "I've got to go change."

He's impatient. "No you don't. I didn't change. Come on, just rip off your shirt and shorts."

It's not the kind of thing I would do, not in a pool full of people. Or even in a pool *not* full of people.

"Hey, Phoenix!" Shane bellows, amplifying his voice with his hands cupped over his mouth. "Quit hiding in your armpit and join the fun."

My head whips over to see that Jay has returned from the gym. He's standing in the kitchen just beyond the open sliding glass doors. I've gotten used to seeing him every day and there shouldn't be a confusing thrill of excitement in my chest. Yet it's there. And I'm ashamed that it's there. I don't aspire to be one of those girls that broods over a guy who treats her like garbage.

Jay looks up. His eyes skate right over me with no reaction. He lifts one hand to half heartedly wave to Shane but refuses to be tempted into joining the party. His attention is on the bowl of fruit he was in the middle of cutting up and he drops pieces into a blender. It's just as well. I feel funny about being with Alden in front of him, which is crazy. Jay doesn't care what I do or who I do it with.

Frustration boils internally and must be what prompts me to rise from my seat, pull my shirt over my head and drop my cutoff shorts. I'm glad I chose the lacy pink bra this morning. And my black bikini panties don't have a thong level of allure but they're still hot.

Alden thinks so. He's practically panting over in the pool.

"Don't stop there, baby," he begs. "Let it all come off."

"Work it, Care!" Lana yells in encouragement. She's always telling me that I'm cuter than I think I am and I shouldn't be afraid to cut loose.

I roll my eyes but I'm also giggling and feeling a little giddy as I approach the pool. The alcohol has helped. I jump right in, stay briefly submerged and break the surface to find Alden right there smiling at me.

Lana's friend Mira hops out of the pool and forages in the cooler. She's got an armful of beers when she returns. Alden holds up a hand

and she tosses him one. Shane doesn't appear to mind that people are drinking in his pool and he yells for a beer himself. Alden passes his drink to me and I'm still thirsty so I drink three quarters of the bottle. I'm not sure if beer is the best way to stay hydrated but a pleasant warmth is spreading in my gut and Alden is impressed.

"I like this side of you," he says and drains the rest of the beer bottle with his arm around me.

Lana remembers that she left a batch of Jello shots in the fridge and she coaxes her boyfriend into taking a trip to the kitchen to retrieve them. Shane doesn't mind. From here I have a view into the house and I don't see Jay standing at the kitchen counter any longer.

Shane returns with a tray filled with rows of small paper cups. He sets it down by the edge of he pool, helps himself to two shots back to back and then cannonballs back into the water.

Alden grabs a cup for each of us before the rest of the crowd can get over here and devour them. I'm not a fan of these things but I take one because Lana might be right about how I ought to cut loose now and then. I avoid gagging as the slippery mess slides down my throat and Alden plucks the empty cup out of my hand, crumples it up and tosses it to the concrete. Then he slides his arms around my waist and pulls me into deeper water.

"You look so fucking hot tonight," he says in my ear and lets his hands roam over my ass.

I don't stop him and slip my arms around his shoulders, pulling him in for a kiss. I really ought to like him more. We've had a casual thing on and off for two years now and though I've never thought of him as my boyfriend he's definitely a friend. Plus we've shared some hot times together and right now being in his arms feels good.

Alden is getting worked up, running his lips down my neck, and pressing close. Meanwhile, I'm starting to realize that I should have eaten something before drinking. There was no time for lunch today and now my stomach has begun to roll around in an unhealthy way. The feel of Alden's hard dick trying to poke a hole in my abdomen isn't helping matters.

"Hold on." I disconnect from Alden and pull myself out of the pool.

Lana calls my name and I wave to say that I'm fine. I just need a minute. Jay is nowhere in sight and I don't feel like walking all the way around the perimeter to get to my apartment. Lana's orange beach towel is draped over a patio chair and I grab it, wrapping it around my waist before I drip my way into the house, charging straight for the door to my apartment in case Jay and his fruit smoothie are lurking nearby.

My senses are fuzzy and my stomach continues to launch a full scale rebellion as I reach my small kitchen. The sleeve of crackers sitting on the counter looks like a safe bet. I pour a glass of cold water and chew crackers while leaning against the wall.

There's a rustling of approaching footsteps outside the door and I tense, wondering if Jay might be the one on the other side.

Alden comes through the door without knocking and I'm relieved.

And disappointed.

And nuts, apparently.

"I got lonely," Alden complains but he's grinning.

I swallow a clump of wet crackers and wash them down with a few sips of water before setting the glass down. "Sorry, I-" The sentence remains unfinished because Alden closes my words off with his lips.

"Alden." I try to step out of his grip but he just pulls me in tighter.

"Don't think I could have waited another minute," he says and he grinds against me while one hand sneaks behind my back and unhooks my bra. "Glad you took the lead."

Huh?

My towel falls and his hands are already trying to yank my panties down. I feel like I missed a crucial piece of communication in the last two minutes. If I were trying to be seductive I wouldn't have been leaning against the kitchen counter and pigging out on salted crackers.

"Wait." I try to yank my panties back up and attempt to slither out of his arms. "I just ran inside because I felt sick for a minute. I feel better now. Let's go back to the pool."

He traces my lower lip with his finger and slides my bra strap off with his other hand. Somewhere along the way he also pushed his wet boxers down. I can feel him, hard and bare against my belly. "You got a condom? I left my wallet outside in my pants but I can go grab it."

I think I've already made it clear I'm not in the mood. "Alden, knock it off. We're not doing this here."

"Let's go to your room then."

"No."

He finally gets the message and his eyes become dim. His hands, however, are still on me and his dick remains hard, pressing into my skin. "Caris, what the hell? I've put in my time with you."

He's whining. He's still touching me. He's pissing me off.

"And you think that means I owe you sex?" I try to push him away. "Fuck right off with that, Alden."

He grabs my wrists just hard enough that I can't struggle. The move shocks me. Alden has never been rough. But I see the anger in his scowl and suddenly I'm afraid.

"What do you think, you've got some kind of golden magic pussy? Who the hell are you saving it for?"

"Let go," I demand through clenched teeth.

Alden hesitates. But then his eyes drift down over my exposed breasts and he smirks.

"There's nothing there worth the effort anyway," he says and releases me with a shove.

I know I should just step back and hope he leaves but my anger and humiliation get the better of me.

"Get out." I push him hard in the chest.

I'm not especially strong but he isn't expecting this move and he stumbles backwards. When he catches his balance the look on his face stops my breath. I've made a mistake. I've poked a rabid bear with a stick.

"Bitch," he spits out. He grabs my unhooked bra and yanks it away. He throws it and seizes me, his fingers digging into my upper arms. I have no idea what he'll do next but I know the time has come to scream for help. The backyard is full of people. Someone will hear me. Hopefully.

But the scream dies in my throat because chaos has erupted. Alden lets go of me with a yelp and the momentum sends me sprawling on the floor. When I get my bearings I see that there's a serious struggling happening a few feet away. The world is slightly blurry without my glasses but I can tell that Jay is somehow here and he's got Alden in a headlock. I remember something Lana told me about Jay. He knows how to fight. He's now going to prove it. He slams Alden's body into the wall so hard that I hear a crack.

Then I hear his voice. Low and guttural. Dangerous and sincere.

"Get the FUCK out of here before I fucking take you apart."

He slams a fist into Alden's belly. Alden is now gasping for air, rolling on the ground, and the man who sent him there looms over his prone body with muscles tensed, ready to strike again.

"Johnny," I whisper and then remember that's wrong, the wrong name. He's someone else now but whoever he is I don't want him to do something that will ruin his life.

Alden coughs and climbs to his hands and knees, crawling away in a hysterical panic, but the sight gives me no pleasure. The trembling begins in my bones and I don't think it will ever stop.

Jay closes the door and flicks the lock in case Alden recovers and returns for retaliation. A second later he's on the floor, inches away, cupping my face in his hands. He looks frantic, stricken.

"Did he hurt you? Caris? *Did he hurt you?*"

Despite the trembling I manage to shake my head back and forth.

"Okay." He breathes and nods in relief. "Thank god."

Then his eyes sweep down and take notice of the fact that I'm pretty much naked. He spots the towel I'd dropped a moment ago and covers me with it. Carefully, tenderly, like I'm a piece of fragile china that might break into pieces. He helps me to my feet and walks me over to the sofa while my teeth chatter.

Jay lays a hand on my back. "Stay here, all right? I'm going to make sure he's gone."

I grip the edges of the towel and shiver. My mind can't quite process what has just happened. I've known Alden for years. Sometimes he's a jerk. But not like that. Never like that. Sometimes he'd pout when I hit the brakes while we fooled around but he's never grabbed me, never tried to force me, never shown a hint of violence. I'm sure I'll never forget the look of fury in his eyes. Maybe I don't know him after all. Maybe no one knows anyone.

Jay must have decided that Lana would be better equipped to comfort me in this situation than he would. I can hear her voice in the hallway, high pitched and anxious.

"What do you mean? What the hell did he do to her?"

She appears in the doorway and her face crumples at the sight of my tears.

"Oh my god, Care, what happened?"

She's next to me, wrapping her arms around me, and I break down into full blown sobbing. Since I have a hard time talking, Jay is the one who quietly explains. He happened to return to the kitchen and Alden had left the connecting door partially open so he heard when we began arguing. As soon as the situation escalated he didn't hesitate to barrel through the door and rip Alden away from me.

Lana is enraged on my behalf. She wants to call the police. She wants Alden arrested. She wants to kill him. I've never seen her so furious.

Shane stands in the doorway and shoots worried glances at all of us. Jay talks to him in a low murmur and Shane nods. There are other voices, Lana's friends, all wanting to know what the commotion is about. She won't leave my side and asks Shane to tell them that the party is over tonight.

Jay departs with Shane and Lana grabs a comfortable sweatshirt for me, helping to pull it over my head because I'm still shaking. And now I'm starting to feel foolish because I needed to be rescued by the last guy I would ever want to be rescued by.

Lana prepares a cup of hot mint tea for me. A few minutes later Jay creeps in silently with his head down. He places an object on the coffee table. My glasses. I'd forgotten they were left outside.

"Thank you so much, Jay," Lana says, giving him a grateful smile. "Really. So glad you were there."

I also need to thank him. There's no telling what would have happened next if he hadn't been around. I wish he'd come sit next to me, just for a minute. I set my mug of tea on the coffee table and pick up my glasses. I feel slightly better once they're back where they belong. But when I look around for Jay he's no longer in the room. He's gone.

JOHNNY, AGE 13

I can't remember how old I was when I found out that my grandfather was a murderer. It feels like something I was born knowing. He died in prison years ago and I only know him from pictures and stories. The pictures are mostly in black and white, although there used to be a family photo album with some that were in color. I don't know what happened to that photo album but it seems like it was something that disappeared about the same time my dad died. We needed to get rid of a lot of things when we had to move from the small house on Wicker Road to the far smaller trailer.

If I want to see a picture of Billy Hempstead now all I need to do is type his name into the internet and his mug shot will be the first image that pops up. He glares out at the camera and there's a bruise under his right eye. He looks wild and dangerous. According to everything I've heard, he was both.

Besides his mug shot, there's always another picture of Billy Hempstead that shows up in an online search. It's his senior prom photo and he's wearing a white blazer while standing in front of a curtain backdrop with a very pretty blonde girl. Her hair is teased up sky high and doesn't even look real but her smile is brilliant. Her name was Nancy Gainey and later she would marry someone other than the boy who took her to the prom. When she died her name was Nancy Chapel. Whenever I see that picture I feel sorry for her. I wish time travel were a thing and that I could go back and warn her what will happen. That someday the boy she poses with so happily beneath the flashy 'Night To Remember' banner will be her killer.

Then again, she probably wouldn't have believed such an awful thing was possible.

My grandmother had something wrong with her legs. That might be why she chose to stay in Arcana with my dad, her only child, after her husband was arrested for the murders of his high school girlfriend and her husband.

A few years back I asked my own mother why we stayed in town after my dad wrapped his car around a tree in the middle of a drunken police chase. She snapped at me, asking, "And where the hell do you think we should go?"

Of course I had no answer because Arcana was all I knew. Someday I'll go somewhere else, a place where people aren't carrying around generations worth of grudges and staring at me with suspicion because of my last name.

The day Caris told me whose granddaughter she was my heart sunk to my knees. A wave of pure misery and shame swept over me because I realized I was stuck. Stuck with the Hempstead name and the Hempstead awful legacy. No one has the power to change terrible crimes committed before they existed but too many people have no common sense. I was sure that the girl who had very quickly become my best friend would now recoil from me in horror.

But Caris isn't like other people. She stared at me with wide eyes for a moment while I waited for her to run away or cry or something. She did none of that. She took a couple of deep breaths, looked up at the sky and then back at me.

"I don't care, Johnny. It's not your fault. We're still gonna be friends, right?"

"Yeah." I felt a glow of hope. "We're still friends."

Then she smiled. And she hugged me. I'd never been hugged by a girl before. My mother doesn't even hug me more than maybe once a year. Caris's arms were soft and she smelled like cupcakes and I understood something about the world and how a guy can lose his head over a girl sometimes. For the first time I can imagine doing the same.

As far as Caris was concerned, nothing else needed to be said about the Hempsteads and the Chapels. We walked down Division Street and when she spotted a stray cat we spent a few minutes trying to coax it out from beneath a truck but the animal glared at us with mistrust and darted across the street. She talked about how someday after she fulfills her dream of becoming a veterinarian she's going to open up an animal sanctuary and all the stray cats in Texas will be allowed to live here. She said I was invited to come stay there too and even though I don't especially want to live in Texas forever I might change my mind if I can live on Caris's sanctuary.

That was two weeks ago and we've hung out every day since then. She doesn't like to talk about her parents, which is fine because I don't like talking about mine either.

My memories of my father are fuzzy and incomplete. He was always gone for long periods of time thanks to his job as a long haul trucker. When he was home he argued a lot with my mother and I remember realizing that the two of them didn't like each other very much. He wasn't a bad father when he was around. He laughed often and played catch with me and Rafe. He took us hiking and would patiently tell us the names of the wildflowers and animals we saw. Sometimes he'd go out drinking with buddies and stay out all night. A few times I saw him with his knuckles bandaged up. I can remember being at the market once with my mother and in the next aisle a woman's voice said, "I swear, no man's as hot tempered as Clay Hempstead but no man ever gave it to me so good either." High pitched laughter erupted. My mother slammed her shopping cart into a tower of cereal boxes, charged to the next aisle and started screaming the word "Slut!"

I was nine when he died. Rafe was twelve. I went to the funeral but Rafe refused and promised to throw a tantrum if anyone tried to force him. Soon after that Rafe started getting into trouble and almost immediately my mom threw up her hands and quit trying to stop him. A few months ago he got hauled into the police station because he stole a car but the football coach paid a visit to the chief and Rafe was released with a warning not to do anything like that again. I worry about my brother. I worry about him even though I can't stand him. It's a weird way to feel.

Once when we were at the meteor crater, Caris asked me if I knew that her mom had grown up in Arcana and I had to think about it for a few minutes. I remember hearing the name Suzanne Chapel and I remember that my parents went to high school with her but they were never friends.

Caris frowned and said her mom was still in a Dallas hospital. When she asked her dad if she could visit he said that wasn't a good idea yet. Then she dropped the subject and said we should go to the museum and get some sodas from the vending machine. We spent the rest of that afternoon in the air conditioned comfort of the museum, looking at dusty rock exhibits.

This morning I'm supposed to meet Caris at the playground at nine. In summertime the days blend together and I've forgotten that it's Saturday. My mom is home and sitting at the kitchen table in her rose colored satin bathroom with a rip on the left sleeve. I think the robe was a gift from my father but I can't remember for sure.

She doesn't look up when I start searching the cabinets.

"Are we out of cereal?" I ask.

She yawns. "Probably."

I wait for a few seconds for her to speak again but she simply looks out the window and puffs on her cigarette. She never washed off her makeup last night and now it's smeared on her face. Her boyfriend works at the oil field ten miles outside town and he never stays over here. She sleeps at his place a lot and the rest of the time she's working at the nail salon so I hardly ever see her.

"Are you going grocery shopping today?" I ask because a search of the cabinets has yielded almost nothing worth eating.

The question annoys her. "I don't know. Maybe, if I have time. There are some graham crackers on the counter. Eat those."

I eat the crackers dry and wash them down with the last of the milk. While I'm wiping my mouth with the back of my hand, Rafe barges in through the door. I'm not surprised that he's just coming home now. When he's around I almost always sleep on the sofa because it's a pain to be stuck in the same tiny room with him. Last night he never came home so I got to sleep in my own bed.

My mother, however, is surprised to see him. Obviously she assumed he was snoring away in his bed. Her eyes narrow as she takes in the disheveled appearance of her oldest son. She likes Rafe far less than she likes me. The fact that he looks more like our dad every day might have something to do with that. She's forever muttering that he's 'such a goddamn Hempstead', which sucks because it's one thing to hear that from people in town but quite another to hear it from your own freaking mother. Rafe never appears to care but I care.

Rafe shoves me out of the way and hunts for a clean glass without greeting anyone and our mother sputters in the background.

"Raiford, what in the hell are you doing? Did you stay out all night?"

He fills the glass with tap water and drinks, ignoring the fact that anyone else is even in the room.

My mother sighs and taps her long fingernails on the table. No matter how tired or messed up she looks, her fingernails are always perfectly manicured and studded with sparkly accents. Rafe still says nothing so she turns her attention back to me.

"You're dressed already. Are you going out today?"

"Soon."

"Where?"

"I'm meeting a friend."

"What friend?" She yawns again.

Rafe decides to join the conversation. "Limp Dick's got himself a girlfriend."

My mother takes interest. A slight smile even crosses her face. "Really, Jonathan?"

"No." I'm sure my face is red. "We're just friends."

"What's her name?"

I'm reluctant to share any details. "Her name's Caris."

"Caris what?"

I have to think for a second and then remember Caris has told me this information before. "Marano."

I'm glad she doesn't have the Chapel last name. That would be tough to explain.

"Is she pretty?"

"God Mom, I don't know."

But I do know. She *is* pretty.

Rafe belches. "Too bad she don't have any tits yet."

"Raiford!" My mother slaps her hand on the table. "Don't use that language!"

He chuckles. "Why, you think I've never seen tits before? I messed around with a few last night. Hell, I bet Limp Dick over here has even seen real tits a time or two."

I don't know why he says things like that. I've never kissed a girl, let alone seen one without her shirt on.

My mother drops her head into her hands. "Why?" she moans. "What did I do to deserve this?"

She's tired. She's tired of this trailer and this life. I'm starting to believe that she's also tired of being a mother.

Rafe decides to remove his shirt right there in the kitchen. He's got hickeys all over his neck and he smells like beer. He tosses the shirt on a chair. It's his football jersey, the new one he got at the end of the school year. It has his nickname printed across the back.

Killer.

That's his nickname.

Because he destroys opponents on the field when he charges into them like a bloodthirsty warrior.

Killer.

Rafe thinks it's funny.

It's not funny.

My mother snatches his shirt and throws it back at him. "Don't leave your damn dirty laundry lying around for me to pick up."

"Fuck you," Rafe spits over his shoulder and leaves the room.

A few seconds later the bathroom door opens and then slams shut.

"That boy," my mother mutters, shaking her head.

Thanks to Rafe she's in a bad mood now but I don't know when we'll run into each other again. She'll probably be at Wayne's house by the time I find my way back here this evening.

"Hey, Mom?" I slide into the chair opposite hers.

"What?" She's pinching the sides of her temples, obviously in the throes of a blossoming headache.

"Can I please have some money? You know, to get food or whatever."

Whenever she leaves money here for us Rafe often finds it first and won't give me any.

The politeness of my request has satisfied her enough to be a little generous. She takes out all the cash in her wallet and hands it over. Three tens and two fives. I stick it all in my back pocket right away. I'm ridiculously happy to have the money. Caris ends up paying for stuff way too often because I'm usually down to nickels and pennies.

"Jonathan, are you having a good summer so far?" she asks.

"Sure." I clear my throat because there's a question I want to ask her and I'm not sure how it will be received. "Hey Mom, did you know Suzanne Chapel in school? The daughter of-"

"I know who she is." Her face has changed, grown pale. "Where'd you hear her name?"

"Uh, I don't know. Just around town I guess."

She grunts. "Someone was shooting their mouth off most likely. Suzanne had a shitty start in life for sure but that doesn't excuse what she tried to do to your father. I guess it was her form of revenge or maybe she's really as crazy as everyone says."

I have no idea what she's talking about. Naturally Suzanne would not have been friendly with the son of her parents' murderer. My mother's tense reaction indicates there's more to the story than that.

She leans forward and fastens her tired eyes on me. "You listen to me, Jonathan. Your father had a hell of a lot of flaws but one thing I'll say about the man is that he always owned up to whatever he did. And when he heard what that girl went around saying about him after all he tried to help her, well, he was outraged. And people believed it of course. It didn't matter that Suzanne never went to the cops and your father was never arrested. Too many people just believed it anyway." She stabs her long fingernail in the air. "Let this be a lesson for you. Don't you believe everything you hear."

I nod. I still haven't a clue what's going on. Or what my father could possibly have done to Caris's mother. "Okay."

She leans back in her chair and ties her belt robe tighter. She's scowling now, looking out the small kitchen window and thinking about things that are probably upsetting.

I push my chair back. "I'm gonna go now."

"Fine." She's still staring out the window and runs a hand through her auburn curls. She dies her hair. She's really a blonde. "You'll behave yourself, won't you?"

"Yeah, sure." I always behave myself. I've never even had detention at school.

After all the family weirdness I can't wait to bolt from the house. I run all the way over to the elementary school playground and find Caris has beaten me there. She's on one of the swings, twisting slowly around so the chain curls up. When she lets go she'll spin in fast circles. I used to do that all the time but haven't done it for years.

"Hi!" She's always so happy to see me. She pulls her foot up and allows herself to spin with her hair fanning out. She laughs the whole time and I laugh too because watching her does something magical inside my chest. I already know I won't say a thing about the mystery my mom hinted about this morning, about my father and her mother.

I plunk down on the empty swing beside her.

"You okay?" Her head's cocked and she's studying me.

"Yeah." I force a grin. "Rafe was just being a dick this morning."

"Oh." She nods knowingly. She's already suffered the misfortune of encountering Rafe. My cheeks burn when I remember the things he said to her, and about her.

"Wouldn't it be funny if someday you guys end up being really close?" she asks.

I snort with laughter because I can't imagine being buddies with Rafe. "That's not likely."

Caris won't stop looking on the bright side. "You never know. After all, a brother is a brother."

I agree grudgingly. "A brother is a brother." Then I remember I've got cash burning a hole in my pocket. "Let's go take the bus to the mall today. I'll buy you lunch since you're always buying stuff for me."

She bites her lip and tucks some loose hair behind one ear. The look she gives me isn't one I'm used to seeing from her. "You're going to take me out to lunch, Johnny?"

She sounds playful, flirty. Suddenly I feel grown up.

"Sure. You pick the place when we get to the mall."

"Great! Let's go now. We'll wait at the bus stop until it shows up."

She hops off the swing and I follow.

Obviously the summer will end eventually and she'll return to Dallas but I have a crazy thought that she'll want to stay here with her aunt in Arcana. We could go to school together, make plans together. I know it's a dumb thought because her parents are the kind of parents who will want her back.

But I wish things could be different.

I wish she would always be with me.

*J*ay hasn't said a word to me about the Alden disaster even though we've been working side by side at the bakery since six o'clock this morning. Of course, Shane was there too plus there was a ton of work to do between all the baking and dealing with customers so an ideal time to discuss psycho ex semi-boyfriends never came up.

Lana told me last night that Shane would understand if I wanted to take the day off. I did not want to take the day off. Sitting home alone and stewing about the malevolent look in Alden's eyes wouldn't do me a bit of good.

Surprisingly, I slept well. Lana and Shane stayed in her bedroom so I wouldn't feel alone and that was nice of them but it was really the idea of Jay being close by on the other side of the house that made me rest more peacefully.

Today, however, Jay is back to being his tight-lipped self. He grunts out a one word answer when I ask him a question and is all business throughout the morning rush.

"Need another batch of chocolate chip cookies," I call back to the kitchen when I notice there is only one left in the bin.

He looks up from the prep counter, delivers a curt nod, and says nothing.

Every now and then I get a little embarrassed when I remember that not only did he need to hurl Alden into a wall but he also saw me naked and shaking and crying.

When there's only an hour left until closing Shane says he needs to run out for a few minutes. I remind him that he still ought to look over the invoices and make sure they're right before I pay them and he bobs his head but I have a prediction that I'll be reminding him again tomorrow.

"You doing okay, Caris?" Shane asks me before leaving.

I smile. "Did Lana tell you to ask me that?"

She's already called twice today to check up on me. It's sweet and I feel loved.

"She did." His grin is slightly sheepish.

"I'm fine. Thanks Shane."

The bakery is currently empty of customers and once Shane closes the door the silence is overpowering. Jay is presumably still back there in the kitchen. He must work very quietly.

I don't want to harass him if he prefers to keep his distance so I start straightening up a few things on the counter. I'm refilling the napkin dispenser when the door opens and I look up to greet the arriving customer.

"Hey."

He's looking sorrowful and exhausted as he stands there with his hands stuffed into the pockets of his khaki shorts. He stays by the door and hesitates to take another step.

My hands crush the pile of napkins. "Alden, what the hell do you want?"

Something crashes in the kitchen. A split second later the door separating the kitchen from the rest of the bakery swings open and Jay thunders into the room.

He makes a beeline for Alden and growls, "I'll give you a three second head start, fucker, and then all bets are off."

"Whoa!" Alden holds up his hands in surrender. "Cool it, I'm not here to cause trouble."

Jay lunges but I stop him by placing a hand on his chest. His rock hard, extremely muscular chest.

"Jay, it's okay. I don't think he'll do anything."

Alden is still holding up his hands, like he's begging someone not to shoot. "No, I'm really not here for another ass kicking." He extends a hand. "No hard feelings dude, okay?"

Jay scowls. "Are you fucking kidding me?"

"Uh." Alden pulls his hand back and switches his gaze to me. "Can we talk?"

Jay spits out an answer first. "You're out of your motherfucking frat boy mind if you think I'm leaving her here alone with you."

Alden winces and raises an eyebrow at me. "Caris?"

I set the crushed napkins down. "We can talk."

I remind myself that this is Alden, who I've spent a lot of time with and almost had sex with on multiple occasions. Sometimes he makes me laugh and sometimes he's annoying but I've never felt uncomfortable with him.

Until yesterday.

The look in his eyes. The things he said. The way his fingers dug into my flesh.

I'll never forget. And I know I'm right never to forget.

"We can talk," I repeat. "But I would prefer if Jay stays in the room."

Jay crosses his arms and stays planted in the same spot. My bodyguard. He glowers at Alden with sheer loathing.

Alden frowns a little over being required to keep Jay eight feet away but recovers and clears his throat. "I tried calling you a bunch of times."

"I blocked you."

He scratches his head and thinks for a moment before speaking. "Look, I'm really so very sorry for how I acted. I had too much to drink. I'm not proud of myself at all."

"You shouldn't be. Jesus, Alden. What the hell?"

He nods and swallows hard. "Yeah. Fuck. I'm sorry."

"You're sorry. All right, you're sorry."

"I never meant for things to go down that way. I really like you a lot, Caris. I've always liked you. Hell, I might even be willing to do the boyfriend thing if you'd just give a little."

My jaw drops. "Are you serious?"

Alden fails to catch the sarcasm, and disgust, in my voice. He flashes a bright smile and closes in.

"Yeah, I'm serious. We could still try that if you think you could let this go."

"I have no desire to be your girlfriend, Alden. I don't even want to be your friend anymore."

His smile vanishes. I tense, waiting for the anger I saw in his face last night, but it doesn't come. He looks genuinely hurt, like he can't believe I'm refusing his generous relationship offer.

"If that's the way you feel…"

"It is."

"Okay." He shoots me one last wounded glance and then exits through the glass door.

I sigh with relief that he's gone and lean against the counter for support.

Jay hasn't moved from his post but now instead of scowling at Alden he's watching me.

"You all right?" he asks and I can hear the same gentleness in his voice that I heard last night. Underneath all the gruff attitude and rude comments he's not a bad guy.

Then again, I already knew that.

I exhale slowly. "Look, I don't know what got into Alden last night. But I just want you to know that I'm not in the habit of spending time with someone who would treat me like garbage. That was the first time he's ever acted like that."

"When there's a first time there won't be a last time, Caris."

He's right of course. And he obviously knows what he's talking about. He's seen more than his fair share of violence.

I don't want this moment to end, not now that we're actually talking for real. His posture has relaxed, his powerful arms no longer tensed up and crossed over his broad chest.

My god, he's gorgeous.

I wonder how seriously messed up it is that right now I'm having all kinds of feelings about the impressive way he fills out his Ruby's Bakery shirt.

I clear my throat and hope he hasn't developed a talent for mind reading.

"Jay, I just wanted to say thanks again for stepping in. I really appreciate it."

His brown eyes continue to watch me intently. "I would have done the same for anyone in trouble."

"Well, I'm glad you were there." I wrinkle my nose. "I do feel kind of weird about the fact that you saw me almost naked."

"Nah, I didn't see a thing."

I smile. "Liar."

He chuckles.

And because we're being so civil and because he's even laughing I feel brave enough to ask him a question.

"Why'd you change your name?"

He doesn't hesitate to fire a question right back at me. "Why didn't you become a veterinarian and open an animal sanctuary?"

I shrug. "Things change. Shit happens."

"Same here. Things change. Shit happens."

I think a lot more shit has happened to him than to me. I want us to keep talking. I want to ask him all of the questions. I want to tell him all of the things. I want to know him. I want my friend back.

And if he decides to take his shirt off and flex his muscles while we talk then I sure as hell won't complain about the view.

"It turned out I wasn't very good at science," I explain. "I still dream of opening up an animal sanctuary someday. And if I can't do that maybe I can at least adopt a cat or two."

He digests this information without comment.

"And as for choosing to be a business major," I add, "that was my dad's suggestion. He told me to major in something practical even if it seemed boring and I can't think of anything more simultaneously boring and practical than accounting, can you?"

Jay resists the attempt to be drawn out and simply shrugs.

"Your turn," I gently tease. "You have a phoenix tattooed on your back. I think it's cool, the symbolism."

But his expression has already shuttered and he edges back toward the kitchen.

"I think that's enough heartfelt sharing for one day," he says once his back is already turned and I'm displeased to hear the asshole factor return to his voice.

A moment ago I was hopeful that maybe we were having a breakthrough. I was thinking about all the things I want to share with him, all the things I crave to know about him. But when he disappears into the kitchen once more I realize I was just kidding myself.

There are so many things I want from Jay Phoenix.

And I can't have any of them.

These days Caris isn't exactly giving me the silent treatment but she's not making an effort either. At work we talk when we need to and at home we rarely pass one another. I get that she's disappointed. Sometimes I even wish that weren't the case and that I could give her what she wants. That day in the bakery when she gave Alden his permanent walking papers I thought about it.

She asked me a few shy questions and raised her eyebrows in the hopes of getting an answer. Caris was trying to open a door that I had kicked closed with all my might.

And I wavered, just for a moment.

When she shyly thanked me once again for coming to her aid I told her I would have done the same for anyone and that's true. I have no patience for a man who mistreats a woman and I would have stepped into a situation like that no matter who she was. But I wouldn't be walking around every day since then with the crushing agony over the fact that she'd been terrorized on my watch.

Caris is destined for something else. Someday she'll find a nice button down kind of guy who comes from a good family and has all the confidence in the world because the road he's traveling in life was already smoothly paved for him. He'll know how to treat her like gold and set the world at her feet.

And I fucking hate his imaginary guts already.

I declined to answer Caris's questions or spill my earnest guts about the shit storm my life became after I left Arcana behind that summer.

Now she's upset. Maybe a little mad. So be it. I'm not interested in handing out history lessons highlighting all that's happened since the night she told me she never wanted to see me again.

That was a bad time. With the cops hot on his heels, Rafe had run off but it was only a matter of time before he was caught. My mother couldn't handle anymore whispers and scandals. Her boyfriend Wayne was moving to Phoenix and she decided it was a better option than Arcana. I was allowed to go with them as long as I promised not to cause any problems. Within months puberty caught up to me in a rage and that's when my mother's attitude toward me was fatally altered.

She'd never been the most loving parent and I was always her favorite son, mostly because I caused the least amount of trouble and seemed to be least inclined to take after the line of troubled and violent men who preceded me. So it wasn't until I began to more closely resemble the strong Hempstead men that I'd catch the watchful, wary way she'd observe me and from then on she let go of what little love remained.

My mother hated the city of Phoenix upon arrival. She complained it was too hot and full of ugly concrete. I liked it fine. It was big and sprawling and nobody was at all interested in anyone else's shit.

Wayne didn't last long. He didn't like Phoenix either and decided to head to South Dakota but we weren't invited to come along. Soon there was a new guy named Forester, which I think was just his last name. I never knew him by any other. He moved into our cruddy two bedroom apartment in south Phoenix and I knew right away we'd never get along. I was used to being smacked around by Rafe so I wasn't surprised the first time Forester cuffed me upside the head. At least by then I was getting big enough to punch back. I'd joined the football team at school and it was a rough team, all of us spending more time fighting than playing. I passed my afternoons in the grimy weight room trying to lift my way to invincibility. Forester was still a lot stronger but he enjoyed when I fought back. He'd been an amateur boxer years before and I picked up a few things while getting my ass beat down. Those would be lessons I would later find useful.

I was shocked the day I arrived home from school and found the apartment empty. Not just empty of people but empty of furniture and things. At first I thought we'd been robbed but the old guy who lived in the neighboring apartment said he'd watched my mother and Forester move everything out during the day while I was at school. He wanted to know why I hadn't gone with them.

My own mother had abandoned me. She didn't even have the guts to say goodbye.

I never tried to find her. I figured there was no point. I remained in the empty apartment, sleeping on the bare floor, until the landlord finally got around to kicking me out because no one was paying the rent. After that I found odd places to stay, sometimes with the equally fucked up families of my football buddies. I earned money in ways I wasn't proud of, by stealing what I could and selling it where I could. My mistake was that I kept going to school. Eventually someone got wise to the fact that I didn't have a regular home and Child Protective Services was summoned.

What followed was a regular circus of temporary living situations. It turns out there are few people willing to invite a surly teenage boy to live in their home. It was after getting shuffled to my third foster family in four months that I started calling myself Jay Phoenix. Nobody presented an argument because what the hell did they care what I called myself? Every day I felt a little less like that skinny kid from Arcana who tried to hope for the best. No longer did I wish to be shackled to his name and all the bad history that accompanied it.

In one house there was a young female tattoo artist who lived in the garage apartment. I gave her fifty bucks that I stole from a neighbor who was dumb enough to leave a purse sitting outside on top of a car and she inked the design on my back.

After my tattoo was finished the girl flashed a wicked grin, unzipped my pants without asking and gave me my first blow job. I allowed it to happen even though I didn't like her much, partly because she had straight blonde hair.

Just like Caris.

And Caris was not a person I dared to think about.

All memories of Caris had to be crushed if little Johnny Hempstead was going to survive as big bad Jay Phoenix.

By the time I reached the place I thought of as Hell House I was big and numb and nearly sixteen. I'd encountered cruelty before but nothing like what I saw at Hell House. There were six or seven other kids there at any one time and the pair in charge looked like an ordinary, slightly overweight middle aged couple. Even their names were full of suburban ordinariness. Mike and Beth. I got a pretty quick education on what they were about. They tormented the kids by withholding food, doling out physical punishments and getting them hopped up on cheap drugs. The first time Mike tried any shit with me I made mincemeat out of his nose. He was unwilling to give up the check the state gave him every month for letting me stay under his roof so after that he let me be.

Twice I placed anonymous phone calls to the cops and warned them to check out what was really happening at Hell House. And twice they came, sniffed around, and left without even talking to any of the kids. Mike got wise to the fact that one of us had been calling the authorities. He and Beth gathered everyone for a meeting in a second floor bedroom promised to slit someone's throat if the cops showed up again. I started making plans to run away.

The lone bright spot of Hell House was Shane. He was the only guy there who was my age. The rest were younger. I preferred being alone and wasn't on the hunt for friends but Shane was a crackup and we got tight pretty fast. I could tell he'd started using because I knew the signs by now, but I had no idea what else was being done to him until one night he curled up in a ball on his bed and cried after blurting out the truth.

And the truth was horrific.

They were *selling* him. They'd dangle drugs in front of his nose and get him to go along with the plan when they rented him out to their drug addled kid rapist buddies.

I saw red. It was the first time, though not the last, that I've ever wanted to kill someone.

Shane was scared but I needed his help. On my own I'd never get anyone to believe this story. At school there was a teacher who seemed all right, always went out of her way to say my English lit essays were fantastic and prodded me to consider college. I could try talking to her to see if she had any ideas about what to do next. Going straight to the cops had been a bust. My case worker already thought I was garbage and would be unlikely to believe me. Maybe that English teacher knew a reporter. It was worth a try.

I never did get to talk to that teacher.

One night Shane refused to do what Mike wanted him to do and Mike started kicking the crap out of him. I heard the commotion from upstairs and raced down. I was able to handle Mike easily enough. His gut was soft and his arms flabby. But once he was down I wanted him to bleed. And bleed he did. It's possible I would have killed him if Shane hadn't pulled me back.

There were a few minutes of relief even though Beth was screaming and calling 911 while Mike sprawled unconscious on the floor. I thought that now we would be believed without question.

That's not what happened.

Shane was sick from drug withdrawal and no one listened to a word he said. The other kids were scared out of their minds. And Beth told anyone who would listen that I was a violent psychopath.

A judge ordered me to go to a juvenile detention center. The fact that Shane got sent there with me was complete bullshit but he said he didn't mind because it sounded like a better option than rolling the dice to possibly wind up with another Mike and Beth.

For the most part the teenage jail wasn't awful. Sometimes people would fuck with you so you'd have to fuck with them worse. Shane was my roommate and we looked out for each other and made all kinds of plans. After a year of living in a prison we decided the experience was no longer charming. Security was minimal so it was no big deal to bust out. And since we were closing in on our eighteenth birthdays when we were scheduled for release anyway, the law did not waste much energy chasing us down.

I was able to buy the documents I needed that identified me as a man named Jay Phoenix. A kindly construction crew foreman took a chance and gave me a job. I was strong and worked hard so he gave me another one. Before long I was making decent money.

Shane was less reliable. He bounced around between jobs and his old demons kept returning to haunt him. He'd get clean, stay that way for a little while, and then inevitably relapse. Drugs were plentiful on the streets of Phoenix and he tried every goddamn one of them in an effort to chase the nightmares away.

He'd been clean for nearly six months when some Texas attorney called him to report Ruby's death and ask when he could claim his inheritance.

And when I agreed to join him here in Hutton for the summer it never once crossed my mind that I might run into *her*.

"Jay."

Caris has appeared in the kitchen. Her hands are on her hips and her lips are slightly pursed as she pointedly looks around.

"Where are the banana muffins?" she asks.

"In the trash can."

"Why?"

"Because I messed up and forgot the eggs. I'll make more."

She sighs and practically starts tapping her foot. "The bin up front is empty."

"Are you expecting a horde of starving people demanding banana muffins?"

"You never know." She begins pulling out ingredients and hijacking the work space.

"What are you doing?" I have to force myself not to stare at her ass, which is cutely wrapped in a pair of white jeans beneath her tucked in shirt. "I said I'd make another batch."

"I'll get it started," she declares as if she's in charge. She begins measuring out ingredients with mathematical precision. "I can hear the bell if someone comes in but you can go out front and watch the counter if you want."

"If I want," I mutter as she nearly runs into me while grabbing for a large spoon.

I should move away from this spot.

I should stop staring at her ass.

I should stop picturing twisting her blonde ponytail around my hand while I ride her from behind like a motherfucking stallion.

I do none of these things.

Caris's head swivels and she peers over her shoulder at me. "You look bored, Jay."

"I am bored. You just barged in here and took my job away."

The urge to rub my hard dick against her tight pants is insane. Fortunately I'm good at being stone faced. She has no clue.

Caris rolls her eyes. "Then why don't you go out front, like I suggested?"

"Are you the new manager?"

She seems surprised that I'm arguing. Ordinarily it's my policy to exchange as few words with her as possible. Otherwise it leads to circumstances like the present one, when my blood starts pumping and my dick begs for attention.

"Oh god, I'm sorry," she mutters, dropping the spoon in the bowl and pivoting around. She sets her palms on the counter and rolls her neck around like it hurts. She's got a hot figure. She's slight but not too thin. I can imagine my hands circling the curve of her waist.

"I didn't mean to be overbearing," she says. "It's just that I promised Shane I'd make sure all the product bins were full because we always get a rush of customers when that afternoon hot yoga class lets out across the street."

"Where is Shane anyway?"

"He seemed kind of agitated and said he had to run out for something."

I lower my head. A suspicion that began blossoming days ago sprouts a dozen new leaves.

"Is Shane okay?" Caris asks and when I look up I see her mouth twisted with concern.

My internal alarm bell goes off and I'm no longer thinking about how sweet her skin would taste. "What do you mean?"

Caris listens for a second to confirm we're alone and then shifts her weight, looking uncomfortable. "Lana's getting worried about him. He hasn't been sleeping, seems keyed up all the time. She saw him pop a pill the other morning and when she asked about it he told her they were the multivitamins she gave him but she found a bag of them in his pants later. They're not vitamins."

"No," I sigh miserably. "I'm sure they're not."

"Look, I know it's none of my business but I also know he's had, um, problems in the past."

"Yeah." I feel defensive all of a sudden and I don't mean to snap at her but that's the way it comes across anyway. "Everyone's got fucking *problems* in their past, don't they, Caris?"

A long moment passes while she just stares at me.

An apology is on the tip of my tongue. I didn't mean to hurt her feelings. I'm just worried about Shane. And obviously so is she. And so is Lana.

"Listen…" I start to say but she cuts me off.

"You can finish the goddamn muffins yourself," she bites back and stalks out of the kitchen.

With a sigh I pick up the spoon she left in the bowl.

"Shit," I mumble to myself.

Right now it's the most fitting sentiment. On so many levels.

CARIS

It's a devil's oven kind of day.

That's my mother's expression for times when summer is raging and the humidity climbs to a nearly intolerable ratio.

The thermometer tops out at ninety five degrees in the mid afternoon and the air outside is better suited to a sauna. Shane tells me to take off and go somewhere cool. The bakery is closing in half an hour anyway.

My jeans and scratchy polo feel positively oppressive. I remember that I'd stuffed a change of clothes in my bag this morning so before leaving I visit the rest room to change to denim cutoffs and a blue tank top.

"See ya, Caris." Shane is in the middle of emptying the trash can but he pauses to wave at me.

"You sure you don't need me to stay?"

"Nah, there's just a few things to do before closing and then I get to go home and get ready to take my lady out."

"That's right, tonight's a big date for you two."

Lana told me Shane got an idea in his head to take her someplace fancy. He made reservations at the priciest steakhouse in town this evening and plans to dress in a suit and tie.

He grins. "Only the best for my princess."

"Have a good time."

I hesitate at the exit for a few seconds and glance at the door leading to the kitchen, knowing Jay is back there and probably waiting for me to leave. We've hardly said a handful of words to each other in days. He's impossible. He shoots hungry glances at me every chance he gets and yet can't bring himself to finish a polite conversation.

Whatever.

If he's determined to remain a brooding, sexy enigma then I have better things to do than waste all my energy reaching out. The guy's got issues. And he certainly doesn't want my help sorting them out.

The air outside is every bit as heinous as I assumed it would be and I'm grateful to be wearing lighter clothing. I crank up my car air conditioning and wait for the blast of coolness to hit.

While I'm sitting there I decide to make a quick call home. My mother answers and she's glad to hear my voice. She's already buying all my favorite foods in preparation for my visit next week. Based on my conversations with my dad I know she's maintaining these days. She's begun seeing her therapist three times a week again instead of two. Her medication has been adjusted and the effects have been encouraging so far.

I'm not prepared when she asks me about the guy I've mentioned dating now and again. I have no intention of telling my parents about what happened with Alden. It's not something they need to hear. I simply tell my mother that we've chosen to go our separate ways and she says nothing more about it. She asks for a reminder about what time my plane gets in. I'm leaving from the small municipal airport right outside Hutton that only offers flights to a handful of destinations. The visit will be short. I fly in on Tuesday, my birthday is on Wednesday, and I'll be flying back to Hutton on Thursday. When the call ends I feel the same way I always feel after a conversation with my mother. Very loved and vaguely worried. She did sound happy. I hope she really is.

With a sigh I pull the car out of the parking lot and then have to stop and think about where to go next. I lied to myself about having better things to do than stew about a certain unfairly sexy non-friend. Here it is on the brink of Friday evening and I have absolutely no plans. Ever since the Alden debacle I've been keeping my social outings to a minimum, partly because I dread running into him. I decide to treat myself to a movie. Movies are air conditioned. Movies are fun. Movies are bound to be Alden free.

There's a brand new adaptation of a Jane Austen novel that I've been planning to see and I nearly buy a ticket before changing my mind and selecting a blockbuster superhero flick instead. The movie is not really up my alley and frankly I'm at a loss when it comes to characters like Water Man and Snake Woman. I sit there in the half full theater chewing popcorn and watching things explode on the screen while remembering another movie theater in another town a long time ago. That day I sat beside a boy who was my friend and I considered holding his hand but lacked the guts to make the first move.

The memory makes me smile even as it makes me sad. The movie isn't over yet but I've lost track of who is trying to kill who with their laser beam eyes and so I just take my popcorn and go.

At home the only other car in sight is Lana's and the house is quiet. She and Shane must have already left in his truck. Jay is most likely hiding at the gym and admiring his muscles.

My hair is stuck to the back of my neck and my denim cutoffs have become sweaty and uncomfortable. Once I'm in my bedroom I peel off the damp shirt and spot my bikini top hanging on a knob of the dresser. The bottom half to my bikini is nowhere to be found but my black panties will be good enough. There's no one around to see me anyway.

It's almost five o'clock but the sun still feels strong. Seizing a towel and a bottle of sunscreen that becomes necessary when I spend more than ten minutes outdoors this time of year, I pad outside in my flip flops. I toss everything, including my glasses, on the nearest lounge chair and jump in with the graceless eagerness of a child. The water is perfect. I allow myself to dip completely under the surface, folding my legs and resting my palms on my knees lotus-style as my body sinks to the bottom. The chlorine burns my eyes but I keep them open anyway, gazing up at the bubbles that disappear one by one under the glare of the sun. The roar of quiet filled my ears and my lungs began to complain. This is a game I used to play as a child, pretending I was descended from a long lost line of mermaids. I was waiting for my power to claim me. I imagined it would if I could pass the test and worship the water correctly.

A tickle teases the back of my throat, emerging in a cough that puts an end to mermaid games. I unfold my legs and shoot to the surface, sputtering and flinging wet hair out of my eyes as I dog paddle to the ladder.

I'm out of the pool and dripping all over the cement before I realize I'm not home alone after all.

Jay is here, standing on the far side of the patio. Those powerful arms of his are crossed as he watches me. He might have just arrived or he might have been watching me since I skipped straight to the water. I never looked in that direction before jumping in.

I slick my hair back with my fingers and discreetly check to make sure nothing important has slipped thanks to my reckless jump. There are few things more disconcerting than thinking you're alone and then discovering you are not. Thankfully, no nipples are peeking out. My panties are sodden but in place.

And what if they weren't? Would Jay Phoenix have just stood there on the patio, mutely observing?

"Hello!" I shout. Loudly. Obnoxiously. Because he remains cemented in the same position with his arms crossed. I can't quite make out his expression without my glasses on but I would bet it's unfriendly.

Shooting him a defiant look I stalk over to the lounge chair where I'd dumped my belongings. I swipe my wet skin with the towel, weighing whether I feel like escaping Jay's scrutiny or reveling in it.

I choose the latter.

I've seen the way he looks at me sometimes. He's not as impenetrable as he pretends to be.

I maneuver the lounge chair until it's flat and I stretch out with a sigh. My body isn't fantastic but it has breasts and hips and once I have my glasses back on my face I sneak a look at Jay to see if he's staring. He hasn't moved. He's a Jay statue over there on the patio. I could probably lie here fingering myself and he'd just continue his impassive vigil.

Minutes passed. Or maybe it's only seconds. My internal clock is off. Everything about me is off and has been since the moment I realized who Jay Phoenix really is. I'm not sure what to expect from him. And he doesn't know how to behave around me. For weeks we've existed at a stalemate and what we need is a showdown.

I close my eyes and wait for something to happen. When nothing happens I crack my right eye open.

"You'll get burned," Jay warns.

I might but probably not. The sun is on its way down.

But the deep sound of his voice has produced ripples of warmth to places aching to become more familiar with him. I drop my arm and retrieve the sunscreen from the ground beside the lounge chair before squirting a generous ration into my palm. If Jay likes to stand around and watch then he's free to stand around and watch *this*.

My hands begin at my belly and move down slowly, rubbing lotion on every visible inch, covering my thighs, raising one leg at a time and rubbing slowly, so slowly.

The air hisses out of his mouth. Along with the word "Jesus".

He shifts, twisting his body in the opposite direction and shaking his head like he's having an argument with someone unseen.

Another squirt of lotion and I begin on my arms before moving to my chest. Jay's head swivels back in time to notice when I briefly cup my breasts. This is uncharted territory for me. I'm not bold like this unless I've been drinking. I'd be too embarrassed. I should be embarrassed now. I like this too much, taunting him, enjoying the loss of his indifferent expression, which is now replaced with something much more primitive.

A fundamental ache rises within me and ignites when he takes a step. And then another. His arms are no longer tightly crossed but fall to his sides in clenched fists. He lacks the ability to mask the desire in his eyes and there's madness in the way we look at each other as he closes the distance. My eyes stray to his hands, his big and excessively masculine hands. They do not look like the same hands that touched the stems of wildflowers or tenderly held baby geckos a million years ago in Arcana. There's nothing gentle about the look of his hands now, and nothing gentle about what I'm thinking they might do to me.

He freezes when I sit up. I'm not going anywhere. I roll over on my belly and hold out the tube of sunscreen.

"I can't reach my back."

This is a defining moment. If we can't have honest conversations then we'll have something else. And if Jay planned to refuse then he wouldn't be plucking the sunscreen out of my hand.

I fold my hands under my chin, willing my body to stop trembling. When he hesitates I wish I could see his face. Seconds pass before he finally drops to his knees and exhales loudly. I hear the top of the sunscreen bottle snap open, feel the cool drops being squeezed onto my back.

I swallow. I try to speak and need to clear my throat to be heard. "You might have to unhook the top."

His next move is unexpected. He brushes aside my wet hair and allows his fingertips to graze the base of my neck before tracing my spine. The shock of his touch yields a deep shiver.

I've figured out what I want from him more than anything else.

Jay hooks a finger into the strap and tugs, silently explaining that this is my chance to push him away. I rise up on my elbows with impatience. The ache that had originated deep in my belly travels low to throb between my legs as I arch my back and press my hips deeper into the lounge cushion. A low moan escapes my lips when he unhooks the strap. An instant later his hands are on me, flattened across my back and slowly roaming up and down in order to rub the lotion in. His strong fingers surround my ribcage. I am aware that he could crush me if he felt the urge but the thought does not make me afraid. Jonathan Hempstead or Jay Phoenix or whatever he feels like calling himself would never hurt me with his hands. Only with his cold words. His indifferent eyes. His granite heart.

He keeps massaging in a downward motion until he reaches the waistband of my wet panties.

Do it. I dare you.

The pulsing need between my legs makes me behave badly. I roll my hips in a slow rhythm, rubbing myself on the chair, urging him to do more to me, to do everything.

"You're fucking playing with fire," he growls. His fingertip slides a mere inch inside the elastic before stopping.

My breath hitches and I dig my hips in harder. If he wants to play games then he can play the dirtiest ones ever invented. I will scream if I don't come soon. And I'm out of patience. I abruptly roll to my back. My unhooked bikini top is discarded.

"Then play *with* me," I demand.

His jaw is tight, his eyes blazing. His shirt comes off.

I'm touching myself, teasing lightly between my legs. A second ago I couldn't wait to come and now I don't want to come yet. Not until he's inside of me. This is surreal lunacy and I don't care. I'm pushing my panties down.

"This is what I want," I whisper and reach for him. "It's what you want too."

He does. He's breathing hard and unsnapping his jeans.

"You want me to fuck you out here on the goddamn patio furniture, huh? That's what you want?"

"Yes."

His hands find me again. One holds my right hip and the other covers my belly and moves lower. It's too much. My eyes roll back in my head and I release the most pornographic of moans as his finger slides inside me, just barely, just enough to make me clench my teeth and shudder with the promise of what's to come.

"Caris, look at me," he demands.

And I obey because right now he's in charge and I'll do anything he says. His red boxers are visible beneath his unzipped jeans and his bare chest is fascinating but there's a troubled expression lurking in his eyes.

"This is not how you want your first time to be," he announces and removes his finger before sliding my panties back into place. "Is it?"

For a second I don't understand how he knows that I've never had sex before and then I remember the scene with Alden. Of course he knows. He heard the words Alden yelled at me. He heard everything.

I need him to touch me again. I trace the muscles of his upper arm and feel him shiver. My fingertips reach his jaw where there's just a hint of rough stubble.

"I want *you*," I say with conviction. "I want it to be with you."

His eyes close and I touch his lips.

"You won't be hurting me," I whisper in case that's what he's worried about. "I mean, I've done…other things before. I know it won't hurt."

When he opens his eyes again he's looking away from me. He spots my towel on the ground and gently covers me with the terrycloth. My eyes feel the sting of mortified tears because I'm certain he's about to turn me down and because I remember the last time he covered me with a towel when I was dazed and crying on the kitchen floor.

What the hell did I think I was doing anyway?

I'm no irresistible seductress. I'm not even close.

Jay stands up.

I expect he'll just dash inside without saying anything because that's how he is.

I'm surprised when he offers his hand. I hold the towel in place as he helps me up.

And then I'm completely astounded when he draws me close, slides his other hand up my back and brushes his lips across mine. Our tongues touch and my knees weaken and I don't even realize I've dropped the towel until my nipples graze his chest.

And then I'm lost.

We both are.

I hear the whimper in the back of my throat as the kiss becomes almost savage in its intensity. There's vanished friendship and squandered years and new passion in that kiss and it's unlike any other in the world.

His hands get tangled in my wet hair and my palms marvel over the muscles of his back. I wouldn't mind passing hours this way. Days. Forever. No one else will ever feel this good.

I love the sensation of being lifted in his arms. I believe he'll carry me to my bedroom. He doesn't. He brings me to his room instead and this makes me irrationally happy, like being allowed to cross the threshold of his bedroom is a hundred times more intimate than feeling my naked skin against his.

His room is so neat it's almost like no one really lives here. Jay is careful when he sets me on top of the bed and even more careful when he removes my panties for good.

I'm trying to get rid of his jeans and he lets me. He kicks them off and kneels between my parted legs in his boxers. He smiles at me and my heart lurches because it's not the first smile he's ever given me. It's just the first one he's given me in so many years. I want to take my glasses off because I know I look prettier without them but I'm not willing to surrender a clear view of him.

He kisses the inside of each of my thighs before reaching inside a one drawer nightstand. He shifts objects around in there until he finds what he's looking for and then he tears the package of the condom off with his teeth.

I'm already naked but he's still wearing his boxers. When I make a grab for them he shoves them down with impatience. Now I can see all of him and there's so much to see that it's intimidating. I hope I'm right about this not hurting. But I don't even care if it does hurt. I've imagined doing this a thousand times in a thousand different ways and none of those fantasies could hold a candle to this reality.

He slides the condom on so expertly and it's obviously something he's done many times. I push the thought away. I don't care what he calls himself or who he's been with before. He's here now. He's mine.

"Jay," I whisper and pull him closer. I've decided that I like this new name of his.

My legs eagerly spread wide and he settles on top of me with care. I would have expected him to be rough if I didn't know he's also the boy who once tore his shirt up so that I could clean my scraped knee. That's who he was then and that's who he is now. The harshness of his life hasn't robbed him of his soul and I groan with bliss when I feel him enter me.

The way he moves is slow and tender at first. With his thumb he brushes a strand of wet hair from my forehead and trails his knuckle down my cheek. I tease his lower lip with my teeth and rake my fingers across his back to let him know I'm not breakable. He can use me harder. I want him to.

Jay knows how to take a hint. He quits holding back and thrusts deeply again and again. I give in and allow the frenzy of pleasure to climb to impossible heights before cresting with a consuming fury that rocks me to the core. I'm gasping. I'm shaking.

And he's not finished. He raises himself up on his forearms, driving his way in so deep and so relentlessly that another wave of tortured pleasure overtakes me and I'm glad the house is otherwise empty because I'm aware that I'm being pretty damn loud.

When Jay finally lets himself come he groans, rearing his head back, and I memorize everything about the way his face looks as the spasms shake him. The surge of tenderness within me is made of so many different emotions. I can't even name them all. This is what other people talk about, what they yearn to find; this fierce, almost instinctive connection with another person.

Jay rolls off to the side so I don't get crushed and we spend a few moments catching our breath. It's odd that my next move makes me feel shy after everything that just happened but nonetheless I do feel shy as I reach for his hand.

Our fingers lace together and the room begins to dim with the approach of twilight.

"Can I stay here all night?" I ask and then bite my lip, worrying that I sound foolish. Needy. Ridiculous.

He doesn't answer with words. He curls his arms around me and buries his face in my neck. As I stroke his sweaty skin and watch the light patterns fade on the wall a tear leaks out of the corner of my eye. It's possible I've never been this happy before.

A short time later when he raises his head to kiss me, he's clearly ready for more.

That's okay because so am I.

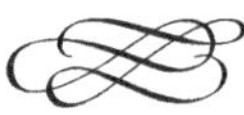

JAY

She's sound asleep when I reach for my phone to check the time. It's a quarter to five in the morning. My alarm is set for fifteen minutes from now and I switch it off to give Caris a few extra minutes of rest.

She needs it after the night we had.

This is what I've been resisting since the moment I recognized her on Shane's back patio. And the instant I touched her last night I knew the battle was over.

I'm not sorry, not even a little bit. Our history is messy, complicated and strange.

Her family.

My family.

Fuck them all.

Maybe they don't need to matter. Maybe we're the only ones who matter in this equation.

Inside of me I've been holding a steel door closed with all of my strength. It crashed open when our lips met. And the world didn't end. Far from it. We teased and screwed and played and fucked until the condoms were gone. I was gentle with her and then I was rough, depending on what we both wanted in the moment.

She stirs ever so slightly and my lips brush her bare shoulder in the darkness. Emotions are coursing through me and most of them are unfamiliar, either long buried or never explored. Deep down I've known this all long, that if I ever took her in my arms then I wouldn't have the willpower to let her go.

There are voices in the kitchen. I must have heard them in my sleep. I can't make out every word but the ones I do hear don't sound good.

Shane's voice is tortured and saying, "Baby."

Lana is distressed, possibly crying. "Have to talk about this," is the fragment that reaches me, and then, "Love you and I'm afraid."

There's a rustling sound and then the opening and closing of a door. Caris continues to sleep. I tuck the covers around her, rise from bed and feel around in my dresser for a pair of shorts to yank on.

I'm quiet when I open the door and as the hallway light bathes her sleeping face my heart flips. She's so fucking beautiful.

Shane is sitting in the kitchen wearing only a pair of wrinkled suit trousers. His head is in his hands. Lana is nowhere in sight.

"You all right?" I ask him as I plug in the blender and begin removing things from the fridge to make a breakfast smoothie.

He lifts his head and I'm alarmed to see how red and sunken his eyes are. He tries to force a smile. "Yeah. Late night, that's all."

I begin cutting up fruit, keeping one eye on him. "You look like you haven't slept."

"I haven't."

"Why don't you go get some sleep now? I'm plenty capable of opening the bakery this morning."

He pauses. "You sure?"

"Absolutely." I drop cut fruit into the blender before adding juice and ice. "Caris will be there too. We can handle it between the two of us."

I don't ask him about the argument with Lana. I have a bad feeling I know what it's about, especially after Caris mentioned how worried Lana has been. I'm worried too. I know Shane. Something needs to be done soon.

He yawns. "I don't like the thought of slacking off but for today I think I'll take you up on that."

I press the button to the blender. When I switch it off I see that Shane is now watching me with a bemused expression.

"You've got someone over," he says, jerking his head in the direction of my bedroom.

I select a pair of tall glasses from the cabinet. "Maybe."

"Maybe my ass." He picks up a random spoon that's sitting on the table and throws it at me. It clatters to the tile, making a racket.

"Keep it down, jackass." I flip him off and pour the blender contents into the two glasses.

He just laughs. "Don't worry. After all the noise you guys made last night, Caris is probably so worn out she won't wake up so easy."

I'm in the middle of taking a sip from one of the glasses and I choke. "What?"

He rolls his eyes. "No point in denying it. Did you really think no one noticed how you guys are always looking at each other like you're two seconds away from boning in public?" He shrugs. "It's cool. You and Caris. It's downright disgustingly adorable."

I set the glass down. "Look, I've got to tell you something."

"What's up?"

"Caris and I, we already knew each other years ago. When we were kids she spent a summer in my hometown."

Shane is surprised. "Arcana, right?"

"Yup."

"Okay, that's definitely news to me. At least it explains why there was so much bizarre electricity between the two of you."

"Yeah, that's not all. Remember how I told you about my grandfather?"

"The murderer. Sure."

"He killed a young couple. Caris's grandparents happened to be the young couple."

"Shit." He says the word slowly and then shakes his head. "Weird world. What are the odds?"

A question I've asked myself a lot lately. I'm not going to ask it anymore. She's here. She's in my life. Let the chips fall where they may.

I'm hoping my confession will prompt Shane to share one of his own.

"Where's Lana?" I ask him carefully.

He shifts his eyes away. "Sleeping." He stands up, stretches and thumps me on the back. "Look, I'm gonna get some shuteye. Thanks for covering this morning."

I'm disappointed that he says no more. "No problem."

I listen to the sound of him shuffling down the hall to his room. Then I take the two glasses and head to mine.

Caris is awake and she's switched on the bedside lamp. Her knees are pulled up and her glasses are on. When she sees me the look on her face is almost timid.

"Good morning," she says, the sweetest voice ever.

"Morning." I raise a glass, close the door with my foot and take a seat on the edge of the bed. "I made you breakfast."

A smile crosses her face. "Is that one of your fruit smoothies?"

"Sure is."

She takes a few sips. "It's good." She sets the glass down on the table and wraps her arms around her knees once more. It's cute the way she's keeping herself modestly covered. After all of last night's dirty deeds there's not once inch of her that I haven't seen or licked or sucked or enjoyed.

She seems to have something on her mind so I silently drink my breakfast and let her sort it out.

"Jay, I wasn't sure how things would be this morning. With us." She takes a deep breath. "When I woke up and saw you weren't here I thought maybe you would just prefer to pretend none of it had happened."

I set my glass down beside hers. It freaking kills me that she assumed I would give her the cold shoulder after the night we shared but I don't blame her. I'm the one who has rudely brushed her off time and again.

The thought occurs to me that I should have kissed her as soon as I walked in. I lean over and kiss her now. Our mouths are cold from our drinks but kissing has a way of warming things up quickly. I want her again. I don't believe I will ever quit wanting her. I back up a few inches and trail my finger over her jawline.

"I've been such an asshole."

"Sometimes," she agrees. She takes my finger and kisses it.

"Caris, I promise you something. I'm not just fucking around for the hell of it. Now that this is where we are I'm all in."

She has my whole hand now. She places it on her breast. I feel the quick thud of her heart beneath my hand.

"Don't you dare break this," she whispers.

"Never."

Caris throws her arms around my neck and hugs me tight. When I hug her back I can almost hear the sound the rest of of my private walls crumbling. They took so much effort to build. Aside from Shane, there hasn't been a single consistent person in my life. Caris is worth the risk. If I can't keep my promise to her then I'll never be capable of keeping it to anyone.

She rests her head on my shoulder and I know this is totally a touching moment and all but I can't help getting hard. I'd have no problem falling back into bed and using her body some more. The condoms are finished but there are plenty of creative ways to have fun. And she'd surely enjoy them all. She has so far.

But there's a bakery to open and a friend to cover for.

I stroke her hair. "We ought to get ready for work. Shane's not going in until later so it's just us this morning."

She nips at my neck. "Should we shower together?"

My dick is all kinds of interested in that idea. I smile.

"You think we'll make it to the bakery before noon if we do?"

She laughs. "Not a chance."

We finish our smoothies and then I give her a t-shirt to wear for the extremely short walk back to her apartment. She suggests driving to the bakery together and the way she says it, like she can't imagine anything more fun, loosens up all kinds of feelings in my chest. Making her happy seems easy.

Half an hour later we're both showered and dressed and leaving for work together like some suburban married couple. Caris is very bright eyed and talkative. I don't know how she has so much energy after last night's endless acrobatics but I give the girl a lot of credit. She points out a bunch of Hutton landmarks on the drive to the bakery and talks about the university. Sunrise is so early this time of year that it's already bright out.

As I pull into the parking lot she grows suddenly silent. I look over to see her tugging on her ponytail and looking out the window. My hand finds her knee and squeezes.

"Hey."

Her head turns at the sound of my voice. I lean over to kiss her, intending just a quick peck because we have twenty minutes before we need to open and even though there's a lot of prepared dough already chilling in the fridge it still needs some oven time.

Caris has other ideas.

She grabs my shirt and escalates the kiss into something rough and passionate. She climbs into my lap, swinging one leg over to straddle me and now the last thing on my mind is baking cupcakes. I pull her shirt up, run my hands all over her skin and sneak my fingers beneath her bra.

"You feel so good," she moans, grinding her hips in a way that's pure fucking torture. "It drives me crazy."

My fingers find the snap of her jeans and then slide the zipper open. I don't give a shit that there's not a single condom left in my possession or that it's light out and boning in the front seat isn't something that wins anyone a good citizenship award.

Apparently my self control is negotiable where she's concerned.

The crunching sound of tires over asphalt causes Caris to freeze. She spots a beige sedan with a white-haired occupant pulling in three spaces down and rolls off me, tucking in her shirt with a red face while I break into laughter.

"What's so funny?" She glares at me, which is adorable.

"You're such a good girl."

"I don't want to get arrested."

"That's why I'm laughing. Because you think you'll get arrested."

"Oh yeah?" She tightens her ponytail and looks me over shrewdly. "Take your dick out."

"What?"

"Your dick. Take it out of your pants."

I have no issue with following her instructions. I unzip and stroke myself in front of her.

"Now what?"

She flashes a sweet smile and leans in to whisper in my ear. "Get ready. Because I'm going to suck you off so hard you'll never dare call me a good girl again."

"Fuck." My hands grip the steering wheel.

"HELLO!"

The old man in the sedan has trundled over here with a walking stick, which he uses to tap on the window.

"I NEED SIX LEMON SCONES!"

He's nearly screaming. He appears to take no notice of my exposed dick and hastily I push it back into my pants.

Caris is cracking up beside me.

"You're gonna make good on that threat later," I vow.

"LEMON SCONES!"

"If you're lucky," Caris giggles and hops out of the truck.

She waits for me to join her outside. The old man is limping to the bakery door. He's still muttering about lemon scones but at a much lower decibel.

Caris is still laughing. She grabs my hand as we walk to the door. It's a simple, affectionate gesture.

And in a heartbeat it causes the past to fold into the present in a way that manages to make me uneasy.

"That's creepy as hell," Johnny says.

He kicks a loose rock and regards me with a worried frown.

"Tell me about it. He stood there outside my door for twenty minutes last night. I could see his shadow. Finally I switched on the light and he disappeared. Then I locked the bedroom door."

"Did you tell your aunt?"

"No."

"Why not?"

Because I feel weird about telling Aunt Vay that her boyfriend was lurking outside my bedroom for the second time in a week.

"I don't know," I sigh. "Let's talk about something else."

Johnny is still bothered but he agrees to move on to a different topic. He says his brother Rafe has been stealing things out of people's houses.

"Not things he could use or sell," Johnny says. "Just random shit. He stole framed pictures and dinner plates and even some kid's stuffed bunny rabbit. I think he just likes to break in and be able to say he took something. Mostly he sets it on fire in a big metal drum right outside the park."

We mull over the weirdness of this development. Johnny thinks it's only a matter of time before Rafe gets into real trouble. This worries him. I guess even if you don't like your brother you don't want to see him in handcuffs.

I take his hand and carefully lace my fingers through his. We've started doing that sometimes, holding hands. It began the day he took me to the mall and bought me a hamburger and fries. I felt very mature ordering food and sitting at a table with him. It was the closest thing to a real date I'd ever had. And later, when we walked around the mall, I finally had the courage to reach for his hand. It felt far better than kissing some grubby boy at a basement party just because everyone expected you to. Holding Johnny's hand gave me butterflies and I was so happy when he didn't pull away. Twice since then he's been the one to reach for my hand and I like that even more. We don't talk about it. It's just something we do.

We get some snacks and sodas from the market and sneak them into the movie theater because the food there is way too expensive. The superhero movie isn't playing anymore. Instead there's a movie about kids who can see ghosts. Shortly after the movie begins I wish we hadn't chosen it because the girl in the movie keeps seeing the ghost of her grandmother. I don't want ghosts to exist. I don't want to think of my own grandmother sadly floating around the grassy field where her life ended.

Johnny can sense that I don't want to watch this. He nudges me.

"Do you want to go?" he whispers and I nod.

When we're outside Johnny says, "I'm glad you wanted to leave. That movie sucked."

The movie didn't really suck but I like him even more for saying that. He reaches for my hand this time and I forget all about ghosts.

We visit the elementary school playground and share the chips and sodas. Johnny finds a small lizard and lets it crawl up his arm and onto his shoulder. He keeps it there for a while, like a pirate would keep a bird. He admitted to me once that he doesn't have many friends at school and I know that's just because they don't understand how awesome he is. The kids at his school must be a pack of idiots. I wish he went to my school instead.

I'm not happy to see the time has come for me to go back to Aunt Vay's house. Every day I dislike being there even more. Whenever I ask my dad when I can come home he promises the day will be here soon. Johnny is the only thing that makes this summer in Arcana bearable.

He holds my hand again until we reach the town square, where we always part ways. I know he watches me to make sure I get safely to the corner of Dunstan Street. Tomorrow we'll meet here in the same place at nine in the morning. Every day when I wake up in my mother's frozen-in-time bedroom I can't wait to get out of there.

I'm not happy to see that Aunt Vay's boyfriend has invited himself for dinner. Gary has been around more and more lately. The only time he's ever laid a hand on me was that day we collided by the side door. He stares at me all the time, though. He's always remarking to Aunt Vay that I look so very much like Suzanne and this makes Aunt Vay smile because she loves my mother so much. She doesn't notice when he stares at me with hooded eyes and I always feel the urge to cross my arms over my chest even though there's hardly anything there. I don't even really need a bra yet.

After dinner I go straight to my room, sit on the bed and look at random things on my phone. I wonder what my mother used to do to pass the time when she was my age and lived in this room. There was no internet in the eighties and Aunt Vay claims she hasn't had a television in her house for thirty years. The first week I was here I found a row of yellowed romance paperbacks in the closet and now I take one out. It's a love story about a teenage couple and the format is unusual. The girl's side is told first on the right hand page. Then you're supposed to flip it over and read the boy's side on the left. It's a cool idea. There's never just one side to any story.

Aunt Vay knocks on the door to tell me she and Gary are leaving. They will be down the street at a neighbor's house for a card game. I'm relieved Gary will be out of the house for a while. I have a plan to wedge a book underneath the door because the little button lock on the knob doesn't seem strong enough. Part of me warns that I'm being paranoid and then I remember the worried look on Johnny's face when I told him about Gary. He doesn't think I'm being paranoid.

Being in this house alone is spooky. I try to skim the pages of the teenage love story but I keep hearing noises and that makes me think about the ghost movie. I'm glad we didn't stay. I'm not sure I want to know how it ends.

I'm beginning to feel drowsy so I set the book aside face down and stretch out, closing my eyes. I'm thinking about Johnny and his temporary pet lizard. Before we left the area he removed it from his shoulder and set it down gently on the sandy ground. Once again I really wish Johnny had a phone but he says his mother doesn't let him use her cell phone and doesn't want to pay for a landline.

The distinct bang of an object falling to the floor makes me sit straight up. The noise sounded as if it were coming from the living room. I'm sure that both Aunt Vay and Gary are gone because I heard the murmured blend of their voices as they walked out the front door a short time ago.

I swing my legs around and slowly approach the bedroom door in my socks. I listen at the door and hear nothing so I crack it open and listen more carefully. My phone is clutched in my palm like a weapon.

"Hello?" I call into the silence.

It's an empty house, I tell myself. The sound I heard was probably just a broom falling over or something.

Yes, it's an empty house.

The house where my mother spent her childhood, the house where my grandparents spent their tragically short newlywed years.

An empty house.

The next sound is a soft kind of scraping noise, barely audible. It has already stopped by the time I recognize it for what it is; a low, malevolent chuckle.

I could call the police. Sure. I could call the police and tell them a ghost is laughing in Aunt Vay's empty living room. Then everyone will say I'm crazier than my mother and they'll sigh over what a shame it is that Suzanne's daughter is nuts; just another misfortune heaped upon the poor Chapel family.

My mother's high school majorette baton is propped up against the desk, exactly where it has likely been hanging out for over twenty years. I grab it, grit my teeth together and fling open the door. I've got the baton raised like a sword when I reach the living room but it's empty.

Of course it is. Because there's no one here.

Exhaling with relief I check every room one by one and nothing seems amiss. The side door was left unlocked and not completely closed but that might be my fault because I was probably the last one to come through there. I push the door closed and firmly lock it.

I spend the rest of the evening in my bedroom. When I hear Aunt Vay and Gary return I double check to make sure the door is locked and then I go to sleep.

Johnny is already waiting for me at nine the following morning. He's got a shopping bag in his arms and he's hugging it to his chest. Even at a distance I can see that something is off about him. When I get closer I notice that his left eye and cheek are swollen and bruised and his hands are cut.

"Rafe did that to you, didn't he?"

I'm furious. Goddamn Rafe. Why doesn't anyone stop him? It's not fair. He's older and far bigger than Johnny.

Johnny doesn't want to show me what's in the bag and when he finally does I can tell that he wants to cry. In a halting voice he says he managed to take it away from Rafe even though his brother kicked the crap out of him for trying.

When I open the bag I can't believe what's inside. It's a small framed photo of my mother. Her senior class picture. It usually sits on an end table in the corner of the living room.

"He took it from your house," Johnny says and coughs, wincing and holding his ribs. "I'm sorry, Caris."

It's not his fault and I tell him so. I'm dumbfounded as to how Rafe could have managed to get into the house and take anything and then

I remember last night. The unlocked door. The crash in the living room. The echo of spiteful laughter.

Tucking the bag under my arm, I escort Johnny to the market. We need to get some antiseptic to clean up his cuts. And maybe we can get an ice pack for his eye and something to wrap up his ribs if they really hurt.

Harold Keyser is working the register and he's very concerned when he sees the condition Johnny's in. He gives us anything we need and takes us to a tiny office behind the counter where he bandages the cuts on Johnny's knuckles himself. I have to stifle a cry of anguish when Johnny lifts his shirt and I see all the purple bruising.

Damn Rafe to hell. I hate him.

Harold looks very sad as he helps Johnny wrap a bandage around his torso. He wants to call the police but Johnny gets upset and makes him promise not to because he doesn't want his brother to go to jail.

Harold bags up some snacks for us and tells Johnny to please come back and see him if there's any more trouble. Funny, but I remember how the day I met Harold he seemed to dislike Johnny but maybe that's just because of the Hempstead family's reputation. Now that he's watched us hanging out together for weeks he seems to like Johnny well enough.

Johnny's in a better mood after getting cleaned up and coming to the realization that I'm not going to blame him for whatever sick things Rafe does. Since the skies look about ready to open up with rain and it's supposed to rain all afternoon we take the bus all the way to the mall. We plunder our bag of snacks from Harold and I keep my mother's photo in the bag. Later on I'll just put it back where it belongs. As for the problem of Rafe walking into the house, I'll just have to make sure all the doors are locked from now on.

We stay at the mall as long as we can and by the time we return to Arcana on the bus I'm late for dinner. We make plans to meet as usual the next morning and Johnny watches me run toward Dunstan Street with the plastic bag over my head.

When I get to Aunt Vay's house I'm glad to see that Gary is nowhere in sight. Aunt Vay is already seated at the dining room table with plates of spaghetti and she calls my name in an angry voice. I don't have time to put my mother's picture back now so I just stick the entire bag under the couch cushion and join her in the dining room.

"I'm really sorry I'm late," I say, wondering if she's angry because I'm late or because my clothes and hair are wet from the rain. I smooth my damp hair back and feel the cold air blowing from the air conditioning vent overhead. "Is it okay if I go change before dinner?"

The flat stare she gives me is worrisome. "No. Stay here."

"I'm sorry, Aunt Vay," I repeat and smile at her. She's never been angry with me before.

There's a fork in her hand and she's squeezing it so hard her knuckles are white. "I went to the market this afternoon."

"Oh." I'm not sure why this is news.

"I spoke to Harold Keyser."

Oh.

"He tells me you have been running around with the youngest Hempstead boy."

I swallow. "Johnny's my friend. We're not dong anything wrong. We're just hanging out together."

The hand holding the fork pounds on table. "He's trash, Caris!"

I'm ready to defend Johnny. "That's not fair and you know it. Do you think Johnny can help who his grandfather was? He's a nice kid. You should meet him."

"I won't be meeting him. And you won't be messing around with him anymore. That family. THAT FUCKING FAMILY!"

I've never heard her curse before. Not even a hissed 'dammit' when she drops something.

I can be stubborn when I want to be and for this I'm ready to take a stand. "Johnny's my friend. And you can't keep me from seeing him."

If I was surprised when she cursed then her next move shocks me to pieces. She slaps me across the face, hard enough to snap my head back and sting my cheek but it's not the pain that brings tears to my eyes.

Aunt Vay immediately realizes she's made a mistake. She cups her hand over her mouth and looks at me wide-eyed.

"I didn't mean to do that," she chokes out.

A tear spills down my cheek. And then another one. But I still have enough courage to defend my friend. Even if my voice quivers when I speak.

"There's nothing wrong with Johnny. Evil can't be inherited. His grandfather was a horrible man but he's dead. He was dead long before Johnny was even born."

Aunt Vay takes her hand away from her mouth. She looks very old right now and her eyes are sunken. "And what about his father?"

"His father?" I try to recall what Johnny has said about his father. Very little. Only that the man died when Johnny was nine. Something about running from the police and a car crash. "What does his father have to do with this?"

"Everything."

"What are you talking about?"

She looks at the ceiling and screams. "IT'S IN THEIR BLOOD!"

My tears have stopped but my cheek still stings.

"Aunt Vay." If I speak softly I might be able to reason with her. "There's no such thing."

She throws me a disgusted look. "Were you aware that Clay Hempstead knew your mother in high school?"

"So?" As far as I can tell everyone knows everyone else in Arcana.

Aunt Vay is breathing hard, her hollow cheeks looking sharper than ever. Yet she pauses and her expression becomes uncertain. She looks around the room. The table and chairs are the only pieces of furniture in here; a long polished table with ten straight backed chairs that no one ever sits in because there are no family gatherings in this house, not anymore.

When she looks at me again the uncertainty has vanished and her eyes are narrow.

"He raped her, Caris. That's why she left Arcana right after high school. It's his fault she won't come back. Clay Hempstead raped your mother!"

My heart seems to stop.

My mother, so gentle and beautiful. She gets hurt so easily. How could anyone do that to her? And why have I never known? Is this the reason for her fragility, her breakdowns? She was only two when her parents were killed. She remembers little, if anything, of them. But being raped in high school is something that would have scarred her deeply.

And the person who did that to her was Clay Hempstead.

Johnny's father.

Johnny.

Johnny, who holds my hand and befriends tiny lizards and understands when I don't want to watch ghost stories.

Johnny is not his father. He is not his grandfather. He is not his brother. Johnny would never hurt anyone.

"That's so horrible," I say, feeling ill. "But it has nothing to do with Johnny. He's my friend and he's going to stay that way. No matter what."

She's tired all of a sudden. She lowers her head in her hands and refuses to look at me.

"Go to your room."

I stand up, ready to be cooperative before another terrible thing is said or done. But I take my bowl of spaghetti with me.

In my bedroom I lock the door and eat sitting cross legged on my bed. I assume that Aunt Vay will come softly knocking on the door at some point to make amends but she never does.

I touch my cheek and wonder if there will be a bruise there tomorrow, like the bruises Johnny often has on his face. I hope he's all right tonight, that his freak show of a brother isn't beating him up again.

I would give a lot to be able to talk to him right now.

The bakery is closed on Mondays so that means Jay and I get to sleep in. Yesterday after work he took me out for a taco dinner and then we went home and fucked like crazy in my bedroom until we couldn't stay awake anymore. All day I'd been pleasantly sore but that didn't stop me from seeking more punishment.

Everything about him turns me on.

I do wish he'd talk more. I already know he's suffered a lot. He likely doesn't wish to be reminded of any of it. But there's this big void between the boy he was and the man he is. And I'm aching to know him better.

Last night over dinner I tried to veer the conversation to a more serious place by asking about the chain of events after he left Arcana. For instance, where is his mother? I don't even know if she's alive or not. Jay shifted in his seat and hailed the waiter to ask for another bowl of tortilla chips. When I tried to ask more questions he casually reached underneath the table and began stroking me in a way that drove all questions of any kind from my head while I gripped the sides of the table, barely able to remain upright.

Afterwards I had to wonder if the smiling waiter had any clue that as he set the overflowing bowl of chips on the table I was busy biting my tongue and trying not to moan as I came on Jay's hand. While I struggled to keep my face neutral, Jay grinned at me in a way that was wicked and triumphant at the same time.

Holy fuck, he's hot.

"What are you doing?" he murmurs now, half asleep, his voice muffled by the arm flung over his face.

My fingers glide over his skin. "I'm measuring your muscles. This part of your upper arm is so big I can't even curl my fingers around it at all."

He opens one eye and lifts his head a few inches to peer at me. I can't stop marveling at the strapping planes of his body. For the last twenty minutes I've been kneeling beside him with a sheet wrapped around me toga-style and admiring him in the soft mid morning light that filters in through the blinds.

Without warning an arm shoots out and tackles me down to the mattress. The sheet has been flung aside and I'm on my belly. He straddles me from behind and I feel the hard length of him pressing against my ass. The feeling is exciting and I arch my body up to urge him on.

Jay groans and slowly rocks back and forth. His hands squeeze my flesh. "Fuck, I don't know if you're ready for that, honey."

I look over my shoulder so I can see him. "Have you done it, um, *that* way before?"

His mouth tilts into a smirk. "I've done everything."

"Oh." I'm not disappointed. Just curious. "You've been with a lot of girls, haven't you?"

A funny expression comes over his face and I wonder if I shouldn't have asked the question. It's very personal. Jay doesn't like to answer personal questions.

"It's never been like it is with you," he says. "Not even close."

On the inside I explode with happiness. Jay climbs off me and pats my rear end.

"Another time," he says, with a slight hint of regret.

I get on my hands and knees and throw him a pouty look. "Be a shame to waste morning wood of that magnitude."

No further invitation is required. Jay rips a condom open, kneels behind me and thrusts into my body so hard that I yelp with surprise. He's concerned, pulling back and asking if he was too rough, if he hurt me. I shake my head and give him an order through clenched teeth.

"Shut up and fuck me harder."

He chuckles and then rides me like a goddamn galloping knight. I like it when he grabs a fistful of my hair, just enough for a sweet little ounce of pain, and I come harder than ever.

After he gets rid of the condom and stretches out on the bed beside me I rest my cheek on his chest. "What should we do today?"

He's stroking my hair gently now. "Anything you want."

"I'm so glad we have a whole day off to spend together. I'm flying to Dallas tomorrow. My folks always expect me to be home for my birthday."

"I know. You already told me."

I kiss his chest. "I'm going to tell them about you."

He snorts. "I'm sure they'll be thrilled."

"They will be once they get to know you."

His hand pauses from stroking my hair and rests on my back. He says nothing. He just sighs.

My stomach begins grumbling and Jay suggests going out to breakfast. I propose enjoying a joint shower first because we didn't get to take one together yesterday. He picks me up, bed sheets and all, and carries me straight to the shower.

And it's magnificent.

Half an hour later I'm towel drying my hair while wrapped in my yellow bathrobe. I'm smiling at my mirrored reflection and wondering if there's a physical limit to how many times a day a girl can experience an orgasm. I plan to test the boundaries.

Jay has retreated to his side of the house to hunt down some clean clothes. I want to look nice for him so I select a light blue dress that I wore to a wedding last year and pair it with white heeled sandals. I curl my hair into long, soft spirals and even add a little bit of makeup; some mascara, a touch of blush and a dash of lip gloss. I examine myself in the mirror and decide I look pretty freaking good, even with my glasses on.

When I step out of the bathroom I see that the connecting door between the apartments is open so I walk right through in search of Jay. There's no one in the kitchen or living room but when I glance outside I notice Lana is on the patio.

She's laying out on one of the lounge chairs. She's got sunglasses on and she's completely still, almost like she's sleeping. I doubt she put on any sunscreen because she never does. With her tan skin she won't burn nearly as easily as I do but she can't stay out there forever.

We haven't really had much of a chance to chat since this whole whirlwind romance started. I open the sliding glass doors and she moves her head at the sound.

"Care," she says, breaking into a smile.

I pull a patio chair close to her, take a seat and primly fold my hands in my lap.

"So," I say. "What's new?"

"What's new?" She cracks up, mimicking me. "I think you have a bigger answer to that question than I do. You and Jay, huh? I'm impressed. You guys have been screwing like you're trying to break a world record."

I feel myself blushing. "He's amazing."

She pokes my leg. "You're more amazing."

My hands twist together in my lap. "Lana, I need to tell you something. I already knew him. I knew him a long time ago, back when we were kids. I probably should have told you but he seemed like he wanted to keep it a secret."

She's already waving her hand. "Doesn't matter. Shane told me all about it." She pushes her sunglasses up and gazes at me wistfully. "It's kind of like fate or something, isn't it?"

"Maybe it is," I say but I'm not really thinking about the question. I'm noticing that her eyes are red and puffy.

"Where's your boy now?" she asks.

"In the house getting dressed." I pause. "Where's yours?"

She shrugs. Then sighs.

"We're going out to breakfast," I tell her. "Why don't you come with us?"

"No thanks, babe. I don't really have much of an appetite and you guys should be alone together."

I'm about to launch a counterargument when Jay appears. He's wearing jeans and a plain black t-shirt. He's freshly shaven and his hair is combed. He looks incredible. He stops in his tracks and gives me a once over. He smiles. I swear my heart can see his smile. It performs a somersault every single time.

When he approaches I automatically reach for him and our fingers connect. He finally notices that Lana is here too. I watch him observe the redness of her eyes and his jaw tightens. But when he speaks he keeps his voice casual.

"Hey Lana. How are you doing?"

"I'm good, Jay." She bobs her head but her smile doesn't reach her eyes. "And you'll be doing good as long as you take care of my girl. Otherwise I'll be personally kicking your ass."

"I'm sure that's more than enough to keep me in line," he says. He glances at me and then back at Lana. "Where's Shane? His truck's gone and he's not answering texts."

Lana plays with a section of her black hair and frowns. "He said he had something he needed to go out and do. I asked him questions and he got mad. So I'm just laying out here until it's time for work."

"You sure you don't want to come out to eat with us?" I ask. "I'll buy you that stuffed French toast that you like so much."

"You guys go ahead." Lana flips her sunglasses down and settles back in her chair. "I'm fine here."

Jay raises an eyebrow at me and I give a helpless little shrug. Whatever is going on with Lana and Shane, she's not willing to talk about it.

Breakfast has become more like brunch and we take our time at the old fashioned eatery close to campus. Summer session at Hutton State is in full swing now and while there aren't nearly as many students milling around as there are during the regular semester, there are still plenty of college kids in sight. A lot of them are girls, pretty girls, but when they shoot interested looks in Jay's direction he doesn't appear to notice them. Jay makes me feel like there's no one else in the room but me.

He's willing to let me pick the day's activities so I choose the butterfly conservatory; a place I've always wanted to go since arriving for school in Hutton. I wouldn't expect a big, gruff guy to be all about butterflies but Jay is intrigued by the idea and looks at the pictures when I pull up the site on my phone. I can't get over how different he seems from the surly character who pretended we'd never met.

The conservatory has a magical feel to it. There are colorful flowerbeds everywhere while butterflies flutter above our heads and then gracefully settle on bright blossoms before taking flight again. Jay remains close to me and touches the small of my back now and then. We stand before a window beneath the words 'Butterfly Nursery' and within the display on the other side are rows of tiny hanging cocoons. While we are watching, an insect face emerges through the end of a cocoon and begins unfolding long wings. Jay wraps his arms around me from behind and pulls me close. I lean into him, more sure by the minute that this is exactly where I'm meant to be.

I know I'm falling hard and fast.

I don't care.

I'm enjoying the ride.

And I refuse to consider the possibility of crashing.

After the butterflies I want him to choose something to do. He suggests the movies. He still likes superhero films. I insist on buying the largest tub of popcorn at the concession stand and wrinkle my nose at him when he laughs that there's no way we'll be able to finish all of that. The movie is the same one that I got bored with and walked out on the other day but Jay doesn't need to know that. I'm not bored now. I rest my head on his shoulder and gobble popcorn while supernaturally powerful heroes save cities from supernaturally powerful villains.

A few times throughout the day I notice him checking his phone and frowning. I don't think for a second that he's contacting another girl. This has something to do with Shane. And with Lana's teary eyes.

For dinner we get giant takeout salads, which is Jay's idea because even though he likes his red meat now and then, he's a healthier eater than I am. Maybe being with him will persuade me to acquire better habits.

At home Shane has returned and Lana is already home from work. They are grilling burgers and they appear to be getting along just fine now. Lana's hugging him around the waist while he flips meat on the grill. We all eat together outside and there's no talk of anything distressing. There are some bookkeeping items I need to discuss with Shane since he has a habit of cheerfully putting me off but I don't want to be a downer and bring up boring business when everyone's having a good time.

Shane likes to tell stories and his stories are always funny. He tells us about the time he set fire to the apartment he was sharing with Jay when he stuck his socks in the microwave to dry them off. And then there was the time he was working on a construction crew and accidentally cemented himself to a brick wall. Jay needed to chisel him free. I'm not real clear on how that's possible and in all likelihood he's embellishing but it's funny anyway.

Dusk has long since settled and someone a few streets away sets off a barrage of illegal fireworks, probably practicing for the Fourth of July in two weeks.

Lana and Shane head inside the house first. They say goodnight and Shane's got his arm around her as they go indoors.

More fireworks light up the sky and I reach for Jay's hand.

"Do you want to go in?" I ask him, already excited about the prospect of spending another night in his arms.

Jay pulls me into his lap. He kisses me long and deep, stroking my jawline with his thumb.

"Your room or mine?" he whispers.

We decide on mine. I haven't done a thing to pack for my short trip to Dallas but I can do that after Jay leaves for work at the bakery early in the morning. My flight isn't until eleven and I've already arranged for a car to pick me up at nine thirty to drive to the small airport for my direct flight to Dallas. I'm looking forward to seeing my parents but at the same time I wish I didn't have to leave him. Two days suddenly seems like an agonizingly long time to spend without his kiss.

Jay removes his shirt and jeans and sits on the bed in his boxers to wait for me while I drag my overnight bag out of the closet. I just want to have it readily available so I can hastily pack in the morning.

"You really like to hang posters, don't you?" he says, surveying my walls.

It's true. My bedroom walls are covered with dog posters and flower posters and Hutton State University posters and a poster of a mermaid lying on an empty beach. The last one is my favorite.

"You could borrow some," I offer. "Since you have absolutely nothing on your walls."

He stretches. "I don't have shit on my walls at my apartment either."

His apartment. The one in Phoenix. The city he really lives in. I'm reminded that his stay in Hutton is only supposed to be temporary. This is an upsetting thought.

"Do you miss it?" I ask him.

"What?"

"Your apartment. Phoenix."

"No. It's not a place to be sentimentally attached to. It's a place to be anonymous in."

"Is your mother still there?"

He looks at a dog poster. I wonder if he's thinking. He doesn't speak so I ask another question.

"That's where you went right after you left Arcana, right?"

"Yeah," he says in a low, flat voice, still looking at the dog poster. Now he's got a slight scowl on his face. "That's where I went."

I drop my overnight bag, kick off my sandals and sit beside him on the bed. I touch his bare muscled thigh.

"You can talk to me," I say, stroking his skin. "I know that painful things have happened to you but you can tell me anything."

He quits looking at the dog poster and kisses me. There's a hard, almost angry level of passion in his kiss and he gets me on my back while shoving the skirt of my dress up over my hips. I'm not complaining because I want him and I open my legs, wrapping them around his body. His lips have moved on to my neck now and he's sucking hard, teasing me with his teeth.

And yes, of course I want him.

It's just that I want him so much that I want more from him than this.

"Wait." I brace my palms on his chest and push. "Jay, let's talk. Let's be real."

He backs off but he's still hovering over me. "You think I'm not being real with you, Caris?"

"I think you're incredible." I slide out from underneath him and sit up on the bed. The strap of my dress has fallen from my shoulder and I move it back in place. "And I am so crazy about you I can hardly breathe. I just don't want there to be secrets between us. We should be able to share things that matter."

"You mean like we used to," he mutters. He rises from the bed and takes a couple of steps away from me before turning around. He's being careful with his expression right now. I can't tell what he's thinking at all.

"Would that be so bad?" I ask. "Two people should be able to confide in each other when they're in a relationship."

"And you know this because of all the relationships you've had? Or did you just read that shit in a book or something?"

I feel my eyes narrow. "You don't have to be rude to get your point across."

"I'm not *him*, Caris."

"Who?" I'm alarmed, thinking he's talking about his grandfather. Or his father. Or his brother. There's a terrible multiple choice selection who could qualify as 'him'.

"I'm not little Johnny fucking Hempstead who's afraid of his own shadow and gets the crap kicked out of him wherever he goes."

His words make me wince.

"No one is the same person they were at age thirteen," I mumble.

"*You* are," he fires back. "I mean, yeah, you're taller and a whole lot sexier now but for the most part you're still the same naïve little girl."

I feel a flash of anger. "That's a bullshit thing to say. You think you're superior because your life has been harder than mine? My childhood wasn't exactly perfect either."

"Then let's just agree not to talk about our shitty childhoods from now on."

I fold my hands in my lap and take a deep breath. "I don't expect you to tell me everything but I don't want you to shut me out either. And I'm afraid that no matter how hard I try you'll only let me in so far."

He rubs his face and shakes his head. "What we have right now is something I've never had with anyone."

My heart lifts. "You have no idea how happy it makes me to hear that."

"Then why isn't it good enough?"

"Because I'm greedy. I don't just want your body. I want to know your heart and your mind too."

He snorts. "So you're saying you don't want to fuck me unless I spill my guts to you three times a day?"

"You're being an asshole again."

"Born and bred, right? No escaping it."

"That's not what I was thinking. I have *never* treated you like a Hempstead."

The words come out wrong. I wish I could take them back.

"Like a Hempstead," he repeats and spits out a nasty laugh. "All of us rapists, murderers and psychos, right?"

"No! I meant that I've never for a second looked at you differently because of crimes that were committed by your grandfather and your father before you were born. And as far as what Rafe did to my aunt, that had nothing to do with you either."

"What Rafe did," he echoes while raking a hand through his short hair. The look he throws my way is full of disbelief. And scorn. "Jesus fucking Christ."

"What's that supposed to mean? What's wrong with you?"

"Nothing's wrong with me." He laughs with no humor. "You're spending all this energy trying to pry my mind open when obviously what you really need to do is to talk to your own goddamn family."

His last sentence throws me for a loop.

"Huh?"

"Talk to your fucking father, Caris! Maybe he'll even tell you the truth."

The words sting even if I don't understand them. I lose my temper. "Oh shut the hell up, Johnny!"

His face turns to granite and it takes me a minute to realize my mistake.

"Jay," I correct myself. "I meant Jay."

"I have an idea." He swoops down and grabs his clothes off the floor. "How about you let me know when you're tired of living in the past? Don't take too long or I might not be waiting anymore."

I should say something.

I should stop him from walking out.

The door shuts behind him and the words I want to say are all still stuck in my throat. They finally emerge in the form of angry tears and I cry on my bed as my mind replays all the terrible things we've ever said to each other.

JAY

Fuck me to hell and back. I couldn't have handled that any worse if I tried.

Instead of surrendering my stubbornness and taking my girl in my arms like I really wanted to, I insulted her and stormed out of her room.

I really am a fucking asshole. She's not the childish one. I am.

I know this and yet I pace around my bedroom for a while before sprawling on my bed to stare at the ceiling. I hear the sound of voices with no distinct words but there's urgency to the way they go back and forth. Shane and Lana are in the middle of an argument. Because that's what you do when you're with someone you really care about. You stay and fight for what you have.

Of course Caris is curious about the details of my life. She was always like that; curious and inquisitive and compassionate. It was part of what drew me to her as a kid. She had this infectious enthusiasm about every little thing. She still does. Like today when we were watching those damn butterflies. She was almost beside herself with excitement when one emerged from its cocoon. And I wrapped my arms around her to draw all that happiness close to my heart.

That's what she is. Caris is happiness. I haven't thought much about being happy until now.

When she first came back into my world I planned to do anything to avoid her. Now I'd do anything to keep her. I already know that resuming my solitary life in a Phoenix apartment and busting my ass every day on a construction crew with nothing to come home to is not for me, not anymore.

And if I need to revisit all the most painful corners of my past in order to give her what she needs then so be it. I know she would tell me anything. I owe her the same consideration.

Hours pass while I mull all of this over with the ceiling. The arguing voices have long since quieted. I haven't slept but I need to be up in the next hour to get ready for work. At least I'm used to these early hours thanks to years in construction.

When I approach Caris's bedroom door there's no light coming from the strip at the bottom. I try the knob and find it unlocked. Then I hesitate. There's nothing I want more than to climb into her bed, hold her and tell her that I lied tonight.

I *am* still Jonathan Hempstead. I tried to deeply bury his soft heart and his gentleness but she's uncovered both and I'm grateful. I haven't been complete in a very long time.

I've been lost.

She's the only one who could have found me.

Eventually I drop my hand from the doorknob. I've already caused her enough anguish for now and she has to get on a plane tomorrow. She needs to sleep. In two days she'll be back and we can sort through everything then.

Her purse has been left on the kitchen table and I take it for a reason. I'll return it in a minute.

While Caris was in the restroom at the conservatory I visited the gift shop and bought her a birthday present. It's silly, like something a high school kid with only a little pocket change would get his girl. I bought it because it practically screamed her name to me and I knew she'd love it.

After retrieving the gift from where I left it in my dresser drawer I wish I'd thought about having something nicer than a brown paper bag to wrap it in but it's too late for that. I find a pen and think for a minute before scrawling some words on the outside of the bag. It's hardly poetry but I hope she smiles just the same. I leave the gift in the front pocket of her purse where she's sure to find it.

I want to learn how to do this; how to be a boyfriend, how to deserve her.

In the meantime she needs to take this trip to Dallas. I feel mildly guilty about dropping a bombshell on her earlier but she's owed the truth and I'm not the one she needs to hear it from.

I'm finally feeling tired but there's not enough time to try for sleep so I suck it up, brew a pot of coffee to keep me awake and get ready for work. I'm ready to leave and wondering why Shane isn't up when he stumbles out of his room. He looks like he might not have showered but he's dressed and he accepts a cup of coffee while stuffing a piece of bread in his mouth for breakfast.

"Let's go make some fucking muffins," he says, pounding me on the back before heading out the door. "I'll meet you there."

At the bakery I try to keep my mind on work but I feel off balance today. I keep thinking I should have gone into Caris's room anyway this morning. I'm not sure what time she's being picked up for her airport ride but at ten I tell Shane that I need to run a quick errand and I'll be right back. He asks no questions.

I drive straight over to the house but she's already gone. It's just as well. She'll find the gift in her purse, if she hasn't already. She'll understand.

It's kind of irrational how much I already miss her. I'm kicking myself for the weeks wasted by being a jackass when I could have been with her sooner. By shutting out the past I didn't just reject the bad parts but also the good. Caris is all good. I'll never make the same mistake again.

Back at the bakery, I begin to notice something about Shane. He's weird today. Weird in a terribly familiar way. Irritable and unable to focus. Luckily Delia is here filling in for Caris. Shane screws up the recipes, drops things in the kitchen and forgets batches in the oven.

Delia soothes him in a motherly way, believing he's just anxious. She doesn't understand that there's something else going on. But I do.

The last few days I've been preoccupied with Caris and I've let my concerns about Shane fall to the wayside. It's time to take action.

A few minutes before closing I tell Delia she can take off. There hasn't been a customer in nearly an hour and I'm just mixing up batter for tomorrow while Shane begins emptying the bins of whatever's left.

The doorbell chime signals Delia's departure and I set the last bowl of batter in the fridge with care. If anyone had ever told me that I'd be stressing out about mixing up the perfect chocolate cupcake and worrying over the texture of scones I would have laughed until my guts hurt.

Shane looks up when I emerge from the kitchen. He's putting most of the uneaten food in reusable plastic containers, which are dropped off a couple of times a week at a nearby homeless shelter. It was Caris's idea. Once a week she collects the food containers.

"You want me to take those down today?" I ask him, going to the door and turning the CLOSED sign out.

"If you want." He snaps a lid, straightens up and rubs his eyes. "I got some shit to do anyway."

"With Lana?"

"No, she's at work."

"Can I come with you?"

He shoots me an odd look. "What the hell for?"

"Because Caris isn't in town and I'm bored. Also because we haven't been hanging out a lot lately."

"Let's go out tonight then," he says and tries to move past me. "I'll see you at the house later."

Shane is surprised when I place a hand on his chest to stop him.

"What's up?" He backs up a step, wary all of a sudden.

I try to get him to look me in the eye. "Where are you going, Shane?"

He huffs and turns his head aside. "Told you I've got shit to do."

"What are you on these days?"

His head snaps to my face, his eyes defiant. "Don't pull this fucking crap on me right now."

"Then don't bullshit me. You're drinking too much and you're popping pills left and right. You've been on this road before, buddy. It's a bad one."

His shoulders slump and he looks at the floor. I reach out and put a hand on his shoulder. He gruffly swats me away.

"Fuck this," he mutters and charges for the door.

I'm bigger. I'm stronger. I can stop him.

I brace my right arm across the door so he can't open it, even when he yanks hard on the handle.

Shane glares, tries to slam into my chest to throw me off balance. I shove him off with ease and he staggers.

"What the fuck's your plan, Jay? To hold me hostage?"

"My plan is to get you help if you need it. And I think you do."

He's angry. In fact I wouldn't be surprised if he takes a swing at my head. This is not really Shane. This is just what that garbage does to him.

"When did you become such a motherfucking life expert?" he growls.

I remain calm but don't move my hand from the door. "I'm no expert on anything. I've just seen this movie before and I don't want to watch it again. I'm worried about you. And so is Lana. You know the house has thin walls, right? I can hear when you guys argue at top volume."

He wilts at the mention of his girlfriend. He no longer looks like he wants to punch me. He sinks right down to the floor and puts his elbows on his knees.

"I'm scaring her," he mutters, sounding as miserable as he's ever sounded. "Fuck, it's the last thing I want to do."

I take my hand away from the door. He won't go running out now. I drop to the floor beside my best friend.

He raises his head and shows me bloodshot eyes. "I'll never really do have it beat, do I?"

My heart cracks. If I could take this burden from him then I would.

"You will, Shane. You will."

He exhales heavily and smacks his leg. "I thought I could juggle it all, man. The girl, the house, the business. And then I stopped sleeping. So now I take shit to help me sleep. And I take shit to help me wake up. And between all that I drink to blur the sharp edges a little."

Of all the demons I've faced, and there are many, addiction has never been one of them. I know from watching others fight their battles that it's a struggle unlike any other. I wouldn't wish it on an enemy.

"Lana wants me to go to rehab again," he sighs. "Maybe she's right. It's the only thing that ever seems to work, at least for a while. I don't want to let this place go but I might have to."

I nudge him. "You don't *have* to do anything. You've got all the help you need for as long as you need it."

He shakes his head. "You can't be my savior forever, Jay. It's not fair to you. None of this is fair to Lana, either."

"Fuck that shit. I'm *not* your savior. Don't you remember back in Hell House? We made a pact and it was you and me. We're brothers, Shane. I learned early in life that blood doesn't count for a thing. You're my brother in every way that counts. So I'm not fucking going anywhere. And you know what else? That sweet girl who's worrying herself to pieces over you isn't going anywhere either. You have people who love you. Get used to it."

He chuckles. "You've always been bossy as hell."

"Just part of my charm." I hold my hand out. "Give it to me."

He doesn't ask what I'm talking about. He reaches into his back pocket and withdraws a plastic bag with a couple of white pills twisted inside a bubble. When I press him, he admits that he's got more at home so that's the next place we need to go.

After dropping off the leftover food at the homeless shelter we go through the house and clear out all the booze. He hands over the rest of his crap and lets me pick apart his bedroom to prove that there's nothing else hidden.

Then we sit down on the back patio and wait for Lana to come home so we can all have a talk about what Shane needs to do to get healthy.

Lana's on board right away and I'm glad I wasn't wrong about her. She holds Shane's hand the entire time and tells him that she's proud of him, that she loves him, that she'll be here when he wins this last battle.

He's worried about the bakery but I'm confident that I can run the bakery with Caris while he's getting well. Delia would likely be willing to work some extra shifts and we could always get some temporary help if necessary to fill in the gaps. Shane does better with inpatient treatment and the good facilities are expensive. Luckily, there's a small life insurance policy from Ruby that Shane just received and the bakery is starting to bring in money again. Lana immediately volunteers to find a nice, reputable place that's not too far away.

Once the emotional flood subsides and we have a plan in place we order Chinese takeout and pig out on the back patio. Shane's yawning by the time dusk settles because he hasn't slept right in weeks. Lana takes him to bed to tuck him in and I don't expect to see her for a while but she returns fifteen minutes later, right after I've finished cleaning up the takeout containers.

"He went out like a light," she says and sinks into a patio chair. She presses fingers to her temples, looking rather tired herself.

I choose the chair across from her and sit back down.

"You holding up okay?" I ask and she stops pressing on her temples.

"I'll be okay if he'll be okay."

"He will be."

She nods. "You really are a brother to him, Jay."

"Always will be."

A tear falls down her cheek but she smiles. "I really love him."

"I know you do."

A slight breeze produces ripples in the pool and we stare out at the water.

"I want to ask you something completely nosy and out of line," she says.

"I probably won't answer but you're free to give it a shot."

"Do you love Caris?"

"Whoa." I shift in my seat. "That's pretty blunt right there."

"Told you I was nosy."

"Caris and I…" I say, and then the words trail away.

"You love her," Lana declares.

I remain silent and without warning she socks me in the shoulder. Of course it doesn't hurt.

"What the hell?" I sputter.

She tilts her chin up with a stubborn expression. "Caris is extremely loveable."

"I know that," I mutter.

She smiles. "So you do love her."

I change the subject slightly. "Have you heard from her today?"

She cocks her head. "Yeah, she texted while I was in there with Shane. I made her promise to tell me when she arrived. I haven't told her what's going on here. Didn't want to say it in a text. She's at her parents' house."

"Good. I mean I'm really glad she got there safe."

"Why don't you just call her?"

"Eh, she's with her folks. Let them have their time together. She knows where to find me and she'll be back soon."

"All right." She shrugs and rises from the chair. "Think I'm gonna start researching rehab places and then join my sweet boy in dreamland."

"Thanks, Lana."

She pats my arm in solidarity before she goes.

The wind continues to pick up. Flashes of lightning slice across the eastern edge of the sky. The idea of calling Caris is a tempting one. There's no other sound I'd rather hear right now than her voice.

Then I remember that she's got some family issues to sort out and that's thanks to me and my big mouth. She should have found the gift in her purse by this time. She'll call me if she wants to talk.

I can hear the thunder now, low and rumbling in the distance. When I was little I was terrified of thunderstorms. I was convinced I'd be struck by lightning. My older brother Rafe knew this and would hassle me about it without mercy. That's what big brothers do, of course, but Rafe was worse than most and he just got more out of control with every passing year. Nine years have gone by since I last spoke to my brother. Anyone else might think it's high time to do something about that.

"A brother is a brother."

But they don't know Rafe like I do.

JOHNNY, AGE 13

"Here." He drops a bag of frozen peas on the sofa beside me.

I pick it up and fling it on the floor. A risky move, considering it's Rafe I'm dealing with.

"I'm not hungry," I announce.

He sighs with irritation, grabs the bag off the floor and throws it directly in my lap.

"It's to put on your face, moron." He sinks down on the opposite end of the sofa, glares at me like I'm the world's biggest loser and shakes his head.

"Thanks," I grumble.

I carefully press the cold bag against my swollen eye. I don't know if it'll help at this point. My eye is already puffy as hell and not likely to go down much tonight. But this is Rafe's half ass way of apologizing for the beating. At least I'm getting better at fighting back. I got in a few good shots before he knocked me to the ground and slammed his boot into my ribs.

He seizes the television remote and I don't care because there's nothing to watch anyway. All we can access are local stations that come in via the spindly antenna and even those are kind of fuzzy.

"Is there anything to eat?" he says. He's wearing his Killer football jersey again. I wonder when he washed it last.

"Go see for yourself," I answer and I must be in a reckless kind of mood because you don't get an attitude with Rafe and walk away intact.

I don't give a shit.

I'm still furious with him for walking into Caris's house and taking her mother's picture. That upsets me a thousand times more than the way my ribs ache with each breath.

Maybe he's tired of hitting things for today because he says nothing, just flips the remote onto the couch cushion and goes scavenging in the kitchen. He finds a box of pasta and then gets mad when he realizes he can't stick it in the microwave so I get up off the couch and start boiling a pot of water so he'll shut up.

I don't like it when he sits on a chair right behind me while I'm stirring the pasta. It's elbow macaroni, like the kind that comes in macaroni and cheese boxes except there's no cheese.

Rafe's quiet for a long time so I keep stirring the pot. I remove the cracked plastic colander from a cabinet and set it in the sink to drain the macaroni.

"I just wanted to see what it was like in there," he finally says. He doesn't sound like himself. He sounds serious. Maybe a little sad.

"Huh? Where?"

"The Chapel house."

My heart freezes. My fists clench.

He doesn't notice. He's playing with a lighter, setting paper napkins on fire and smacking out the flames with the palm of his hand. "There's all this old crap all over the place. You know, pictures of dead people on the walls. Hey, you never said that little girlfriend of yours is one of them. That's some sick shit. Her mother's such a lying bitch. I'm sure she is too so watch your ass."

I look down into the pot of boiling water. "Leave her alone, Rafe. Please."

He snorts with laughter. "You think I'm gonna touch that little bag of bones? Not interested. You can keep it for yourself."

I'm shaking on the inside as I pour the boiling hot contents of the pot into the colander. For a second I thought about doing something terrible. If Rafe had said the wrong thing then I might have.

And then I'd be just like the rest of them.

Maybe that can't be helped no matter what.

"Hey, get two bowls," Rafe says. "There's enough mac there for us to split it."

I don't feel like sitting down at the table and eating a bowl of macaroni with him but it's about as generous an offer as Rafe ever extends and besides, I'm hungry.

I get two bowls and two spoons and Rafe grabs the salt shaker. He becomes almost cheerful as we sit there eating bowls of salted pasta, almost as if we're two regular brothers having regular dinner.

He talks about football, about how he's tired of being on the offensive line and he wants to be the quarterback. He says the minute he graduates from high school he's getting the hell out of Arcana. He's always thought that Las Vegas would be a cool place to live.

Even after my bowl is empty I keep sitting at the table because it's not often that Rafe behaves like a person you wouldn't mind having a conversation with. I'm still pissed at him for the whole thing with the picture of Caris's mother but it seems like just one of those dumb stunts that he pulls because he thinks it makes him a badass. He doesn't sound like he's interested in bothering Caris and that's all I care about.

We're still sitting there at the table when my mother walks in. I haven't seen her in a couple of days. She must have just come from work because she's still wearing her salon smock. Her dry lips are painted red and they look like angry gashes in her tired face. She sees Rafe first and scowls. Then she notices me and her eyes widen.

"Jonathan." She drops her purse on the floor and flies over to examine me. "Oh my god, what the hell happened?" She checks out my eye, looks at my cut up hand, notices when her hand lands on my back that I yelp because my ribs are still sore.

It's not like this is the first time I have bruises but I'm in worse shape than usual and I see from the grim set of her mouth that she's going to make a big deal out of it.

"You did this to him, didn't you?" she accuses Rafe.

For once Rafe appears uncertain. He looks at her and then at me.

"Get out of here," she whispers.

Rafe doesn't move an inch.

"Get out!" she screams. She picks up my dinner bowl and hurls it against the wall. "GET OUT! Get out for good!"

Rafe now reacts. He rolls his eyes and then laughs but somehow I don't think he finds this the least bit funny. I certainly don't find it funny. For all the times I sort of wished my mother would kick him out I never thought she'd actually do it.

"Be gone by the time I'm out of the shower," she says, already walking out of the kitchen. "Or I'll have you arrested for what you did to your brother."

The bathroom door opens and shuts. I guess mothering time is over. Rafe and I just stare at each other for a minute.

"Crazy ass bitch," he mutters and gets up from the table.

I find him in our room, stuffing clothes and things into his school backpack.

"I don't think she means it," I say but I'm not convinced.

"I don't fucking care." He pushes more clothes into the bag. "I'm done with this shit. I'll find a way to get some money and then I'm getting the fuck out of here."

I shouldn't feel like crying. Rafe is someone I avoid at all costs.

"A brother is a brother."

Caris told me that. I can't remember why. But it's true.

Rafe is still packing while I dash into the kitchen. I find the purse my mother left on the floor. Her wallet has ninety two dollars inside and I take it all.

"Here," I say a minute later, pushing the money into my brother's hand.

He looks at it and his mouth tilts up in a smirk. He pockets the money and then reaches into his bag to pull out a pack of cigarettes.

This is a strange time to casually light up a smoke. But he hands the pack over to me.

"To remember me by," he says and he zips his backpack closed.

I stare at the cigarette pack. Half of the cigarettes are gone and there's a lighter stuffed inside.

Rafe hauls his backpack over his shoulder and starts for the door.

"Maybe I'll see you again someday, Limp Dick." He turns and gives me a grin. "But probably not."

I'm still standing there holding the cigarette pack when I hear the front door open and close. I don't smoke and don't especially want to start but I put them in my back pocket anyway because it's the only thing my brother has ever given me.

I sit on the edge of Rafe's bed with a hollow feeling in my gut. All at once it seems like the world is ending. My world, anyway. My brother is gone. My mother barely notices that I exist. And the summer is nearly over, which means Caris will be leaving soon. Caris is the best friend I've ever had. She's the only person who makes me happy. But she's leaving. And when she's gone I'll be more alone than ever.

It's not fucking fair!

I pound on the bed with my fist even though it's something a kindergartener would do.

Nothing is fair. Nothing ever has been. Knowing this makes no difference at all.

All it does is make me angry.

CARIS, AGE 13

*J*ohnny is late today and I'm starting to worry when I finally see him come around the corner. He's walking more slowly than usual, almost trudging. I run over to close the distance between us. I've been keyed up, pacing around the town square while I wait. There's something I need to tell him.

He sees me coming and stops. "Hey," he says but his voice is flat.

"Are you okay?" I touch his arm, hoping to hold his hand, but he doesn't want that right now. He twists away the second my fingers graze his skin.

"I'm fine."

He doesn't look at me. His face looks much better today. The skin around his eye is still discolored but far less swollen. I'm sure his ribs still hurt. He leans against the thick trunk of a shade tree and lowers his head. I notice that he's wearing the same clothes that he wore yesterday.

The tree trunk isn't wide enough for me to lean beside him so I just kind of stand there awkwardly and fidget. He's not going to be happy to hear the thing I need to tell him.

"Rafe was at my house this morning," I say and Johnny's head immediately snaps up.

"Rafe was in your house?"

"Not *in* my house. Outside. I was eating breakfast and I heard yelling so went out through the side door to see what was going on. Aunt Vay was bringing a bag of garbage out and it looked like she found him coming out of the shed in the backyard. He just stood there glaring at her while she shouted about how he was trespassing and she was going to call the cops. Then he reached into the shed, grabbed a black backpack and gave Aunt Vay the middle finger before walking away."

I'm expecting Johnny to become furious at his brother, like he was furious when he found out Rafe had been sneaking around the house and stealing pictures.

He just stares at me. "And what did *you* do?"

"Nothing. I just stood there watching. I don't think Rafe even saw me."

He makes a face. "Bet you told your aunt about the picture thing."

"No, I didn't. I probably should. But she just would have been all upset. I put the picture back on the table where it belongs and she never noticed it was gone."

I don't tell him the rest of it. How Aunt Vay slapped me. What she said about his father. How she ordered me to stop being friends with him. I won't do that and I don't care if she wants to slap me every day. She said nothing when I told her I was going to town and I'd be back for dinner. She stayed on the couch and kept folding clothes from a basket of laundry. I don't think she likes me very much anymore. That's fine. I don't like her very much either.

"What was Rafe doing in our shed?" I ask Johnny.

To my shock, he snaps at me angrily.

"How the fuck should I know, Caris?"

I swallow and my throat feels thick. Being yelled at by Johnny is worse than being smacked by Aunt Vay.

"What's wrong?" I ask him in a quiet voice because I'm sure that something really is very wrong. He's not acting like himself at all.

"Nothing."

"You can tell me."

"All right." The look he gives me now is different, full of disdain, like the sight of me irritates him. "My mom kicked Rafe out last night. He was probably sleeping in your shed."

"Why'd your mom kick him out?"

"Because she's a crazy bitch."

I'm stunned to hear him refer to his mother this way. I know she's not a good mother. She's always running off with her boyfriend and leaving him to fend for himself at home where he's abused by his violent brother. But he's never talked about her like that before.

Suddenly he slumps against the tree. "I'm sorry. I know I'm being a jerk."

"It's okay." I want so badly to hug him. I'm not sure he wants me to, though.

He looks completely miserable. "I don't think I can hang out today."

"Maybe you'd feel better if we went somewhere else. We could take the bus to the mall again."

"No. I've got to go look for Rafe. Maybe if I talk to my mom I can convince her to let him come back to the house before he gets into trouble."

"You'd do that for Rafe? Even after everything he's done to you?"

Johnny looks at me. His brown eyes are beyond sad. "A brother is a brother."

I've heard that before. Actually, I've said that before, although I didn't know what I was talking about because I have no brothers and never will.

"It seems like Rafe might be the exception." My only fear is that Johnny's brother will hurt him again but somehow my words make him furious.

"You don't know anything," he says and even though I'd just been thinking that exact thing a few seconds earlier I'm stung when he says it.

"I can help you," I offer. "We can look for him together."

"No." He refuses without a pause and peels himself away from the tree trunk. "I'm going alone."

I'm hurt. I know he's hurting more. I only want to help him. There's nothing I wouldn't do for him.

I take a deep breath so I don't start crying. "Can we meet here tomorrow?"

"Yeah, I guess so." He's already walking away and he hasn't even said goodbye. His head is down and his hands are jammed in his pockets.

"Johnny!"

He turns at the sound of my shout. I don't really have anything important to say. I don't want him to go.

"Be careful," I call to him.

The slightest of smiles skates across his bruised face and he nods. Then he turns around and keeps walking.

I watch him until he disappears and then I lean against the same tree Johnny was leaning against. I don't really have anything to do in town without him around. My dad sent me some more money and I was going to treat Johnny to ice cream today. I could still go and get a butter pecan cone but I just don't want to, not by myself.

I end up wandering around the aisles of the market. Harold Keyser spots me and calls me over when he's between customers.

"How's your friend? Is he doing okay today?" He seems honestly concerned about Johnny. Then I remember that he's the one who told Aunt Vay that I was hanging out with the grandson of Billy Hempstead. Harold probably didn't mean any harm but now I'm annoyed.

"What do you care?" I say and then leave without buying anything.

As lonely as it is wandering around town by myself, I really dislike the idea of returning to Aunt Vay's house. Even without the disturbing presence of Gary it's uncomfortable, especially now that Aunt Vay is mad at me.

I decide that if I walk around Arcana for long enough then I might run into Johnny. Maybe he already found Rafe. And if he can straighten out this mess with his brother perhaps he'll be in a better mood. I want him to come visit me in Dallas. If I talk to my dad about it he might agree and even pay for Johnny's trip.

Then I remember one critical fact.

Johnny is a Hempstead. His grandfather killed my grandparents. There's no way my folks will invite him to our house.

I walk out to the meteor crater, thinking all the while. In a few years I'll have my driver's license. So will he. Then no one can stop us from seeing each other. I wonder if I'll be prettier by then. My parents tell me I'm pretty all the time but that doesn't count. Johnny will be really good looking when he gets older. I can tell already. He'll probably have all kinds of girls deciding they like him. I'm jealous of them, the girls his age in Arcana.

He's not at the meteor crater. No one is. The museum is closed today and it's kind of spooky walking around the edge of the crater while the wind whistles in my ears and not a soul is in sight. I don't stay there long but before I go I look through my phone to find the picture I took of us the day we met. Looking at it makes me feel depressed so I stick the phone back in my pocket.

On the way back I take a different route. Usually I avoid going this way and so does Johnny. I'm not sure about the exact spot on this road where their car broke down. It might be right where I'm standing. Richard would have pulled it to the side and Nancy probably stood nearby, watching and asking if there was anything she could do to help fix the flat tire.

I stop in my tracks when I see the field. The grass is long and yellowed from being scorched beneath the summer sun all season. It probably looked the same way when my grandmother was killed in this spot.

A sour taste rises in my throat. I'm going to vomit if I stay here for one more second. I shouldn't have come. I turn on my heel and run as fast as I can back to the road and the comfortable civilization of downtown Arcana. I keep going all the way to Dunstan Street and when I get to the door I'm panting so hard I feel faint. There's a dull pain in my chest and my heart hammers away. The side door is unlocked and I go right to the sink and fill a glass of water. I drink two more glasses after that and finally begin to feel better.

I'm surprised that Aunt Vay hasn't called out like she usually does when she hears me come home. She must be here if the side door was unlocked. Plus I saw her car outside. On the other hand, sometimes she walks around and visits neighbors. The house has an empty feeling to it so that's probably the explanation.

Now that I'm not dying of thirst I feel better. In the living room there's no sign of anything amiss. The photo of my mother that I replaced on the end table is still there. She smiles at me from the past. I wonder if the photo was taken before she was raped by Clay Hempstead. I'm sure Johnny doesn't know anything about that.

The wall clock ticks the seconds away and it's the only sound.

Something feels off and I don't know why or how to explain it. I'm struck by the horrible thought that maybe Rafe Hempstead has come back. If Aunt Vay left the door unlocked before visiting neighbors then he might have returned and sneaked in.

I stand frozen in place and listening for endless seconds.

There's nothing.

There's no one.

I'm paranoid.

With a sigh I start down the hall toward my bedroom. I'm tired after running so much. I feel like taking a nap.

I'm all the way inside my room before I see her. She's crumpled up on the floor between the bed and the dresser and there are dark red splashes on the beige carpet. Her bare legs are splayed out at an uncomfortable angle and she doesn't move.

"Aunt Vay!" I'm down on the floor in an instant. I touch her shoulder but she still doesn't move. I heard somewhere that you're not supposed to move a person who has been injured in case their spine is affected but I have to make sure she can breathe.

Using as much care as possible I turn her over and what I see makes me gasp out loud. Her face is covered with blood and is so swollen I can hardly recognize her. A sizeable gash is on her right temple. This isn't from a fall. Someone did this to her. A wheezing sound escapes her mouth and I'm beyond relieved to know that she's alive.

"Don't worry, Aunt Vay. I'm calling for help."

My fingers shake and I'm hyperventilating as I call 911. I'm crying as I explain the need for an ambulance. The operator keeps me on the phone and asks me questions in a kind voice but I can't answer them because I can't think correctly.

Within minutes I hear the first sirens.

The police arrive first and then the paramedics. They load Aunt Vay onto a stretcher and she's moaning now. One of the officers tells me to go sit in the living room and then another officer arrives to talk to me. He finds a box of tissues and gives them to me. He asks me questions and tells me it's okay to answer them. He's probably a dad. He has that dad tone to his voice.

"Caris, I know this has been an awful shock but your aunt is on her way to the hospital and the doctors there will take good care of her."

I blow my nose and focus on taking deep breaths.

The officer's eyes are gentle. "Can you tell me if there is anyone who would threaten your aunt? Have you seen anyone hanging around the house who shouldn't be?"

I keep breathing deeply so I can manage to talk.

And then I tell him.

I tell him about Rafe Hempstead stealing my mother's picture.

And about Rafe coming out of our shed this morning.

The office's mouth sets in a thin line and he nods. He says not to worry. He's going to make sure my parents are called and someone will take me to the hospital shortly.

Then he needs to get off the couch and leave the room to talk into his radio.

While I'm sitting there alone with my hands in my lap people keep coming in and out of the house. A few of them glance at me but their faces are all determined and grim.

I know my thoughts should be all about Aunt Vay and many of them are. But I also think about Johnny. I hope he can forgive me for telling the police about his brother.

I wish he were here, holding my hand.

But somehow I don't believe he will ever hold my hand again.

CARIS

here's something both comforting and unnerving about waking up in my childhood bedroom. When I open my eyes I see the purple accent wall with the butterfly curtains that I picked out when I was eleven.

Since I left for college my parents only venture into this room to dust. When some of my friends come home from school they find their rooms stuffed with exercise equipment or repurposed as a craft room. The sight of the cheerful butterflies on my curtains makes me smile and I reach underneath my pillow for the object I put there before I fell asleep.

I sit up to snatch my glasses from the nightstand the then touch the block printed letters on the brown paper bag in my hand. I was on the plane and halfway to Dallas by the time I found the bag. I'm sure it was not there when I left my purse on the kitchen table after we got home last night. Jay must have put it there later, after we argued.

Reminds me of the day we met.

I do remember everything, Caris.

And I want to tell you about it.

Happy birthday.

Love, Jay

I reach into the bag and remove the delicate silver butterfly necklace that he obviously bought the other day at the butterfly conservatory. On the day we met, a Monarch butterfly surprised us on the walk back to the Arcana town square. That was my thirteenth birthday and I remember thinking that my best present was meeting a new friend named Johnny. I remember it all now as clearly as if it happened yesterday.

He remembers. This is his way of admitting that there are some pieces of the past he's not willing to forfeit after all.

Love, Jay

I fasten the chain around my neck. My phone is plugged in on my desk and I grab it to fire off a text before I can think twice. He'll be working at the bakery right now so I don't expect he can answer but I feel an urgent desire to tell him what's on my mind.

Thank you for my gift. I miss you.

I pause and add something else.

Love, Caris

Less than ten seconds pass before there's a ping from my phone.

Miss you more. Happy Birthday.

In all likelihood he's elbow deep in muffin batter but I need to hear his voice. He answers on the first ring.

"Happy birthday," he greets me. He's smiling. I can tell.

"Thank you for the necklace." I touch the silver butterfly beneath the hollow of my throat.

He takes a deep breath. "The other night was my fault. I should never have said those things and walked out of your room and-"

I'm shaking my head as I cut him off. "No, we don't need to talk about that right now, not on the phone. I just woke up and all I wanted was to hear your voice for a minute."

"I really do miss you like hell, Caris."

"I miss you too." A smile spreads across my face. "I might have had a dirty dream about you last night. Are you working?"

"Somebody's got to make the banana muffins." He pauses. "Got to tell you something. After we close later, Lana and I are bringing Shane to a rehab facility. It's about forty miles from here. Looks like a nice place."

"Oh." I'm saddened to hear this. I suppose it has to happen, though. Lana's been worried sick about Shane.

"It's a good thing," Jay assures me. "He'll get the help he needs."

"You're right. It's a good thing."

There's a long pause.

"How are your folks?" he asks, slowly and carefully.

"Talk to your fucking father. Maybe he'll even tell you the truth."

I have not done that yet. My parents were so overjoyed to see me yesterday, especially my mother. We went out to dinner together and then we watched one of the original Star Wars movies in the living room. They went to bed early.

"They're fine," I tell him. "But I think I hear them lurking around outside my door, eagerly waiting for the birthday girl to get up."

"You should go put in an appearance then."

"And you should get back to your banana muffins."

"I want to hear more about this dirty dream when you get home."

Home.

Yes, the house in Hutton is home now. *He's* my home.

"You will. I plan to act out the particulars for you."

He groans. "Now I have to finish making banana muffins with a boner."

"I'm sure it's been done before."

"Happy birthday, baby."

I keep touching the butterfly around my neck. "And Happy First Day We Met Anniversary."

"That too."

I want to tell him I love him. He's infuriating and sexy and tender and protective and I don't need to know anything about his past that's too painful to share. I just want to know that he's mine.

There are voices on the other side of my door.

"She's still asleep, Suzanne," my fathers stage whispers.

"No, I heard her voice," my mother insists. "Caris?"

"I got to go," I tell Jay. "But I'll be home tomorrow. My flight is supposed to land at four thirty so if it's on time I should be home a little after five."

"I'll be waiting," he says. "In case you have any doubt, I'd wait for you forever."

This boy. He doesn't know what he does to me.

Half a second after I set the phone down my parents crack open the door.

My mother beams when she sees me sitting up in bed.

"Happy birthday, sunshine!" She strolls into the room carrying a bouquet of pink and purple balloons.

"For my sweet girl." She hands me the balloons and then sits on my bed before folding me in the softest of hugs. I breathe in the smell of her gardenia perfume. She pulls away, moves a strand of hair off my forehead and peers into my eyes with a gentle smile.

Suzanne Chapel Marano has always been beautiful. When I was little and other kids met my mother for the first time they would often exclaim over how pretty she was and I would be puzzled because it had not occurred to me to see her like that. She was just Mom. And mothers are always beautiful, aren't they?

"Happy birthday, peanut." My dad leans in and plants a kiss on the top of my head.

"Twenty two years old," my mother sighs.

"Hard to believe," my dad agrees in his scratchy baritone. "Don't know where the times goes. Feels like yesterday I was watching your mother rock you in a chair right over in that corner the day we brought you home from the hospital."

His hand lands on my mother's shoulder and she rewards him with a smile. He lives for her smiles. I know he does.

My parents met when my mother was in her first year at the University of Texas. He was twelve years older and a frequent customer at the electronics store where she worked as a cashier. From the little I've been told about their romance it was a slow burn. They were married three years later, chose to settle down in Dallas and eventually I came along. For years they tried to give me a sibling and it seemed like a miracle when my mother finally became pregnant again. But it was not to be.

He must have known about her mental health issues before they married. There was never a time in my own memory when I was not aware of 'Mommy's sadness'. That's what my father would call it when she was in the middle of a bad spell that would send her to bed for days, sometimes weeks, on end.

They've suffered their ups and downs but I admire them. They're still together. They love each another. And love is so much more than the easy thrills of romance. Love is also the hard stuff that must be overcome.

They insist that I need to open my presents immediately. I receive a new Kindle reader along with a generous Amazon gift card. There are also boxes of cute clothes picked out by my mother and an adorable hand painted porcelain cat that I can't wait to add to the shelf above my desk in my bedroom. I feel spoiled and loved and grateful. I'm so lucky to have my parents. So many people don't have this. My own mother didn't have this. Jay doesn't have this.

I can't really think straight in the morning before a shower so I set my gifts aside, accept another round of enthusiastic hugs, and promise to come to the kitchen for a pancake breakfast as soon as I am showered and dressed.

"Don't forget we have to go see Aunt Vay this afternoon," my mother says as she follows my father out of the room. "She's looking forward to it."

I nod because it's become tradition to go visit Aunt Vay in the nursing home on my birthday. She suffered brain damage as a result of her brutal attack and was thereafter unable to care for herself. My parents moved her to a nursing home nearby so they could assist with whatever she needs. The Arcana house, originally Nancy and Richard's house, was sold. It's changed hands a couple of times since then. I found pictures of it online at a realtor site. It's been renovated and looks nothing like the house I remember.

Even though we always go see Aunt Vay on my birthday it's unlikely she's looking forward to the visit. She doesn't remember things from one day to the next and for the last few years the only person she consistently recognizes is her niece. Suzanne. The little girl she raised after her brother's murder.

The smell of apple cinnamon pancakes greets me after my shower. As I pass through the living room en route to the kitchen I pause to look at the small, framed photo on the end table. It's my mother's senior photo, the very same photo that Rafe Hempstead once stole from the house in Arcana. When the house was sold some neighbors offered to help pack it up so my folks wouldn't need to do it themselves. The furniture was all sold but the personal effects, like the photo, were shipped here. In the corridor that leads to my parents' bedroom hangs the picture that I used to stare at in Aunt Vay's house. The last family photo of Richard, Nancy and baby Suzanne.

While I look around the living room, another object catches my eye. It's a small figurine of a sleeping angel. Inscribed at the base is the name Ella. The name of my sister, who was born sleeping. I think about her often. She'd be nine now. I don't know how it's possible to desperately miss someone you never even got to meet but it is.

I find my mother in the kitchen, busily putting the finishing touches on my birthday breakfast. There is a stack of pancakes covered in whipped cream waiting in front of my seat at the table. She's cut up some strawberries and arranged the slices in a heart shape in the whipped cream.

"Sit down," she urges and pours me a glass of juice. I watch her closely for any sign of distress but today she seems happy.

"Where's Dad?"

"He had to run to the store real quick to get a part for the sprinkler system. Apparently it's leaking again."

My mom takes a seat across from me and happily watches me dig into my breakfast. She's wearing a cute lemon colored dress that I'm sure I'd fit into with no problem because we have the same figure. She hasn't dyed her blonde hair lately and it's noticeably streaked with gray, which on her manages to look glamorous, especially with the way it's pulled back into a chic bun at the nape of her neck.

"How pretty," she exclaims and reaches out to touch my butterfly necklace.

"It was a birthday gift. From Jay."

Her eyes sparkle with interest. "You haven't mentioned him before. He must be someone special."

"He's *very* special. I care about him very much."

I take a deep breath. I need to tell her everything.

"Mom, we first met when we were kids, during the summer I spent in Arcana. He's changed his last name but it used to be Hempstead."

She doesn't get upset. Her eyes become thoughtful. "Oh. Is he Clay Hempstead's son?"

I would think the name would be too painful for her to utter. "Yes, he is."

She nods. "I knew Clay in high school. He was kind of a hothead but he meant well."

My mouth falls open. "But…"

She looks at me. "What, sunshine?"

"But he hurt you, Mom. Didn't he?"

Her eyebrows lift. "Clay? No. Clay never hurt me." She frowns. "I hope Aunt Vay didn't tell you that. At a party in high school I had too much to drink. There was this football player named, oh, I forgot his name but he kept trying to get me to come outside with him. Clay got angry and told him to back off, that I was much too drunk to mess around. Then he grumbled that I shouldn't have come to the party and helped me to his car. He drove me straight home and that's the only time we were ever alone together. A lot of people saw him escort me to his car. They saw that I could hardly walk and they made up stories. They said I was passed out. They said I was naked. Aunt Vay heard the rumors and got upset. She wouldn't listen when I told her the truth. Clay Hempstead drove me home from a party and that's all."

"He didn't hurt you," I say, trying to come to terms with something that has been haunting me for years and was never even true.

"No. Clay didn't hurt me." Her tone has changed, softening to a near whisper. Her chin quivers. "He wasn't the one."

Clay Hempstead never hurt her. But *someone* did.

My mother sighs and when she raises her eyes again they are a little teary but she smiles.

"What's Jay like? Is he nice?"

"He's perfect. I can't wait for you to meet him."

"Yes, I would like that. I would very much like to meet him."

I can feel my own tears starting. "I love you so much, Mom."

"Oh, Caris." Her arms open. "I love you too, baby girl."

I'm happy to climb right into a long hug. My father has returned from the store and when he walks into the kitchen he smiles at the sight of us embracing. My mother pats my back and reminds me that I ought to eat my breakfast now because we need to leave soon.

Aunt Vay is expecting us.

CARIS

The long term care facility looks like a happy place from the outside. The building is a wide, sprawling structure similar to a single story hotel and the exterior is painted red and white. A tiered fountain bubbles in the front courtyard and the multi acre grounds are immaculate.

Aunt Vay's room is meant for two people but she is currently without a roommate ever since her last one died in her sleep a few months back. When we arrive, Aunt Vay is asleep in her comfortable armchair and there's a fleece blanket draped across her knees even though the temperature outside is over ninety degrees.

My mother gently calls her name and she stirs, opening her eyes in confusion. At first her gaze lands on me and there's no light of recognition. Then she sees my mother and her face, so gaunt and creased, breaks into pure happiness.

"Suzanne." Varina Chapel lifts her thin arms to embrace the one person her damaged mind never forgets.

"Aunt Vay, look. Caris is here. It's her birthday today. Isn't she beautiful?"

My aunt's eyes shift back to me and are not impressed. There's a scar on her right temple, plainly visible amid the wispy white hair remaining on her frail scalp.

She doesn't remember the details of her attack. She doesn't remember slapping me or spitting out the terrible news that my mother was raped as a teenager. She doesn't remember me at all.

My mother fusses over her aunt, helping her select a soft cardigan to drape over her shoulders and then picking out one of the pretty hats in her closet.

Aunt Vay has absolutely no interest in either me or my father. Her eyes only land on Suzanne. She only smiles at Suzanne.

We usually stay for at least an hour when we visit and this seems like an opportunity. My father and I are overdue for an important conversation.

"Hey Dad, why don't we go out and get something to bring back for lunch so Mom can visit with Aunt Vay a little longer?"

He clearly likes the thought of getting out of here and running an errand together. "Great idea. What do you want for lunch, Suz?"

It's decided that the Mexican food restaurant right down the street will do nicely. I suggest walking since it's so close. After we exit the front door of the nursing home I point to an empty bench.

"Dad, can we sit and talk for a minute?"

"Sure, peanut."

Once we're sitting side by side I try to puzzle through what I want to ask him. As far as I know, my father has never lied to me. Sometimes he paints a rosier picture of the world than it really is but he doesn't lie. At least I don't think he does.

"I need to ask you about something. It has to do with Arcana."

He sighs loudly. "Is that reporter bothering you again? I told her to quit calling. We're not interested in reopening those wounds."

"Reporter?" I have to think for a moment. "You mean the one who wanted to talk about the show she was working on about the murders?"

"Yes. She's trying to get the case reopened."

The news is unexpected. "I don't understand. Why?"

"There was a man from El Paso who made a deathbed confession to his son. He claimed to have been the one who really killed Nancy and Richard."

I'm shocked. "Wait, so she's saying that Billy Hempstead didn't kill them?"

"I'm sure Billy Hempstead really *did* kill them. He was convicted. He was given the death penalty. This guy who confessed was either delusional or trying to make himself infamous. The authorities consider the case closed. But supposedly there is still some evidence in storage. Nancy's dress, I think, among other things. The man's son has provided a DNA sample and it's been suggested that testing ought to be performed on the murder evidence to see if there's a match. Since law enforcement has no interest in pursuing hearsay leads on a murder that was solved decades ago, they would need a relative to sign a consent form to access the evidence."

I need a moment to process this. My mind rattles off the memorized details of the grisly case.

Billy Hempstead never confessed. His conviction was based on multiple witness testimonies. He did engage in a fistfight with Richard Chapel at the Roundabout Bar. He was drunk and furious. Around the time of the murders he was seen on the very road where Richard and Nancy's car broke down. He was known to still carry a torch for Nancy, his high school girlfriend. Those who knew him say he never recovered from their breakup, not even after he married and had a son.

There was no DNA testing at the time. There were no other suspects. Billy had a violent temper at times and he had both motive and opportunity.

The fact that he insisted on his innocence was not considered important. After all, murderers do that all the time.

And so do people who really *are* innocent.

All my life I've known that Billy Hempstead killed my grandparents.

And most likely he did.

But maybe not.

Maybe not.

My mouth has gone dry. "What does Mom think about all of this?"

My dad looks down and toys with his wedding ring. "I don't see any reason to bother your mother with this ugliness."

"You don't? They were *her* parents. Don't you think she deserves to know what really happened to them?"

He sighs and looks off into the distance. "This would upset her."

"Oh for god's sake, she's not a child, Dad!"

The outburst surprises me. And him. His eyes widen and then become wounded.

"From the day I met your mother I've always done everything in my power to protect her."

"I know." I lower my voice. "I know you have. But it's her decision whether or not to pursue this."

He sighs. "You're right. But the past still hurts her. Arcana still hurts her. I'm not sure she's ever forgiven me for sending you there when she was in the hospital."

"What do you mean?"

"Your mother didn't know you were in Arcana. She thought her aunt had come to Dallas to stay at the house with you."

"Why wouldn't you want her to know that I was there, staying with Aunt Vay?""

"Because she hates that place so much. Even hearing the name Arcana would set her off. And at the time, after Ella… She was in such fragile shape, Caris. I refrained from mentioning anything that would upset her." He gives me a pleading look. "I thought she hated her hometown only because of what happened to her parents. She loves Varina and Varina was always so devoted to her. It never crossed my mind that sending you to Arcana would place you in any danger. Then I had to tell her about Varina's attack. I'd already brought you home by then but she freaked when she found out you'd been staying in Arcana. You see, honey, she never told me about Gary."

A terrible suspicion begins to take root.

The way my aunt's boyfriend would look at me. The way he would lurk outside my bedroom door.

"Clay didn't hurt me. He wasn't the one."

I try to swallow but I can't. "Never told you *what* about Gary?"

He rubs a hand over his face. He's struggling not to cry. "I asked you about him, remember? You shrugged and said you thought he was creepy but you didn't seem distraught."

I do remember that. I remember sitting at the kitchen table with my father and eating pizza a few weeks after he brought me home from Arcana. It was soon after my mother's discharge from the hospital and she was tired. She slept upstairs while we ate dinner and he asked me questions as his pizza sat untouched in front of him. His voice sounded strange and his eyes were bloodshot but that was understandable after everything our family had been through.

"Did Gary come around the house often? Did he bother you? You can tell me, sweetheart."

And I had swallowed a bite of my pizza before saying, "He's just a weirdo. I didn't really talk to him." I saw no point in bringing up the fact that my aunt's boyfriend frightened me. My father would have been troubled. Instead he visibly relaxed. After that I forgot all about the conversation. Until now.

A sob rips out of my father and he drops his head into his hands. "I swear I would have killed him myself if he'd done to you what he did to your mother."

A girl about my own age wearing pink nursing scrubs walks briskly past. She glances at us with curiosity but keeps moving into the building. Sobbing relatives probably aren't an uncommon sight around here.

"Gary raped her." I feel the need to say it out loud and it sounds even more terrible than it did inside my head.

He raises his head and nods. "Her senior year of high school. She never told me. She carried that pain alone. My beautiful Suzanne. For so many years I never knew."

"Did Aunt Vay know?"

"No. She loves your mother more than anything. And she loves you too. She had no idea about Gary. Not until that day."

I assume he means the day Aunt Vay was attacked. Presumably by Rafe Hempstead.

I finally manage to swallow the lump in my throat. "Dad, you need to tell me what happened."

He gathers his thoughts for a moment and when he begins talking his voice is clear. Maybe he's relieved to be releasing this burden.

"After your mother told me about what Gary had done to her I got suspicious about Varina's attack. I called the police in Arcana but they were so sure the Hempstead boy was responsible. And they already had him in jail awaiting trial so they dismissed any other possibility. So I went there and confronted him myself. For backup I flew out a couple of tough guys from my old Brooklyn neighborhood. Good friends, though. The kind who will stand by your side when your family is threatened."

This shocks me. My father has always been a man who avoids conflict. But I suppose when it comes to protecting the people you love, all bets are off.

"We didn't have to work on him for long." My father looks off into the distance, remembering the details. "He broke down and cried. He said Varina had found him in your bedroom. He was stealing your underwear from the piles of freshly washed laundry she'd placed on your bed. Of course Varina was irate. Whatever she said to him was enough to send him into a rage. He struck her in the face repeatedly and she fell, hitting her head on the corner of the dresser."

"My god." I cover my mouth, thinking about poor Aunt Vay. And then I think about Rafe, about what I'd told the police.

"Dad, the cops picked up Rafe because I told them he was hanging around the yard that day and that Aunt Vay had yelled at him. I told them he'd broken into the house before. It's because of me that they thought he was Aunt Vay's attacker."

"You only told the truth, Caris. After all the awful history between the Chapels and the Hempsteads, they believed Rafe was responsible because it made sense. And they didn't investigate too carefully."

"Is Gary in prison?"

"No. He killed himself in his cell a few weeks after he was arrested."

I'm glad to hear that he's not alive.

And I'm sad about everything else.

"What about Rafe?"

I think of the tall, strong boy with the cold eyes who was scary as hell at age sixteen. By now he's likely to be a terrifying and far stronger man.

My father nods. "We hauled Gary down to the police station and Rafe Hempstead was released only hours after Gary confessed. Rafe's mother and brother had already left the state. She was called but she didn't have much interest in retrieving her troubled son. I really don't know what happened to him after that, to any of them."

It's almost too much to take in at once.

How much of this does Jay know?

Some of it, obviously.

He was likely still living with his mother when she got the call from the Arcana police that Rafe had been released. She was almost certainly told why. Jay knew all along that Rafe didn't attack Aunt Vay. Until the other night he must have assumed that I knew it too.

"Why didn't you ever tell me?" I ask.

There's a touch of bitterness in the question.

Secrets.

Why do families keep them from each other?

Even though I was a child I was old enough to be told the truth.

He doesn't make excuses. "I should have. I'm sorry."

We share a long moment of silence. The courtyard fountain continues its steady music as the water recycles itself and keeps flowing.

When I look at my father his face wears a miserable expression.

"Daddy?" I haven't called him that in a long time.

He smiles a little. "Yeah, honey?"

"You said you didn't know what happened to any of the Hempsteads."

"That's right."

"I know what happened to one of them."

He listens as I tell him about Jay. At first I can see his skepticism, like he's wondering if Jay, formerly Jonathan Hempstead, is seeking revenge or something. But the more I talk the more accepting he seems. Especially when I tell him that Mom already knows.

"We should go get lunch before Mom sends out a search party." I rise from the bench and reach out to help him up because he has bad knees and sometimes they cause him pain.

My father is relieved that I'm not angry with him. We buy a ton of food and bring it back to Aunt Vay's room. The rest of the visit is pleasant and Aunt Vay even expresses a little bit of curiosity about me. When I hug her goodbye she hugs me back and asks me to visit again. Perhaps she remembers me sometimes after all.

At home my father is the one who cooks my birthday dinner; chicken parmesan, a family favorite that his long dead grandmother used to make for him.

I find a few minutes to give Lana a call. She's glad to talk to me on my birthday but she's also preoccupied. She and Jay will be bringing Shane to rehab this evening. This will be tough for all of them. I'm glad I will be back tomorrow. They need me.

After dinner my mom asks me what I want to do for the rest of the evening and I decide I want to take a walk by the duck pond they used to bring me to as a child. It's not far from our house and I have lovely memories of strolling along the shore and watching the birds splash in the water while my parents walk hand in hand right behind me.

I'm still reeling a bit from all the news that was dropped in my lap this afternoon but I'm not at all sorry that I know the truth. I'll tell Jay everything tomorrow. Some of it he surely knows. And some of it he likely doesn't.

"Look, Caris," my mother calls from behind me. "A swan!"

The beautiful birds glides with confidence on the surface of the water, like it's aware of being admired.

This visit has been nice. But later on as I fall asleep in my old bed with my birthday necklace under my pillow once more I'm already looking forward to leaving.

I'm eager to get home.

To him.

And to the life I'm hoping we'll share together from now on.

JAY

*L*ana is good at putting on a cheerful face for Shane's sake but once we leave Reflections, the facility where Shane will be staying, she's uncharacteristically silent.

"He'll be okay," I assure her because she's just sitting there miserably in my passenger seat. "He can do this."

She bobs her head. "I know he can." She discreetly wipes a tear from her cheek. "It's just that I feel as if I left my heart behind when I had to kiss him goodbye."

There was a time not too long when I wouldn't have had the slightest understanding about how she feels. Now I do. I would be crushed if I had to watch Caris struggle the way Lana sees Shane fighting an intense battle with himself.

"Do you mind if I sleep in his room?" she asks. "I mean it's really your side of the house so I don't want to seem strange but I feel closer to him in there."

"Won't bother me a bit."

The house is rather depressing with both Shane and Caris missing. Lana announces she's going to retreat to Shane's room and go to sleep early so I'm left on my own to sit beside the pool and think about all kinds of things.

Rafe has been on my mind.

A few weeks after we landed in Phoenix, my mother got a call from the Arcana PD. Rafe, who'd been arrested for the violent attack on Varina Chapel and was going to be charged as an adult, had been released. He was innocent of the crime. The real culprit was Varina's shady boyfriend, Gary. The one Caris would complain about, saying he used to stand outside her bedroom door and watch her as she slept. Caris's father was the one who traveled to Arcana and wrestled a confession out of Gary.

It never occurred to me that Caris was unaware of the circumstances surrounding her aunt's attack. She was still under the assumption that Rafe was to blame.

I have a longstanding habit of refusing to examine the past. It's difficult to break. There was a time when I needed that buffer in order to get through each day without losing my mind.

I still think you can't move forward if you're always looking behind you. But finding Caris again made me realize that you also can't forge ahead if you refuse to acknowledge where you've been.

I'm ready to try to find out what became of my brother.

There's an old boss of mine whose wife used to be in the bail bonds business. About a year ago they both left their jobs and opened up a private investigation company.

He answers my call but when I explain what I'm looking for he gives me the number for his wife since she's better suited to the search. Her name is Amy Blunt and this seems very fitting. She speaks quickly, asks pointed questions and then declares that she'll likely be giving me a call within the next day or two with some answers.

I'm stunned over how easy it is. I hope I'm ready to hear whatever Amy Blunt finds.

It's still not very late but I've run out of things to do and besides, I need to get up earlier than usual to go to the bakery since I'll only have Delia to help me handle everything tomorrow.

In order to tire myself out I take a shower and jerk off like a madman while I pretend I'm fucking Caris rough and hard, the way she sometimes likes it. After that I'm ready to collapse into bed and once I close my eyes I don't open them again until my alarm starts howling.

After spending two hours mixing and baking, Delia arrives in time for the doors to open for the day. And bless her heart, she's brought her sister along to help out while we're so short handed.

I feel my phone go off in my pocket but after I check it and see that it's not Caris I just stuff it back in there without answering. When I'm this busy anyone other than Caris can wait.

The customers thin out after noon and I finally get a chance to breathe and check my phone. There's a voicemail from Amy Blunt.

The office is the size of a small closet and the only one who really goes in there is Caris to take care of bookkeeping tasks but it's a good place to make a private phone call. Amy answers her phone right away and gets right down to business.

"Your brother is currently living in Houston. He's required to supply his parole officer with current contact information. I have his cell phone number."

This has moved faster than I thought possible. I wouldn't have believed I'd have Rafe's direct line in hand just like that. I jot down the number on the back of an invoice and thank Amy for her quick response.

After the call ends I stare at the number that will presumably connect me to my brother. I don't spend any time thinking about what I should do next. I punch the numbers in and wait for the line on the other end to begin ringing.

Chances are he won't answer. He won't recognize the number and it's the middle of the day.

Then I hear a click and a voice says, "Yeah, what?"

It's shocking the way his voice is slightly deeper but pretty much the same.

"Rafe," I croak.

He's annoyed. "The fuck you want, asshole? Who are you?"

I exhale slowly. "It's Jonathan."

There's a moment of stunned silence. Then a cough. Then some more silence.

"Limp Dick," he finally says in a tone of sheer disbelief. "Is that really you?"

"It's me."

"Well I'll be fucked. Never thought I'd hear from you again. How the hell are you?"

"I'm good."

"And what about that crazy old bat who calls herself our mother?"

"Don't know. She took off not long after we moved to Phoenix. Haven't seen her since."

He chuckles. "Not surprised."

"What about you, Rafe? Are you all right?"

He thinks the question is funny. "Sure. I've got plenty of cash in my pocket and ten minutes ago I had a pretty mouth on my cock. I think I'm doing okay."

Amy Blunt had said he's been in and out of prison a few times. Robbery. Multiple counts of assault. To me, that's not okay at all but then again I'm not Rafe.

"Hey, where are you living now?" he asks. "I could come crash with you next time I get bored. We'll raise hell together, live up to our name."

I'm not interested in raising Rafe's version of hell. And I don't want to tell him the truth about how to find me. Rafe was always a powder keg. It doesn't sound as if he's changed. He might even be worse than what I remember. I can't take that risk, especially not now that I have Caris.

"I'm in Phoenix," I lie. "Got a tiny apartment in a really shitty neighborhood."

"Huh." The way he grunts out the sound confirms that he knows I'm lying.

"I'm glad you're doing okay," I tell him.

"Why'd you call?" he asks, not sounding hostile. Simply curious.

"I just got to thinking about you. And I was worried."

He snorts. "Just not worried enough to give out your address, eh?"

There's no point in lying again. "No."

"Don't blame you. But keep checking your rearview mirror, kid. Maybe one of these days I'll be right there behind you."

An ominous thought.

"You take care of yourself, Rafe."

"You do the same, Jonathan."

He ends the call before I can. I'm unsure if I just made a mistake by placing myself back on his radar. I hope not. I hope somewhere deep in Rafe there lurks a heart and that his heart is satisfied to hear that his only brother is alive and well.

I check my watch. There are only a few hours left until the bakery closes and then I can go get my girl. Caris plans to take a car home from the airport. She has no idea that I plan to meet her there. I'll buy her some flowers to make up for the fact that I didn't get to see her for her birthday. I'm convinced there's only one girl in the whole wide world who has the power to turn me into a romantic fool.

How lucky I am to have found her again.

JAY

I've heard that there was a time when it was possible to meet someone at the airport gate but I'll have to settle for hanging out beyond the security clearance line with a handful of yellow daisies and a smile on my face.

I probably look like a fucking goofball.

I don't even care.

She's staring at her phone when she appears, squinting behind her glasses, and I unleash a loud whistle to get her attention. A few of the airport staff shoot me some side eye for the disturbance.

Caris looks up and her face changes. It's a common expression to say that someone 'lights up' but Caris really does. She's the most alive thing in this entire freaking terminal. She's the still point in my world. She's the sunshine.

"Jay!" she squeals and runs the last few steps, dropping her overnight bag and jumping into my arms. I'm in love.

When I kiss her I'm not bashful about it. The hand not holding the flowers twists all up in her hair and she gets all the tongue she can handle. I can't wait to get her alone and peel off that hot little sundress she's wearing.

But first thing's first.

After we're done kissing to the point of being obscene I hand over the flowers, pick up her overnight bag and hold her free hand all the way to my truck.

I hold the door for her and toss her bag in the back before coming around to the driver's side. She hasn't stopped smiling since she caught sight of me in the terminal and I'm pretty sure the grin on my face looks like it was tattooed there as well.

"I can't believe how much I missed you." She takes my hand and places it in her lap, stroking my palm.

"I missed you too."

That summer dress is doing things to my dick. Her bare legs tease me and I have a crazy fleeting thought about what we ought to do right here in the front seat behind the truck's tinted windows. I want to talk to her in the worst way but I also want to get between her legs and wear her out until she begs to come.

It's a fantastic dilemma to have.

Since there might be some kind of federal law about fucking in the parking garage beside an airport I start up the truck and suggest going out for some food instead.

On the drive back to Hutton, Caris gives Lana a call. From what I can gather via Caris's side of the conversation, Lana remains understandably emotional about Shane's rehab stay but she's determined to be positive. Caris says all the right things that one friend ought to say to another in this situation. She offers to grab some takeout for Lana on the way home but it sounds like Lana declines and chooses to test out her cooking skills in the kitchen instead.

Caris is in the mood for pizza and I would have taken her someplace nicer, especially since it's a birthday celebration dinner, but she insists on pizza so twenty minutes later we're sitting inside a back corner booth at Pesto's, a little Italian place not far from the university.

Her mood has become more subdued since sitting down and I can tell she has something she wants to talk about. I wait until after the waiter has taken our order before I move over to her side of the booth and slide my arm around her shoulders.

Her hand moves to my leg. "I told them about you. Everything."

I have no idea how Caris's parents will feel about their daughter being in a relationship with a member of the Hempstead family. Whatever the answer is, I'm determined to win them over.

"How'd they handle that news?"

She smiles. "They're happy that I'm happy." Then her smile fades. "There's a lot I need to tell you."

I tighten my arm around her. "I'm listening."

She now knows that Rafe was not her aunt's attacker. She's also learned something important about my father. He wasn't such a bad guy after all. It's true that her mother suffered terribly but not at the hands of my father. I'm relieved to hear this, that the man with the laughing blue eyes who lives only in my memory was not a monster.

Her last revelation almost knocks me out of my seat.

"Your grandparents weren't killed by Billy Hempstead?"

"Not necessarily. I don't know much about this man who supposedly confessed to their killing. The authorities don't think much of his story. My mother has decided she's going to sign whatever they need her to sign in order to access the evidence and run the necessary DNA tests if there's anything they can test. The evidence was all circumstantial. It's possible that Billy Hempstead was not the killer."

I try to let this possibility sink in but I don't really believe it.

Caris is toying with her butterfly necklace and watching me. "Are you okay with all of this?"

Of course I'm okay. Whatever the verdict, I'm okay. I've got her.

The waiter arrives with our food and Caris digs in.

"I'm starving." She takes an impressively large bite of a folded slice.

I take a slice for myself. "Then eat up. You'll need energy for everything I plan to do to you later."

She swallows and takes a sip of soda. "I'll eat fast."

My hand strays to her thigh and sneaks beneath the hem of her dress. "You do that."

She shuts her eyes. "You have no idea how much you turn me on."

I stroke the inside of her thigh and move higher. "I'll need some details."

Now she's really squirming. "Fuck. Don't make me come at the table again."

"Then don't tempt me by talking dirty."

Caris pulls back suddenly and gives me a serious look. "Are you my boyfriend?"

As if that's a question even worth asking.

I plant a kiss on her lips. "I'm your forever."

She reaches out and traces my lips with her fingertip. "I hope I'm never without you again, Jay."

I pull her close. We both know this conversation is a long awaited conclusion to something that was begun long ago.

"You never will be, Caris."

With the craziness of running the bakery and falling more in love every day, we don't get around to fulfilling an important errand for a couple of weeks.

It's Monday and with the bakery closed and nothing else requiring immediate attention, we're able to leave early for the long drive to Arcana. Lana declined the invitation to come along. She thinks this is something the two of us need to do alone and she's right.

Rainfall was lower than average this summer, the temperatures hotter. The sun scorched damage is in evidence along the highway. We begin seeing signs for Arcana when we're fifty miles away.

We're less than ten miles outside town when we come across the oil drill machinery. At the moment the drills are idle, resembling prehistoric metal monsters on the quiet horizon.

When we pass the shabby green and white 'Welcome to Arcana' sign I reach instinctively for Jay's hand and find it waiting to accept mine. A familiar landscape looms ahead. I spent less than a single season of my life in this place and yet it's burned into my memory like no other.

"It looks the same from here," Jay says, echoing my thoughts.

The sun is high in the sky. It's early afternoon. "Yes, it does."

Jay drives slowly through the streets. We don't stop in the town square yet. I want to see Dunstan Street first. Even though I already knew the house had been remodeled I'm still surprised when I need to check the number hung beside the front door to confirm it's the same one.

The truck idles beside the curb but Jay doesn't cut the engine.

"You want to go knock on the door?" he asks.

I don't know what I'd say. Perhaps the home's current owners know the whole history. Or maybe they don't and don't want to.

"No," I tell him and squeeze his arm. "We can go."

Jay has no desire to see the trailer park where he lived with his mother and brother. He's glad he was able to get in touch with Rafe and yet their conversation unnerved him. I know that Rafe was proven to be not as deadly as I'd once thought. But I still shudder when I think of him.

We decide to return to the center of town and park in the nearly empty lot of what used to be the Arcana Market and is now a chain drugstore. Harold Keyser died six years ago and his brother was gone before that. I looked it up and was sad to know that the friendly old man who was a local icon would never know the fate of the two children who wandered through his store aisles and gladly accepted the snacks and kindnesses he generously offered them. I think the sight of us together today would please him.

Now that we're in the heart of downtown I can see that the town has changed in other ways. The movie theater is shuttered. The ice cream parlor is a hair salon. The beautiful mountain laurels that used to bracket the town square have all been cut down and replaced with anemic flowerbeds.

We hold hands as we walk slowly up the street to the spot where we met. There aren't many people around. It's a weekday afternoon and it's hot. The ones we do see don't give us a second glance. They have their own missions to complete, their own histories to be preoccupied with.

The DNA tests that might exonerate Billy Hempstead will never happen. My mother signed the paperwork but when an attempt was made to access the evidence it was missing. The box where it was supposed to be was opened and was empty. The man who confessed was also linked to two other murders in this part of the state at around the same time. So it's possible he told the truth as he lay dying. But we'll never know. It will remain a question without an answer.

For once I wish for ghosts. Or at least for the possibility of brief visits from those whose time here on earth is finished. I would love to think that Richard and Nancy are watching, that they can see their granddaughter's happiness. I hope they are proud of their legacy.

"What's your name? I'm Caris."

"Jonathan."

"And you live here?"

The shiver I feel across the back of my neck is not unpleasant. Jay might have felt it too because he draws me closer into the protection of his arms and props his chin atop my head while I rest my cheek against his chest. It's hard to believe that I was once taller than him. A lot of things are hard to believe. But that doesn't mean they are unbelievable.

The Hempsteads. The Chapels.

We are neither. And we are both.

We are the long lost remnants.

We are the conclusion to their story.

"I love you," I tell him. I close my eyes and draw strength from his warmth. He holds me tighter.

"I love you too."

"I'm ready to leave now, Jay."

Before leading me away he takes my hand, lacing our fingers together.

And that simple gesture makes me just as happy as it did the first time he ever made it.

EPILOGUE

JAY

The following spring

"What time's the graduation?" Shane asks from where he sits beside the pool as he tests the chlorine level.

"Not until six but we're supposed to meet her parents for dinner first."

"Maybe Lana and I will stop by and watch you squirm under the glare of Caris's dad."

"No need. He's reached the stage of acceptance where I'm concerned."

It's true that Caris's father kind of eyeballed me in the beginning but we've visited them in Dallas a few times now and he's decided to relax after seeing how happy his daughter is. The man has no need to worry. I'll treat his daughter like a queen every day of my life.

Her mother never seemed to harbor similar reservations. She was delighted to meet me for the first time and her enthusiasm never wavered. Once she pulled me aside just to tell me that I'm as handsome as my father was. I didn't really know how to answer that prop-

215

erly so I just mumbled something and nodded. She beams every time she sees me put my arm around Caris and I understand why her daughter has such a generous heart.

Lana pokes her head through the sliding glass door. She zeroes in on her boyfriend and grins.

"Oh, lover boy. Are you planning on feeding me before we crash Caris's graduation?"

He answers with a wicked smile. "I've got something you can put in your mouth if you can't wait."

"Guys," I complain. "Seriously."

Shane hops to his feet. "Oh, like you're not twenty times more oversexed. Remember how you told me the walls are thin? You were right."

Lana smirks at me. "Like rabbits, the two of you."

"Do me a favor. Don't make those kind of jokes in front of her folks when we're all together later."

Shane reaches his girlfriend's side and slips an arm around her waist. Lana kisses his cheek and then issues a warning.

"I know better than that. He might not."

"I might not," Shane agrees. "But it's possible to muzzle me if someone tempts me with a reward."

"Tempt him," I say to Lana, rolling my eyes. "Please."

She laughs and drags her boyfriend into the house. It's nice to see Shane on solid ground. He's worked hard to stay clean after his relapse last summer. And with some help he's turned the bakery into a profitable venture and become a regular upstanding local business-man. A member of the Hutton Chamber of Commerce. Enthusiastic sponsor of a little league team. Ruby would be glad to know that her gift to her godson was not wasted.

As for me, once Shane learned the ropes at the bakery I decided that mixing batter in a kitchen all day was not to my liking. I was going stir crazy. I need to work with my hands more. So with Caris's assistance I crafted a business proposal, obtained a small loan from the bank and started my own carpentry business. Thanks to everyone watching all those home improvement shows and wanting built-in this and custom made that I've had no problems getting more business than I can handle. At some point I expect I'll be employing a crew of my own.

Carris will be starting her new job in the accounting department at the university in a few weeks. Between the two of us we'll be able to afford a nice place here in Hutton real soon.

We agree that living with close friends is nice. But what would be nicer? Being able to fuck our ever loving brains out in the room of our choice without anyone complaining that we're making too much noise.

"Hey," I call through an open bedroom window. "We've gotta go or we'll be late to meet your folks."

"I'll be right there," she calls back.

Five minutes pass and finally she emerges with a small bundle in her arms. "Say goodbye to Daddy," she croons to the blanket.

A pair of furry heads pop up and four little eyes blink at me. Two days ago I visited the local animal shelter and adopted two gray kittens, both female and from the same litter. Caris fell in love the instant they were placed in her arms. If they weren't so cute and fluffy I might be a little jealous of all the attention she lavishes on them.

I reach out and scratch the nearest kitten behind the ears. "Did you decide what to name them yet?"

She kisses the head of the second kitten and gives me one of her heart melting smiles. "I'm working on it."

"Now you have your cat sanctuary."

She laughs.

This girl.

I'm going to marry her.

Discreetly I pat the lump in my back pocket to ensure the ring is still there. I've been doing that all day. I already spoke to Caris's parents. Not because their permission is needed. But because I wanted their blessing. I know Caris would too. They did not hesitate to give it.

Well, her mother didn't hesitate. Her father looked a little forlorn for a moment before he reached out and shook my hand. He squeezed harder than he needed to. That's okay. If I ever have a daughter I'm sure I'll be the same way.

I'm asking Caris tonight, after her graduation ceremony.

She uses a lot of baby talk as she carries the kittens back indoors. When she returns a moment later she's got her cap and gown in hand.

"Are you ready?" she asks me.

To answer her question I reach for her hand.

I'm going to do that every chance I get for as long as I'm breathing.

FIRED

NAILED

Stand Alones

UNRULY

IN THIS LIFE

HICKEY

THE HERMIT

SYLER MCKNIGHT